He opened his eyes... ...there.

"What are you doing in my bed?" he asked.

There was enough light that he could see her smile. "I couldn't sleep in my room. I just...wanted to be with you. To feel safe."

He stiffened against the emotion those familiar words invoked. *I will keep you safe, my dearest heart,* he'd once told her. Now he only said, "You better go before somebody finds you here."

"I told you," she said, "I don't care who knows."

"Your brother might."

"It's *my* life, Rio. I—"

"Look, Anne, I'm not the kind of man you need," he interrupted, his voice almost harsh. "I *can't* be that man." He had nothing to offer her but his love, and he was realistic enough to know that was never enough.

Anne held his eyes, and this time he let her see what he normally hid. Surety. And denial. Without speaking, she got up from the bed, and Rio turned his eyes to the ceiling. He didn't want to watch her. The image of Anne leaving him was not a memory he wanted to keep....

Dear Reader,

Although we were both born and bred in Alabama, my husband and I were fortunate enough to live for several years in West Texas, very near the Rio Grande. Accustomed to the fertile black soil and virgin forests of the Appalachian foothills, we were both surprised by how quickly and passionately we fell in love with the border and the desert. The truly unique blend of cultures and the unhurried pace of life there enchanted us as much as the magnificence of the country that surrounds the river. We have always vowed to return, and now, in this HOME TO TEXAS trilogy, I have in some small way fulfilled that vow.

The three heroes in this trilogy—the McCullars—are strong men who love the rugged, desolate land they've inherited with the same passion I felt for the desert. With roots deep in the land they love, they choose to fight the increasing lawlessness that threatens both the ranch and the people they love. I think you'll find that the women who stand beside them are well matched with these lawmen heroes. And I also hope you will see a reflection of your own family in the sense of family strength, pride and unity I've tried to instill in these three books.

Thank you for allowing me to show you the McCullars and the border country I still consider a second home. I sincerely hope you enjoy these stories as much as I enjoyed creating them for you!

Much love,

Gayle Wilson

Whisper My Love
Gayle Wilson

Harlequin Books

TORONTO • NEW YORK • LONDON
AMSTERDAM • PARIS • SYDNEY • HAMBURG
STOCKHOLM • ATHENS • TOKYO • MILAN
MADRID • WARSAW • BUDAPEST • AUCKLAND

For Tabitha,
with my friendship and admiration
(You already have the best hero I have ever created!)

ISBN 0-373-22466-4

WHISPER MY LOVE

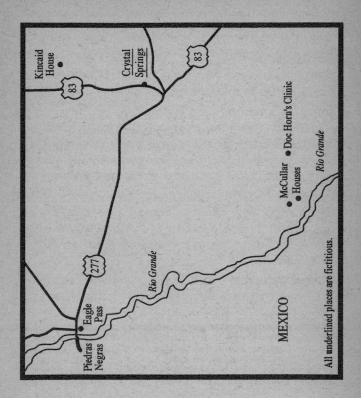

Kincaid
House

83

Crystal
Springs

83

McCullar
● Doc Horn's Clinic
● Houses

Rio Grande

277

Rio Grande

Eagle
Pass

Piedras
Negras

MEXICO

Rio Grande

All underlined places are fictitious.

CAST OF CHARACTERS

Rio Delgado—Five years ago, he was sent to prison for a crime he didn't commit. Is he now being set up to take the fall for another murder?

Anne Richardson—She has always had in abundance everything Rio Delgado lacks: family, position, wealth. She is wise enough to recognize, however, that this border outcast is the only man who can heal her spirit and erase the terrifying memories that haunt her.

Chase McCullar—Rio has come home to South Texas for only one reason—to even the score with Chase McCullar, the man responsible for sending him to prison.

Trent Richardson—How far is Texas state senator Trent Richardson willing to go to stop his sister's relationship with Rio?

Jenny McCullar—She has never been certain that Rio had any part in her husband's murder, but will she protect him from a community determined to make him pay for that crime?

Buck Elkins—Mac McCullar was his best friend. Is he out for revenge against the man who killed him?

Raymond Morales—Sheriff Elkins's deputy knows too well the angry mood of the county he protects and the dangers their anger represents for Rio Delgado.

Doc Horn—The one man in South Texas who has never doubted Rio's innocence.

Prologue

"Mac McCullar's going down. You can count on it."

The words drifted out of the haze of smoke that filled the small Mexican cantina. Sometime during the early-morning hours, the windows had been closed against the growing chill of the December night, and the cigarette smoke had built upward from a low cloud that had hovered just above the floor until, like fog, it had crept into all the dark corners of the room.

Rio Delgado wasn't sure where those words had come from. They had only been audible, he knew, because the *norteña* blaring from the jukebox had momentarily been silenced by the ending of one record and the short, mechanical delay before the beginning of the next.

He had been sitting at a single table, his back to the wall. That was an old gunfighter caution, which he followed unthinkingly. Both long-fingered hands had been wrapped around the beer he'd been nursing for the last hour.

Rio's eyes slowly lifted from his glass to survey those sitting at the tables around him. He hadn't paid much attention to the other patrons who had crowded into the warmth of the border bar tonight because his thoughts had been directed inward and because he wasn't a sociable man by nature.

Suddenly the music began again, and the surrounding conversations faded back into a low, subliminal murmur.

There was no one near him who looked suspicious. No furtive eyes had been raised to see if that dangerously revealing snatch of conversation had been overheard.

Mac McCullar's going down. There had been other indications that someone was out to get the popular sheriff of the Texas county that lay just across the shallow river that was the international border. McCullar was too good at his job. He had been too successful at keeping out of his county the lawless elements that seethed northward along other stretches of the virtually unprotected boundary.

It seemed that Mexico might go the way of her South American neighbors, poor nations who suffered the same societal ills, the same sharp class divisions. Drug money spoke loudly to the impoverished, promising them all the things they had before only dreamed about. The violence that went along with the trafficking had already begun here, and those to the north shivered at the threat and were now attempting to close the back door, which had long been tacitly left open, against their southern neighbor.

In places like this isolated, rural stretch of border only men like Mac McCullar stood in the way. Men who said with determination, *It won't happen here, not on my watch.* Men who were willing to say no to the enormous sums of money the drug lords offered and brave enough to face the consequences of that refusal.

That had been the other rumor he had heard about Mac. That he had already been warned. *Pesos or bullets.* The classic threat had been issued. Take the money and look the other way or pay with your life or the lives of your family.

Rio looked back down into the amber liquid in the bottom of the glass he held. He didn't owe the McCullars anything. They certainly had given him nothing.

"You're staying late tonight," the waitress said, interrupting that almost-habitual bitterness. She had stopped beside his table again, although he'd refused another beer the last three times she'd asked.

The desire to give good service wasn't the reason she kept coming back. She had made her interest obvious all evening. She was new here, attractive in a soft, overblown way, like a rose at the very end of its late-summer beauty.

"Are you sure I can't get you anything…else?" she asked softly. The meaning behind the question was as obvious as her other attempts at flirtation had been.

"I'm fine, thanks," Rio said, shaking his head. He wasn't looking for a woman tonight, and if he had been, there were a dozen others in the village who would be just as accommodating. And more familiar. That was the one thing in his hard existence that had always come easy. Attracting women. Given his looks, that was hardly surprising.

The dark, obviously Latino beauty of Rio Delgado's face had been inherited from his mother, whose family had once proudly traced its ancestry to the Spanish colonials who settled the northern part of Mexico.

Although Marcella Delgado had grown up, as her son had, in the grinding poverty of this small Mexican village, she had once been celebrated as the most beautiful woman in the north. Her son's aquiline features mirrored hers, in a totally masculine representation.

But there was also something of the other side of his parentage stamped indelibly in those perfect features. Andrew McCullar, a big brawling man with a hair-trigger temper and a reputation for drunken cruelty, had fathered a bastard son on his Mexican mistress and then had never bothered to acknowledge the boy's existence. The most unforgivable aspect of that—to Rio, at least—was that his mother had never demanded that acknowledgment. She had welcomed Drew McCullar into her bed until her sudden and unexpected death from a virulent strain of pneumonia.

Rio had been eleven when his mother died, and still his father had made no effort to see to his welfare. After all, McCullar had two other sons—Mac and Chase—two very legitimate sons. He had no need, and apparently even less desire, to claim his mistress's half-breed by-blow.

Mac McCullar's going down. The words echoed again in his head as he watched the deliberately seductive sway of the waitress's hips moving away from his table. Rio knew he should forget what he'd heard, walk out of the bar into the winter night and travel the short distance to his aunt's house where his bed was waiting. That would be the smart thing to do.

Except he liked Mac McCullar. He even admired him, and in his short life he had encountered too few people worthy of his admiration. And there was also the fact that Mac was his half brother.

Rio got to his feet and threw a wad of pesos down on the table. As he walked to the door, he still hadn't decided what to do. There hadn't been much to go on—just a few words, overheard in a setting that didn't lend credence to much that was said there.

The clear, cold desert air outside was welcome after the smoke-filled room. He pulled in a couple of deep lungfuls, trying to clear his head, and then he began walking down the dirt street toward his aunt's. He knew he would make one more stop before he turned in. A habitual one. A late-night visit with The Devil. The sensuous line of Rio's mouth tilted upward in pleasure at that thought.

He had bought the stallion several years ago in a small Mexican stock auction because no one else had wanted him. No one involved in the sale had attempted to hide the black's viciousness, probably because it was blatantly apparent whenever a human came near. The horse had savaged a handler, and if there had been no offer for the big black, he would have been put down and his carcass sold for dog food.

No one had questioned the sale to the slender boy. They hadn't even questioned the lowness of Rio's bid, all the money he'd had in the world. They had all known that Rio

Delgado had the gift, that strange affinity with animals that was unexplainable in any sort of logical terms.

Even as a child Rio could approach the feral village dogs. He was absolutely fearless in dealing with the most vicious of them. That was perhaps part of the magic he wrought. No one, not even Rio, could explain exactly what he did, but his gift guaranteed that he would never be without work along the border ranches, if for no other reason than that he could break colts or even wild mustangs more efficiently than anyone else.

He always started by crooning Spanish endearments to the frightened horse. The process was apparently fascinating to even the most hardened rancher—fascinating to watch the wild, rolling eyes calm as they focused on the whispering kid. The agitation seemed to melt out of the animal's tense muscles at his first touch. Rio had been in demand since he'd turned fifteen, tall and lean and as beautiful then as he was now.

When he'd bought the stallion, he had just turned eighteen, and he had certainly known enough about horses to suspect what had caused the black's wildness. The stallion had been mistreated. The signs were all there, just as the physical ones had been when he'd gotten him home and had finally had an opportunity to examine him.

That hadn't been for a while, of course. Over his aunt's protests, Rio had first fenced in a patch of dirt behind the tar-paper shack they lived in. He had built a temporary lean-to to shelter the stallion, and then he had begun the slow, painstaking process of winning the horse's trust.

Of course, he hadn't had much else to do. He had finished what schooling the village offered, and there were few opportunities here for any kind of employment. He could have found permanent work on one of the ranches in the States, but the decision to remain in Mexico had been deliberate—a rejection of his birthright and his citizenship, a determined denial of his father's blood.

In the last few years the stallion had more than repaid

his pittance of a purchase price and had even begun to repay the patient hours of training. They were building a reputation on the rodeo circuit and beginning to win prizes with surprising regularity. They hadn't ventured yet into the larger cities where the winnings were more substantial, but they were learning, and he knew that would come in time.

Rio stepped into the narrow wooden stall of the stable he'd eventually built to replace the lean-to and closed its low gate behind him. Even now, no one else would have dared invade the stallion's domain. He still trusted no one but the soft-spoken man who had taught him that human hands could do more than cause pain.

The horse harrumphed softly in welcome, releasing a fog of warm breath into the cold, predawn darkness. He lowered his nose, pushing it into his master's chest. Rio put his cheek against the big head. He ran his hands caressingly down the sides of the powerful neck.

He whispered the familiar Spanish love words, and Diablo's ears flickered in interest. There was no one else in this world that Rio Delgado loved, but he loved this black-hearted, black-hided brute with all the emotion he was capable of, with all the love that had been left in his soul after his mother's death and his father's betrayal.

"Would you like to make a run, my heart?" he asked softly. In answer, Diablo butted his chest. "To ride the wind into the night."

Rio crooned the suggestion to the stallion, trying it out. He still had made no decision. It was none of his business what happened to Mac McCullar. It was nothing to him, his logic argued, the words unconvincing, somehow, against the prodding of his conscience.

It had been nothing to Mac, he acknowledged, when, years before, he had been the one to catch the small group of Mexican adolescents who had broken into the barn on the McCullar ranch to steal agricultural chemicals, for which there was always a strong and profitable black market on both sides of the border.

It had been Rio's suggestion, of course, that they hit the McCullar place. At thirteen, he probably hadn't even been aware of all his motives in selecting his father's ranch to burglarize. It had seemed a relatively safe method of thumbing his nose at his Texas relatives. It was a crime the boys had successfully carried out several times at other border ranches.

And it had seemed to be going well until Mac McCullar had suddenly appeared in the double doors, a powerful flashlight in one hand and a shotgun in the other. To the terrified kids, he had loomed out of the shadows, seeming immensely tall and broad-shouldered. He hadn't used the gun, of course, and he had finally let them go without calling the county sheriff, but only after he'd scared them to death with warnings of what would happen the next time he caught them on McCullar property.

The other twelve- and thirteen-year-olds had not hesitated in exiting through the barn's double doors when Mac had finally indicated the scathing lecture was over. However, his big hand had closed uncompromisingly around the back of Rio's skinny neck, and he had had no choice but to remain behind. He had been wondering at the time how Mac could possibly know he was the leader, and then he realized that wasn't why Mac had stopped him.

"McCullars don't steal," Mac had said, "especially from each other."

"I'm no McCullar," Rio answered sullenly.

Mac laughed, his mustache lifting over a flash of white teeth. "Yeah? Well, that's not what your birth certificate says. And looking at you, there isn't much doubt that your mama was right about what she put down."

"How do you know what my birth certificate says?"

"I looked it up at the county courthouse."

"Why?" Rio had asked.

"Because I don't have that many brothers. Not so many that I can afford to lose track of 'em."

"Half brother."

"Blood's thicker than water," Mac said, and his deep voice was suddenly touched with humor when he added, "even if it's river water. Don't you ever forget that, little brother. And from now on, you stay the hell out of this barn."

He had turned away, fading into the night where Rio's friends had already disappeared, grateful for the opportunity to escape. Rio, however, had stood in the sweet, hay-scented darkness thinking about what Mac had said. Thinking about it now.

Blood's thicker than water. Maybe that was why he felt the urge to mount Diablo and ride to the McCullar place and warn Mac about what he'd overheard. Maybe those words, uttered more than ten years before, had made a bigger impression than he'd realized.

There had been other occasions when Rio suspected his big brother had used his authority on his behalf—minor scrapes with the law that had resulted in warnings rather than the arrests they had probably warranted. *Someone* had spoken in his defense, and the only person he knew who might have that kind of influence, and that kind of concern for him, was Mac.

Diablo butted him again, bringing him back to the reality of the present. Should he tell Mac McCullar about the vague threat he'd overheard or let it go, consider it only drunken bravado?

Blood's thicker than water. Even river water. Rio's beautiful mouth again curved into a slight smile. Maybe Mac was right. He had nothing to lose, and besides, it would give him an excuse to take Diablo for a run. A quick trip across the river and then he would sleep—better, he knew, than if he didn't make the effort to pass on that warning.

THE NATURAL FORD WAS closer to the smaller of the two McCullar houses, nearer the one that belonged to Chase

McCullar. The few times Rio had encountered his other half brother, their meetings had not been cordial.

The first time he'd been aware of that brother's existence—the first time he'd been aware of his parentage at all—had been when a group of hooting teenagers had taken delight in pointing Rio and his mother out to Chase McCullar and detailing in explicit terms their relationship to him. Rio had been only a child, maybe five years old, and he and his mother had come into Crystal Springs, the small south-Texas community nearest his father's ranch, to shop.

The boys' derisive comments had caused the stain of blood to rush under Marcella's olive cheeks. She had held her head high, seeming to ignore the catcalls, but the sapphire eyes of ten-year-old Chase McCullar had met his, filled with the same embarrassment and pain that Rio was feeling.

He thought that was probably the first time he had associated the word *bastard* with himself, certainly the first time he'd been aware of its meaning, of the stigma of his birth. But it had not been the last, of course.

He had learned to hide whatever he felt about his father under a cold layer of indifference and hostility, but the pain had never gone away. He had also pretended that he didn't care about the contempt revealed in Chase McCullar's eyes whenever they ran into each other during the next couple of decades, but he was honest enough with himself at least to know that wasn't true. He still cared what the McCullars thought of him, he realized. Maybe that was what had compelled him to make this foolhardy journey tonight.

For some reason he had stopped Diablo in the elongated shadows under the old cottonwood that stood in the yard, spending an unnecessary moment contemplating Chase McCullar's home. There were two cars parked before the house tonight and that was unusual. Chase no longer lived here, he knew. He was working with the DEA and the small house had sat empty for almost four years. But it wasn't empty tonight.

McCullar land, Rio thought, his eyes scanning the neatly maintained spread and unwillingly comparing it to the shack and the village where he lived. At his death, his father's land had been divided between his sons, the ranch evenly split between Mac and Chase. There had been nothing for Rio. His only inheritance was that unmistakable and unwanted McCullar resemblance.

He had already begun to turn the stallion when the door of the small ranch house suddenly swung open. Chase McCullar stepped out on the porch, his size leaving no doubt as to his identity, even in the darkness. He moved purposefully out into the revealing silver moonlight of the winter night.

Rio would never be sure of the impulse that prompted the exchange that followed. Perhaps it was simply an unacknowledged desire to replace the customary contempt in his half brother's eyes with some other emotion. Whatever the reason, giving Chase the warning he had intended to deliver to Mac would be the worst mistake of Rio's life— a mistake he would have ample time and more than ample opportunity to regret in the years to come.

"Give your brother a message," Rio said, his voice raised only enough to travel through the short distance that separated them. "Maybe save his life."

"What message?" Chase asked.

Since Chase hadn't questioned the identity of the speaker, Rio knew he'd been recognized. "Maybe he doesn't know who he's dealing with," he suggested, wondering if that could be true.

"And you're going to tell him?" Chase asked.

"Pesos or bullets," Rio said. "*You* tell him."

His half brother laughed, the sound dismissive and again contemptuous. "That's supposed to scare Mac off? You don't know my brother very well."

"*Your* brother," Rio said, emphasizing the pronoun.

Who is also my brother, he thought bitterly, *no matter how much you might wish to deny that relationship.*

"Tell *your* brother what I said," Rio repeated, feeling the surge of self-disgust flood his body. He knew it had been a mistake to come. This was a journey he had made only for Mac, he reminded himself. Not because he owed anything to this man. And so he added, hoping to convince Chase of the seriousness of that threat, "His life depends on it."

"You go to hell, you bastard," Chase said angrily. He descended the remaining steps and paused for a moment, looking into the shadows where Rio and Diablo stood before he added the final insult. "And get off McCullar land. You don't belong here. You've got no right to be here."

Bastard. The word reverberated with the old agonies. That was all Rio was and all he would ever be to this man. A bastard who didn't belong on McCullar land.

Fighting his fury, Rio turned the stallion. Behind him, the sound traveling clearly, he heard a woman's voice. "Who was that?"

And his half brother's answer. "No one. No one who matters."

Rio's hands were shaking with anger as he headed Diablo back to where they belonged, back toward their side of the border. Behind him he heard the sound of a car starting, and he turned in the saddle to watch Chase drive out of the yard and down the road that led to his brother's house. *His* brother, Rio thought bitterly, remembering Chase's words. To hell with the McCullars, he decided. To hell with thinking he could change anything about their relationship.

Just before Diablo stepped into the cold water of the river, Rio stopped him. Despite his fury, he realized that he had not done what he had come here tonight to do. Speaking to Chase had been a mistake, but it did not negate the importance of passing his warning on to Mac, the one to whom he owed the debt.

And so in the silver moonlight, he turned the horse, directing him again to his original destination. When he neared the ranch house, he could see his brothers, both of them. Mac was sitting in his pickup, the driver's-side door still open. It was obvious he had been waiting for Chase to join him.

They were talking to one another as Chase walked across the yard, closing the distance between them. The sound of their voices, but not the sense of the words reached out into the darkness. And then finally Rio was close enough to hear the last of the exchange.

"Rio have anything to do with that?" Chase asked.

"Not to my knowledge," Mac said decisively. He shifted his big body to the right, more inside the truck. Rio was close enough now that he could even see when Mac reached down to turn the key in the ignition.

And then the night exploded, the pickup seeming to mushroom upward into a shaft of fire, shooting sparks and debris high into the clear, cold desert air. Diablo reared in reaction, so that horse and rider were silhouetted against the red-tinged inferno of the sky.

By the time the stallion's reaching hooves touched down again, it was over. Mac McCullar's burning body had been thrown out onto the ground, and Chase was kneeling over him, trying to beat out the flames with his bare hands.

Too late, Rio thought again. He had been too late. *My brother,* he remembered thinking as he watched, paralyzed by horror. *My brother.* The words had formed again, this time echoing in loss and in grief.

Chapter One

Almost five years later

"You're sure you'll be all right out here?" Trent asked, his brow wrinkling as it always did when he was worried. Luckily, that habitual furrowing hadn't diminished his attractiveness. Someone had called Senator Trent Richardson the state's most eligible bachelor, and Anne knew he'd secretly been pleased by the flattering sobriquet. She loved her brother, but that didn't prevent her from recognizing his perhaps-justifiable lack of modesty.

"Of course, I'll be all right," Anne said. "What do you think's going to happen to me out here?"

Trent hadn't answered, but the look, that mixture of compassion and concern she had grown to hate, was in his eyes.

"I'll be fine," she reiterated. "I have Rommel for company, and frankly I'm looking forward to some peace and quiet. You and Jenny have a good time and don't worry about me."

"Are you sure that—"

"I don't want to go with you to Austin. And I don't want to go back home. Honestly, Trent, you'd think I was three years old, the way you're acting."

"I just thought you might have changed your mind," he said defensively. He bent to pick up Jenny's suitcases. "After all, there's not much to do around here. Jenny will tell you that.''

"Great," Anne said, but she softened the trace of sarcasm with a smile. "That's the whole point, in case you've forgotten. It's a vacation. You remember those. That's where you *don't* work for twenty-four hours a day. You ought to try one sometime.''

"I just wanted you to be sure—"

"I'm sure. Pack the car and stop worrying about me. Please, just stop worrying.''

Anne wanted to add more, but as always, she resisted the urge. She knew that whatever Trent said or did was motivated by love. More than ten years her senior, he had helped raise her and that had always made him overprotective. And now...

"Men," Jenny said softly, when Trent had finally gone outside. In her dark eyes was a conspiratorial glint of amusement instead of that unwelcome concern.

Anne liked Jenny McCullar. Maybe that sensitivity was one of the reasons. Of all the women her brother had dated, Jenny was also the least sophisticated and the most down-to-earth and therefore the one Anne would have once said was least likely to become a permanent fixture in his life.

Their relationship, however, had lasted now for almost a year, moving as slowly toward romance as Jenny had demanded. Trent joked that if he ever got Jenny McCullar to the altar, it would be by dragging her there, probably kicking and screaming. It had been the first time in her life Anne had ever heard her brother mention marriage, and despite the fact that he was thirty-six, she had to admit his use of the word had been a little shocking.

"I'm glad you're going to have to deal with him for a while," Anne said honestly.

She was tired of being hovered over. And she was just plain tired. That was one reason why, when Jenny had invited her for a visit to the ranch, she had accepted, surprising even herself.

She had made arrangements with the San Antonio Mission Museum where she was assistant curator to take the time off. She had ignored her boss's look of concern and the unasked questions in *his* eyes. That was something she had become adept at during the last few months. Peace and isolation had never before been high on Anne Richardson's list of priorities, but now she found she was really looking forward to spending some time alone. Maybe a chance to rethink everything. To reevaluate her life.

"Just for a couple of weeks," Jenny warned, "and then you get him back, I promise. If I can stand being social for two whole weeks."

"You'll have a wonderful time. That's one thing I truthfully can say about Trent. He knows how to show a girl a good time."

"And I'm not sure I like the sound of that," Jenny said.

"It'll be great," Anne assured her, smiling at the doubt in her voice. "Besides, you'll get a chance to meet all the important movers and shakers in Texas," she teased.

One of Jenny's dark brows arched, implying that she wasn't exactly sure that was an inducement.

Privately, Anne had wondered how Trent's cronies in the capital would react to Jenny. There wasn't an ounce of pretense or pretension in her small body. She was as open and honest as anyone Anne had ever met, and sometimes, she knew, those qualities weren't considered attributes in a political wife. But Jenny McCullar also carried the legacy of her martyred husband, and that was probably enough to overcome any shortcomings Texas society might find.

"Remember, if you need anything," Jenny said, "call Chase. He's five minutes away. He'll probably look in on you when he comes over to check on the horses. If he gets to be a nuisance, tell him to back off. Samantha knows where I keep everything. If you can't find something you need, call her. I taped their number on the receiver," Jenny reminded.

"I know. I'll be fine," Anne said again, fighting her

smile, thinking that Jenny might prove to be almost as bad as Trent, despite her disclaimer about men.

"I know you will. *I've* been fine out here for the last five years. It's just that sometimes…" Jenny hesitated. Her dark eyes, locked on Anne's, were full of understanding. "Sometimes it gets a little lonely. Some nights are so quiet, you feel like you're the only person in the world."

"That's good. I think maybe 'lonely' is what I'm looking for," Anne said softly.

Jenny nodded, but her eyes were suddenly considering. "I want to show you something before we go," she said. "While Trent's outside might be a good time."

Obediently Anne followed her hostess into her bedroom, wondering what this was about. It wasn't like Jenny to be mysterious. She watched as Jenny took a small key out of the jewelry box on the top of her bureau and used it to open the drawer of the table beside the bed. She pulled the drawer out, revealing its contents.

"It's one of Mac's guns," she said. "I gave the others away to people I thought might like to have them, some of his friends who I knew would value them." There was a small pause before she raised her eyes from the drawer to meet Anne's. "Maybe it's just the remnants of my Wild West ancestry, but I feel more comfortable knowing this is here. I've never taken it out of the drawer since I put it there. I know you won't need it, but I just wanted you to…know that it's here," she finished with a slight shrug.

"You're right," Anne said. "I won't need it, but I appreciate your showing it to me. Don't worry, Jenny. I feel very safe in your house."

Again Jenny's dark eyes considered her, but she didn't offer any of the platitudes Anne had come to dread.

"You *do* know how to use it?" she asked instead.

"That was one of the things…" Her voice faded suddenly. "Yes," she finished simply.

Surprisingly, Jenny leaned forward and pressed her

cheek against Anne's. Her small hands found the younger woman's shoulders and squeezed them gently.

"You're right. You'll be fine. See you in two weeks— *if* I can survive being a social butterfly that long."

Jenny turned and left the bedroom, thoughtfully leaving her alone. Anne looked down on the big revolver resting in the drawer. She resisted the urge to touch it, instead closing the drawer and using the key Jenny had left on the top of the table to relock it. She returned the key to the jewelry box and stood for a moment, trying not to remember.

From the bedroom window she could see Trent loading Jenny's bags into the trunk of his car. Rommel, her German shepherd, was eagerly circling him, excited by the activity. The dog had taken to the desert as if he had been born here, and after the cramped suburban grounds surrounding their house in San Antonio, she knew he was relishing the chance to enjoy the unlimited space.

We'll be fine here alone, she thought, wondering who she was trying to convince now. *Just fine,* she repeated determinedly in the face of her sudden self-mockery.

"THANKS FOR THE LIFT," Rio said softly to the rancher who had given him a ride out from town. For some reason he had found it hard to voice his gratitude. Maybe because "thanks" was a word he hadn't had much occasion to use in the last few years.

Surprisingly, Ben Pirkle hadn't recognized him, and he supposed he should be grateful for that as much as for the transport the rancher had offered. Rio had known he'd changed. He just hadn't realized how much until now.

He had aged, of course. After all, nearly five years was an endlessly long time—especially when you were faced, at twenty-three, with the prospect of serving that time in the most notorious prison in Texas. The beautiful features that had been almost boyish when Rio had begun his sentence had matured. And they had hardened. He was a man now. There was no doubt about that, given the unforgiving crucible in which his maturation had taken place.

"You sure this is the right place?" Pirkle asked dubiously. "Don't look like there's nothing out here."

"It's close enough," Rio said.

The dirt road that led to the McCullar ranch—ranches, he amended—was about four miles from here, traveling cross-country. He intended to walk the rest of the way until he reached the bluff that looked down on the two houses.

He didn't know why he had to come here, but he had acknowledged that this pilgrimage was necessary before he went back to his aunt's. Although crossing into Mexico would technically violate his parole, the border here was fluid enough that no one would ever know. Rio intended to be there only long enough to get Diablo and bring him back across.

"If you say so," the rancher said, still sounding puzzled, despite Rio's assurance, at the desolation that surrounded them. "You take care now, you hear?"

"Thanks," Rio said again. He shouldered his pack and waited until the pickup had bounced far enough down the one-lane for the dust cloud to provide cover, and then he began to move across the empty, arid grassland of south Texas.

For someone accustomed to this vista of cloudless blue that again stretched above him, to the endless sweep of the desert, and to the panorama of distant, haze-topped hills across the horizon, confinement itself had been one of the hardest things to bear. Locked behind bars like a trapped and hopeless animal. That was exactly what it had felt like.

He had found ways to occupy himself during those years, ways to prevent thinking. He had known it was either that or insanity. The weights had helped. He had taken out his anger by challenging the physical boundaries of his own body when he could challenge no others. He had worked mindlessly until his slender frame had gradually thickened with hard-packed, powerful muscle.

And then, like a miracle, he had discovered the prison library. Usually he had the place to himself, except for the section of law texts where the jailhouse lawyers toiled away, filing appeal after appeal.

There would be no appeal for Rio Delgado because he had known it would do no good. He had believed he would serve out his full sentence. He had resigned himself to that, nursing his bitterness over the injustice like a shield.

His own brother had called due every favor, every ounce of goodwill of the Texas law establishment, and had used it to ram through Rio's quick trial and conviction. The only concession the court-appointed defense lawyer had achieved was a change of venue, but even that had had little effect on the outcome.

Chase McCullar had used the natural horror of south Texans over what had happened to Mac as a bludgeon, an instrument of revenge against the man he held responsible, the man they all believed had been part of the conspiracy to kill the sheriff. Apparently, only Rio knew he had had nothing to do with Mac's death—and, of course, whoever had really planned that murder.

The parole board's decision to release him had been a shock, but then so had the fact that no one had come to the hearing to petition against it. After those first few brutal weeks of adjustment, he had been a model prisoner, knowing by then that he couldn't afford any incident that might lengthen his sentence. He recognized now that he couldn't have served any longer, couldn't have spent another day locked up like an animal.

Eventually his stride lengthened as he walked, thinking about it all again. Finally he was allowing himself to think about what had happened. He found a rhythm, and the strong muscles of his legs began eating up the distance. He found himself breathing more deeply, not from exertion, but savoring the hot, dry heat that again surrounded him, as familiar from his birth as his own heartbeat.

The two houses lay below, peaceful in the afternoon stillness. There had been additions to Chase McCullar's spread, he noticed. Some pretty elaborate stables had been added near the house. He smiled slightly, remembering the simple wooden box he'd built for Diablo. Quite a contrast. The same contrast between their possessions that had always existed.

His eyes eventually focused on the house where Mac had lived with his wife, Jenny. It was the original ranch house, the one where his own father had once lived. Unconsciously Rio's gaze moved across the ribbon of river to the convenient pass that led through the low hills of Mexico and then on to the village where his mother had grown up. Such a short distance for the endless gap that loomed between Andrew McCullar's three sons.

He didn't know why he had come up here, but he knew it was time to leave. He wondered briefly if the McCullars were even aware that he'd been released, if Chase or Mac's widow had kept up with the date. He had thought they would have been notified of the hearing, but maybe that wasn't the way it worked. Maybe that was why no one had come to speak against his parole.

It didn't matter, of course, whether or not his half brother was expecting him. He'd know soon enough that Rio was back. That was why he'd come home—to settle the score. If he didn't know it now, Chase McCullar would understand that soon enough.

"BUT THE PRIEST WROTE you a letter," his aunt's neighbor said again. As if that explained it all. As if that made any difference in what had happened.

Rio turned away from the tar-paper shack, hiding his feelings behind a rigid control he'd refined in prison. Someone else was living in the small house now. Apparently it hadn't taken their landlord long to rent it out again. His aunt had been dead more than three months, and Rio hadn't even known.

There had been a letter or two from her at the beginning,

but he hadn't been surprised when she had stopped writing to him. They hadn't really been close—his fault maybe, because he had always known she had never wanted the responsibility of her sister's wild, half-grown son. It was just that there had been no one else to take him in, nowhere else for him to go.

"And my horse?" He made himself voice the question, not daring to hope. Hope led only to disappointment. That was another lesson he'd learned too well. Besides, he already knew that the news about Diablo couldn't be good.

The small stable he'd built had been empty. He had gone there first, even before he'd tried to enter his aunt's house. He had disturbed a couple of chickens who had taken up residence inside the stall, nesting in the old hay.

"Dolores hadn't been able to work for a long time because she was so sick. There were many debts. We sold the black to pay those and for the funeral. Besides, we didn't know what else to do with him," the man said plaintively.

"Who bought him?" Rio asked.

He had closed his mind to Diablo's reaction to strange hands. The stallion had tolerated Dolores only because Rio had told him to, or more logically, others would say, because he associated her with his master. Rio had worried about whether the black would allow his aunt to care for him while he was in prison, but Dolores's death had not been something he had ever considered. His aunt had been young, younger than his mother, and now she was dead, too, and the black was gone.

"The lady from across the river," the man said. "She came to buy him."

"What lady?" Rio asked sharply. Most men were justifiably terrified of the black. He couldn't imagine why a woman would take on the stallion.

"McCullar. Señora McCullar," the man said. "She knows horses, so she wanted him, despite his reputation. I thought she might back out. They had a hell of a time loading him. I was afraid..."

The man hesitated because he didn't understand what was happening in Rio's eyes. They were so different now than they had been when he had gone away. They were black and opaque, as if all the light had gone out of them. And seeing the coldness in them, the man shivered. He wasn't sorry when Rio Delgado shouldered his pack again and turned away without asking any other questions.

After all, the man thought, there had been nothing else he could tell Dolores's nephew. He had known how much the boy loved that horse. They had all known, but still there had been nothing else they could do with the stallion. Shaking his head, he watched the tall, muscled body disappear into the shimmer of late-afternoon heat, heading back in the direction from which he'd come. Back toward the river.

"YOU JUST WENT OUT," Anne Richardson said when the cold nose of her shepherd pushed under her elbow. "Right before it got dark. I'm not letting you out again. Not until bedtime. You'll just have to wait."

The big dog sat down beside the couch where she was lying. Even as she had talked to him, Anne had kept her gaze locked on the print of the book she was pretending to read, but she knew that the eyes of the shepherd had not left her face. She could feel his concentration on her, willing her to obey.

Except I'm the one who's supposed to be in charge, she thought, holding her eyes on the page in front of her through sheer determination.

That was something they had taught her in the obedience classes she and Rommel had attended. Let the dog know from the first who's in charge. The only trouble was that in Rom's case she had never been entirely sure just who that was.

She glanced at the waiting dog. It was a mistake, of course, because it signaled his success. Having acquired her attention, he barked once, short and sharp, but as articulate as a command.

"You just want to chase something," she said. Almost without her volition, her fingers reached out to caress him. "You'll be gone half the night chasing some jackrabbit, and I won't get a bit of sleep worrying about you."

That was a joke, she thought, rubbing the deep softness behind his ear. She wouldn't sleep anyway, whether the dog was here or not. Despite her repeated assurances to her brother and to Jenny, she had known she probably wasn't going to sleep. Not the first few nights, anyway. She didn't sleep too well anywhere, but all alone in a strange house, there was about a snowball's chance in hell she'd be able to get a good night's sleep.

She should certainly feel safe enough with the shepherd around. He had been trained to attack at her command. Although it had been Trent's idea to get the dog, she'd gone along, not because she'd believed it would solve anything, but because she'd always loved animals, and it had been easier than not to give in. Keeping things uncomplicated had been important at the time.

The dog barked again and placed his big paw on her arm.

"I said *no*," she said, turning resolutely back to her book. She couldn't even remember what had been happening in the story. Not much, she guessed, or she'd have some clue about what she'd read.

Rommel turned around, the movement of his powerful body cramped between the coffee table and the couch, and then he headed for the back door. She could hear him in the kitchen, shuffling and whining. Twice he barked as sharply as he had when he'd sat down beside her.

"All right," she said under her breath. Maybe he really *did* need to go out. She'd be a pretty poor houseguest if she let her dog have an accident in her prospective sister-in-law's kitchen. Trent would never forgive her even if Jenny did.

"I'm coming. I'm coming," she muttered as she put her book facedown on the coffee table and crawled out of the depths of the low couch. "Don't scratch Jenny's door, you big nitwit," she ordered loudly, talking to him as she always did, as if he understood every word she said.

Maybe he had, because by the time she got to the back door, the scratching and whining had stopped. He was sitting at attention, looking expectantly at the door.

"There's nothing out there," she assured him. But even as she said it, her hand hesitated, hovering just over the knob. *Nothing out there?* she thought. *How can I really be sure of that?*

"*Damn* it," she said softly, again under her breath. She closed her eyes, willing herself not to think about that possibility. She was not a coward, she told herself angrily. She never had been. She hadn't been raised that way, and she damn sure wasn't going to start now. It was no excuse that she was in an unfamiliar place.

She opened her eyes, determined not to give in to her fear. The dog was still waiting for her to turn the handle. Except now...

"Just a minute, Bozo," she said softly, looking down into the dark, intelligent eyes. "You're just going to have to wait one more minute."

She turned away and walked quickly down the dark hallway. Trent had warned her that Jenny's house was a little rustic, but she had loved the ranch. It might be simple, but everything was tasteful and comfortable.

Everything, she thought again, except the paper that covered the walls of this narrow hall. The red and pink roses were overblown and cheap looking, out of keeping with the rest of the house, and Anne almost cringed whenever she encountered them. They weren't so bad tonight. Not too garish in the dark.

When she entered Jenny's unlighted bedroom, she felt like an intruder. Using the key Jenny had shown her, Anne opened the drawer of the small table beside the bed. Mac

McCullar's revolver was still there, of course, right where it was supposed to be, where it had been this afternoon. She picked it up without hesitation, confident in handling it, and checked to make sure it was loaded.

The gun was a big .45. Mac had been this county's sheriff, and she remembered that in the Old West, lawmen used a Colt they called the Peacemaker. If the bad guys *weren't* peaceful, one shot from that and they would be. This gun would have the same kind of power, powerful enough that it wouldn't even demand dead-on accuracy. If you shot somebody with this thing, even in an extremity, they weren't going to get very far.

She did hesitate when she noticed the phone number Jenny had taped to the receiver. *"Call Chase if you have any trouble,"* Jenny had offered. It was tempting. Only, the dog wanting to go for a run didn't exactly qualify in most people's minds as "trouble." And therefore, it shouldn't in hers, she decided.

Resolutely, she turned away from the easy temptation of calling for help and headed back to the kitchen. It didn't look as if the shepherd had moved, his attention still focused intently on the doorknob. Maybe he was thinking he could will it to turn, Anne thought. He hadn't had such a tough time getting her to do what he'd wanted.

"Don't you dare run off," she ordered, reaching for the knob. Again her hand hesitated, the fingers suddenly trembling. Her lips tightened with her determination, and she made herself fasten her hand over the old-fashioned glass knob and turn it. Then she forced herself to open the door.

The shepherd shot through the narrow opening and into the outside darkness like a black-and-silver shadow. Her eyes followed his path across the moonlit yard. There wasn't any doubt where he was headed. Even from here she could see the slit between the double doors of the barn. *And no jackrabbit opened those,* she thought.

She had known there was more to the dog's agitation than the need to visit the nearest tree, which, considering the countryside that surrounded the ranch, might be several miles away. She wasn't amused by that errant thought, of course. She was scared. The cold, black ice of her fear was edging up from the frozen knot that had already formed in her stomach, but she fought it. She was *not* a coward, she reminded herself like a litany, and she had options.

She could call Jenny's brother-in-law. *And look like a fool if there is no one out there,* she acknowledged. She could picture Trent's face when he got back and heard the story. She knew she wasn't up to facing that.

Or she could just close and lock the kitchen door and leave the dog in the barn with whoever was out there. Except he was her dog and her responsibility.

And the other option? She hefted the reassuring weight of Mac McCullar's big revolver in her hand. Nobody was going to bother her as long as she held this. That was one thing she was absolutely certain of. Nobody was ever going to get close enough to hurt her as long as she had this in her hand.

Chapter Two

The black wasn't in Jenny McCullar's barn. It had taken Rio only about five minutes to be sure of that, but of course, he had already had an orientation with the building's layout—a long time ago. He glanced back at the double doors and could almost see Mac McCullar standing in them, looking larger than life and terrifying to the kid he had been then.

Rio put his hand against the wooden post that supported the last stall and leaned his forehead against the back of it. He closed his eyes, thinking about the loss of the black. It completed the loss of everything he had ever cared about.

Somehow, that realization opened the floodgates, also letting in the memories of the last time he'd been in this barn. He could almost taste the copper tinge of the fear he'd felt then, and he even remembered his initial bitterness at Mac's warning.

It was, however, the other that had stayed with him during the hard years of his growing up. *"Blood's thicker than water,"* Mac had told him. But now, standing in his dead brother's barn, surrounded by that memory, he knew Mac had been wrong. Chase McCullar had proved that.

The sound he heard was very soft, almost hidden by the animal noises that had surrounded him since he'd entered the barn's scented darkness. He lifted his head in response and watched with fascinated horror as the crack he'd left between the double doors slowly began to widen. The moonlight was strong enough to create a distinct demarcation between the shadowed interior and the outside.

The hair lifted on the back of Rio's neck, and he held his breath, dreading the sight of whatever appeared in that opening. He resisted the sudden superstitious urge to cross himself, knowing logically that his memories couldn't possibly conjure up Mac McCullar's ghost.

The slight figure that appeared in the doorway was not his brother—not either one of them, Rio acknowledged, relief washing through him. His heart had begun beating again, and his lips tilted, mocking his own irrational fear.

It was a woman. She held a gun in her right hand. The moonlight glinted off its metallic surface, just as it played in the lightness of her hair. She was wearing something dark and loose, maybe a nightshirt, and her legs, revealed below its short length, seemed endless. Heartbreakingly long. Slim and yet beautifully shaped.

"I know you're in here," she said. There was no tremor in her voice. No trace of fear. Her other hand had moved to support the right one around the grip of the big handgun. Despite its size, she held it competently. And confidently.

Rio felt nothing but admiration, in spite of all the unpleasant elements of his situation—elements he was just beginning to realize. Like the fact that he was trespassing, a convicted felon out on parole for only one day and trespassing in the last place on earth he should be.

And the fact that that was a damn big gun and she had every right to use it. Even he acknowledged that. A woman living alone out here had every right to protect herself. Coming out to face him in the darkness had been foolish, maybe, but incredibly brave.

"Step out into the light," she ordered.

So you can put a bullet into my heart? he thought, his lips curving again, almost in amusement, despite his predicament. Instead of obeying, he eased backward, moving more deeply into the shadows. The horse that was occupying the stall shifted uneasily, the sound too revealing of the intruder's position.

"Come out *now,*" the woman ordered in response to those sounds.

She had taken a step farther into the shadowed interior. It was harder to see her since she had moved out of the light filtering in through the open door. Which meant, he realized, that she probably couldn't see him at all. And she wouldn't shoot blindly, not with her livestock around. *Stalemate,* he decided, leaning back against the wooden wall of the stall he was now sharing with the mare.

With one hand, he found her nose and gave a reassuring rub along the jaw. She lowered her head into his caress and again he smiled. He had always had a way with women. Apparently he hadn't lost his touch.

There was something about that thought that disturbed him. Maybe because it had been a hell of a long time since he'd had a woman. Too long. Nearly five years too long. But he couldn't allow himself to think that way about the one who was standing in the center of the barn. There were plenty of other women who would welcome Rio Delgado into their beds—*back* into their beds.

He fought to block the unwanted thoughts of *this* woman. His hand unconsciously continued its unthinking seduction of the mare, but his eyes again examined, almost against his will, the length of slender leg revealed by whatever the woman was wearing.

He took a breath, fighting the effects of that examination. She was his brother's widow, he reminded himself. Who else would be guarding this ranch tonight? Somehow that realization had the desired effect. He leaned his head against the roughness of the planks behind him and closed his eyes. The heat that had invaded his groin faded into regret.

Mac McCullar's widow was standing between him and the door, very efficiently holding a gun pointed in his direction, and there was probably not another soul in this world that she'd rather use it on. She would shoot him in a heartbeat if she recognized him.

"Looking at you," Mac had said, *"there isn't much doubt that your mama was right about what she put down."* There still wasn't, he knew, despite the changes prison had etched in him like acid.

He opened his eyes again, knowing that shutting them wasn't going to make the predicament he'd gotten himself into go away. He and Mac's widow could stand here until dawn, he supposed, and when the sun rose, she'd recognize him and shoot him. Or he could try to overpower her and take the gun away. Only she looked like that wouldn't be as easy as it sounded, not with the way she was handling the weapon, and he didn't relish taking a bullet in the gut.

Or he could tell her the truth. Tell her why he was here and finally tell her that he hadn't had anything to do with her husband's death. She wouldn't shoot blindly, not with her horses in here, he reminded himself. At least he hoped not.

So he took a breath. "Mrs. McCullar," he said softly.

There was silence for a moment. Even the animals had responded to his voice, waiting in the darkness, momentarily unmoving.

"I'm not Mrs. McCullar," she said after a moment. "Who are you and what do you want?"

Not Jenny McCullar. Not Mac's wife. *Then who the hell are you?* Rio mentally repeated her question, trying to work it out. Maybe Jenny had sold the ranch after her husband's death. But his aunt's neighbor had said Mrs. McCullar had bought the stallion, so that must mean…

"I came to find my horse," he said. It didn't make much sense, but he realized that only after he'd confessed it. It was simply the truth.

"Your horse?" the woman repeated. "You're trying to find *your* horse in Jenny's barn? I don't think so."

"She bought him," Rio explained. He had been released

from prison yesterday and here he was, breaking into some-one's barn to retrieve a horse that he no longer owned.

"Then he's not *your* horse," she said reasonably.

"He shouldn't have been sold. It was a mistake. Some-one else sold him."

There had been a minute relaxation about her stance. She was no longer totally focused on the threat he represented, no longer so careful. The relaxation of her guard had been so subtle that Rio probably couldn't have articulated how he had been aware of it. Reading body language had been a survival skill in the last few brutal years, and he *was* aware.

Talking to him had made him real to her, he supposed. He was a person now and not just a menacing figure in the shadows. That was to his advantage, of course, that small relaxation, that acknowledgment that he was a fellow hu-man being. It might mean a split-second delay in her de-cision to pull that trigger her finger was still competently resting against.

"So you just came here to steal him," she suggested.

He hesitated, wondering if that was what he had in-tended. That would have been a hell of a violation of his parole, he thought, his mouth tilting in recognition of how stupid this entire escapade had been. He hadn't done any-thing this stupid since, at age thirteen, he'd broken into this barn the first time. Except the night he'd tried to tell Chase McCullar about the threat against his brother's life.

"I needed to see him," he said. Again, surprisingly, he realized he had told her the truth.

There was another hesitation, a silence as she thought about that. "Why?" she asked.

"Because…it's been a long time."

"You were away," she suggested, "and someone sold your horse."

"Yes," he agreed.

"And you just wanted to…visit him?" There was mock-ery in her tone.

"Yes," he said again, knowing suddenly that that was the total reality of why he was here. Sentiment. Stupid sentiment.

"You must think I'm a fool," she said. The relaxation had disappeared.

"I guess I'm the fool," he said softly. That was certainly true. "But I'm not here to hurt you. My horse isn't here. Apparently what I was told about the sale wasn't true."

"Someone told you Jenny bought your horse."

"Mrs. McCullar," he agreed.

"Maybe..." the woman began, and then the sentence was cut off. The word hung in the air between them. "Maybe you just better go," she suggested instead of finishing whatever she'd begun. "If the horse isn't here, there isn't any reason for you to be here, either."

"You're letting me go?" Rio asked. He straightened in surprise, pulling his shoulders away from the wall of the stall.

"Why not?" she asked. "You found out that what you're looking for isn't here. I certainly don't want you to be here, but I don't particularly want to have to shoot you. So I guess the best thing would be if you just...leave. Just get off McCullar land."

Rio laughed, the sound harsh and bitter. He couldn't help it. That was the same "invitation" Chase had issued before he'd had him railroaded. *"Get off McCullar land. You don't belong here."* He still didn't, but at least now he had accepted that he never would.

"You think this is funny?" she said angrily. "Breaking and entering? You think this is something to laugh at?"

"No, ma'am," Rio acknowledged softly. He didn't. He'd had enough of living dangerously for one night. He couldn't go back to prison. He knew that. Breathing desert air again had made him know that he would never survive another incarceration, would never be able to endure it again, no matter what he told himself. He wouldn't ever go back, so, trying to mollify her, he simply agreed with her. "I don't think it's funny."

"Okay," she said, sounding satisfied that she had forced the admission from him. "I'm going to back out of the barn, but I'll be watching you as you leave."

It was a good plan, simple but effective. He wouldn't know where she was, but he'd be aware that she—and the gun—were watching his every move. He was luckier than he had any right to be that she was going to let him go.

He watched her back through the opening, her long, fair hair once more reflecting the moonlight. When she had disappeared into the outside darkness, he obediently started across the empty space between the stall where he had been hiding and the double doors. He had almost reached them when the whole thing fell apart.

"Help me," a woman's voice begged hoarsely in Spanish. The entreaty had come from the back of one of the empty stalls he'd ignored in his initial search for the black. "For the love of God, please help me," the plea came again.

Against his will, Rio glanced to the side, into the darkness where the agonized voice had come from. He swallowed, fighting his natural inclination to respond. His gaze moved back to the opening. Escape. He had been given an unexpected—and considering his stupidity, an undeserved—chance to melt away into the desert night. No one would ever be able to prove he had been here. No one would ever know he'd been foolish enough to set foot on Mac McCullar's land.

"Please," the voice said again, the sound abruptly becoming a gasp.

Was that pain? he wondered. And even if it was, he told himself, it was none of his business. Her pain was not his concern. He had enough trouble of his own without taking on someone else's. *"For the love of God,"* she had begged. Only the love of God wasn't anything Rio Delgado acknowledged anymore. That had all been destroyed, burned out of him, and whatever was going on here was nothing to him. Less than nothing.

Three steps and he could be through the doors that beckoned and away from the danger his sentimentality had already gotten him into. He took one of those steps, and the sound from the stall came again, inarticulate this time. Guttural and animalistic in its agony.

Rio closed his eyes, fighting its pull, but despite everything that had happened to him as a result of the last time he'd tried to help someone, he still couldn't force himself to take that next step. He had never in his life walked away from a creature in pain. He took a deep breath, knowing he was a fool, and then, instead of taking the escape the woman with the gun had offered him, he turned to his right, toward the shadowed darkness of the stall.

Rio was unaware until the shepherd growled that the dog was there. The sound came from low in the animal's throat and was clearly menacing, a warning. Rio couldn't see him, nothing beyond the shape of his big body standing guard, alert and poised to attack.

"She asked me to help her," Rio explained, speaking to the dog in Spanish. "But I can't help her if you don't let me get closer. I'm not going to hurt you. Or her. I don't like to hurt things. I'm not that kind of man. You know that, little one."

The shepherd made another sound, but the quality was different. Obviously different. In the darkness, Rio stretched out his hand and held it absolutely motionless as the coldness of the dog's nose brushed across his knuckles and then down over his fingers. He still couldn't see much about the animal beyond its size.

"I told you," Rio said, "and now you have seen that it is true. These are not hands that hurt."

The dog whined softly in response, and Rio took a step farther into the stall. But then the dog growled, and again the man stopped in recognition of that command.

"She needs help," he said. "You have tried to help her,

but you know that what you can do is not enough. You will have to let me help. You'll know that if you think about it.''

''The problem might be that he doesn't speak Spanish.''

The voice came from behind him, but Rio didn't turn around. His entire attention was focused on willing the dog to let him get to whoever had called for help. Now, apparently, the woman with the gun had come back inside to see what was keeping him.

''It doesn't matter,'' Rio said. It didn't, of course. They spoke the same language, whatever language he was speaking. His tone was what the dog heard and responded to. And to whatever else was in Rio's seductive voice, to the magic that had always been there.

''For the love of God, help me,'' the voice from the stall begged again.

''Let him by, Rom,'' Anne ordered. Her own Spanish was sketchy, but she had recognized enough of what had been said to know that someone was begging for help.

''Call him,'' Rio suggested.

She didn't have much faith that the dog would obey, not if he'd made up his mind he was supposed to guard the woman in the stall. *Just exactly who's in charge here?* she thought again, this time in resignation, waiting to be disappointed.

''Heel, Rommel,'' she commanded.

The shepherd moved out of the stall, brushing past the waiting man, and then sat down on his haunches beside her. Anne reached down and touched his head. ''Good boy,'' she said disbelievingly.

The man had already begun moving. He disappeared into the blacker shadows at the back of the enclosure, and Anne listened breathlessly to the conversation that whispered out of that darkness. She caught an occasional word, but they were speaking too softly and too rapidly for her to understand even the gist of what was being said.

''What's wrong?'' she asked finally. They had stopped

talking and she could hear the gasping breathing of the woman beginning again. And then again the agonized moaning. "What's going on?" Anne asked over the climbing horror of the sound.

"I don't suppose you know anything about delivering babies?" the man's softly pleasant voice asked, its tone such a contrast to the other.

Babies? My God, did he say babies?

"No," Anne whispered, trying to marshall what she did know. Hot water. Scissors. Towels. "No," she said again, just in case he thought that because she was a woman she could do something to help.

"I was afraid of that," he said, and she heard a thread of amusement in his resignation.

"Do you?" she asked hopefully.

"Horses. Dogs. Not people," he admitted. And then he added, "At least not yet."

There was nothing else for a few moments. More breathing. Almost panting now. A low, heartfelt moan of pain.

"So what do we do?" Anne asked. She had finally remembered to lower the gun she had been directing toward the sound of the man's voice. She didn't think she was going to shoot him. Not unless he tried to leave her here alone with the woman who was in labor. If he did that...*then* she might.

"You have a car?" he asked. He had been whispering to the woman again, the sound of whatever he was saying subtly comforting Anne's fears, too, although that had certainly not been his intent. He hadn't been talking to her and she didn't understand Spanish, but still there was something about his voice...

"A truck. Jenny's pickup. The keys are in the house."

"Get them," he ordered. "And lock the dog inside."

"Why?" she asked, wary again of his intentions.

"So he won't follow us."

"But...where are we going? I mean, I don't know anything about the local hospitals, about what's close enough."

"There's only one place close enough. I'll show you the way. Just get the keys."

She stood there thinking about it, about getting into the truck with a couple of strangers, and then the low moan came again. This time it seemed to grow and expand until it filled the darkness with its pain, and through the crescendo of suffering, she could still hear his voice, soft and yet remarkably powerful in its compassion. Comforting. Reassuring.

"Now," he ordered sharply. The single English word was directed at her, of course, and then the compelling tone slipped back into Spanish.

Anne turned and ran out of the barn toward the ranch house. She had to stop halfway there and call Rommel to come with her. She was surprised again when, after a short delay at one of Jenny's shrubs, he obeyed her. Probably because the man had told him to, she thought. In Spanish, no doubt, she acknowledged in amused disgust, as she again began to run toward the house, the shepherd at her heels.

THEY WERE ALL THREE packed into the seat of the pickup. Anne had found herself behind the wheel, and of course, that was because he was still helping the woman. He had brought her out of the barn after Anne had pulled the truck up beside the double doors. He had carried her effortlessly, it seemed. That had been the first time she'd gotten a good look at him, and she hadn't been able to stop looking at him since.

He was... She hesitated, trying to find a more acceptable term, but she had already recognized that there wasn't one. He was *beautiful*. That was the only word that fit. He was Mexican, Anne thought. Latino, she amended. It was the politically correct term, since she couldn't really know his nationality.

His features were incredibly fine drawn. Beautifully aligned. The face was put together with compelling perfection, like some Renaissance drawing. Da Vinci, maybe. A sketch for an angel for one of those remarkable frescoes. He ought to be making movies. Modeling. Doing magazine ads. Doing something besides sneaking into someone else's barn to steal a horse.

Her cheeks flamed with heat when she remembered that his eyes had lifted suddenly from the pregnant woman to find Anne's fascinated gaze on his face. Those dark eyes, surrounded by their sweep of incredibly long, black lashes, had revealed only amusement at her gaping fascination.

He was probably used to that reaction, she thought—the unthinking reaction she had had to his face. Someone who looked like he did had probably grown up accustomed to the adulation of women.

Except she wasn't one of them. Beauty was only skin-deep. She had more than ample reason to understand that. She should be the last person in the world to be attracted to a man because of his looks.

"The next right," he directed, breaking into her reverie.

His remarks to her had all been made in English. The rest of the time he talked softly to the woman in Spanish. Anne was aware that his dark, long-fingered hand was cupped low on the woman's protruding abdomen. Occasionally, out of the corner of her eye, she could see it move over the thin, tightly stretched cotton of the shapeless dress the woman wore, caressing an accompaniment to the words he continued to whisper.

It should be wrong that he was touching the woman in such an intimate way. And yet it wasn't. It didn't seem any more inappropriate than a doctor's examination. Or a mother's touch of her frightened child. Whatever he was doing was asexual. He wasn't a man touching a woman. He was simply a voice. A caressing hand. A reassuring human contact.

Resolutely, Anne pulled her mind away from the image

of that strong, dark hand moving over the woman's belly and back to the narrow, unpaved road he'd directed her to turn down. A small adobe building appeared suddenly in the beams of the truck's headlights.

"That's it," he said.

Anne parked in front and then hurried around to the other side of the pickup. He was already lifting the woman from the seat. The muscles in his shoulders bunched with the strain, but he was apparently far stronger than he looked. She tried the door of the building and found it was locked.

"Knock," he ordered. "Doc's here. He lives here."

She knocked, too softly at first to arouse anybody. And then louder. Finally she pounded the flat of her hand against the wood. Still there was no response.

"Move," he said.

Despite the burden he carried, he raised his knee and kicked the door with the bottom of his boot. The sound reverberated in the desert stillness. "Doc!" he shouted. The contrast between the shout and the unceasing whispering caress that had been his voice was a shock, but it had the desired effect.

The lights came on, shining out through the front windows into the darkness where they stood together. She glanced at her unknown companion again. Profile this time. It was as perfect as the other view. And again she forced her eyes away. This wasn't like her. She had no explanation for why she couldn't seem to stop looking at him.

She was thankful when the door opened and the old man appeared. His white hair was wildly disordered and his pupils were dilated. It was obvious he had been asleep.

"What the *hell?*" he asked softly, his eyes making the same fascinated appraisal of her companion's face that her own had made.

"She's in labor," the man from the barn said. "But something's gone wrong."

"Bring her inside," the old man ordered, moving out of the doorway.

Anne trailed them in, but neither paid any attention to her. She closed the outer door and then followed the exodus into the examination room. The man was laying the woman on the table as she came into the room.

She stood in the doorway, silently watching, just as he did, while Doc scrubbed his hands and began his examination. Somehow that didn't seem wrong, either—for them to be here, watching that examination. Somehow they had a part in whatever was going to happen.

"Breech," the doctor said.

"I thought so." The man's soft agreement was in English.

"I didn't know you were back," the old man said.

"Today."

"You do what they said you did?" the doctor asked, his eyes moving for the first time from his patient to the man who had brought her in, even as his hands were still occupied with the examination of the baby's position.

"No."

The denial was only one word, but its tone caused the old man to nod in agreement. "I didn't think so," he said. "I never thought so, if that's any comfort."

There was no response from the dark man, so the doctor nodded to himself again before he asked, "How'd you get mixed up in *this?*"

Anne wondered if he thought the man had something to do with the baby. And then *she* wondered. Was it possible that this was his baby? Was that why he'd stopped to help the woman? Had she followed him into the barn?

"I was looking for my horse."

"I should have known," the old man said, gentle amusement in his voice. "I think I'm going to need you."

"You know I don't know anything about delivering babies. Not human ones, anyway."

"You just talk, hotshot. I'll do all the work—as always."

"Talking's what I do best," the man said, but there was a hint of amusement in that, too.

"Second best is what I heard. Who are *you?*" the old man asked, and it took Anne a second to realize he was talking to her.

"I'm Anne Richardson," she said.

The old man's head came up again at that, and he took time to look at her, over his shoulder as he worked, so she knew he had recognized her name. She wondered what he knew about her—other than the fact she was Senator Richardson's sister. She glanced toward the dark man, but there had been no reaction to her name in his perfect features.

The old man's eyes also moved to the other man and then came back to her face. "Senator Richardson's sister?"

"Yes," she acknowledged softly.

"I'm Tom Horn. I'm not even going to ask how *you* got mixed up in this," he said.

"It was Jenny McCullar's barn he was looking for his horse in."

"You're staying at Jenny's?"

"She and my brother are in Austin. I'm...ranch-sitting, I guess."

"Got a little bit more than you bargained for," Doc Horn suggested.

"Yes," she said truthfully.

"You know who he is?"

The man she'd found in Jenny's barn moved slightly in response to that, so that Anne's gaze was attracted toward him again. He wasn't looking at her, but at the old man.

"No," she said, her eyes coming back to the doctor.

He nodded. "I didn't think you did. His name's Rio, but you might want to forget you heard it. You gonna stand there all night?" he asked. And Anne realized he wasn't talking to her anymore.

"What do you want me to do?" the man named Rio asked. He still hadn't looked at Anne.

"It's too late for a C-section. I can't take a chance on putting her under, not with what's going on with this baby. I'm gonna have to turn him and get him out in a hurry. I'll take care of the baby. Looking after *her* is up to you. Let's see how good you really are. See if you live up to your billing,'' the old man suggested, his hands beginning the procedure he had told them about. ''Why don't you just start talking.''

Chapter Three

"Know anything about babies?" Doc Horn asked Anne after it was over. It was the same question that Rio had asked her in the barn, so she gave the answer she had given then.

"No," she whispered. What she did know was that she had just witnessed a miracle, and she found it a little hard to talk after the experience. Mother and son both seemed to be doing fine. Against all expectations. Against all the odds.

"At least know how to hold one, don't you?"

She nodded, her blue eyes moving from his to the small bundle he was holding out to her. Doc had wrapped the baby in a clean towel after he'd done the necessary things for him.

"One of you needs to hold him while I finish up with his mother. I thought you might like to. If not..." He waited, his dark eyes searching her face, assessing her hesitation.

"I'll hold him," she said finally.

The baby felt a little cold, despite the towel and the warmth of the clinic. She cuddled him against her breasts. With her right hand, she moved the towel aside, revealing small, rounded features and eyes that seemed as black as those of the man she'd found in the barn. Unconsciously, she smiled down into their unfocused darkness.

"Looks good," Doc said, and she glanced up to find him watching her.

"He's going to be all right?" she asked, her gaze falling again to the baby. "Isn't he?"

"Far as I can tell," Doc agreed, turning back to the mother. "There's no guarantee, but I think we were in time. She'd never have delivered that baby on her own. It was lucky the two of you found her."

"Lucky she was in the barn," Anne said unthinkingly. And then she asked the pertinent question. "Why *was* she in Jenny's barn?"

"You tell her," Doc suggested, his hands already involved in the remaining tasks of the delivery.

"She wanted the baby to be born here," Rio complied. "At this clinic."

"This side of the border."

"She crossed the river just so the baby could be born in the States?"

"Just?" Rio repeated softly.

It had been a foolish question. This baby was a U.S. citizen. Doc would fill out the birth certificate to that effect.

"It just seems so dangerous for her to be alone," she defended. "Why didn't her husband come with her?"

"She says her husband came north more than five months ago. Someone had promised him work—good work for top wages. He was supposed to send for her as soon as he found a place for them to live, but...apparently something happened. She doesn't know what."

"She hasn't heard from him?" she asked.

"Not since he left."

"Now that ain't the first time I've heard that story," Doc said. The words were muttered under his breath, almost musingly, as he worked.

"They'd agreed that the baby should be born here," Rio continued, "and when he didn't send for her, she didn't know anything else to do."

"So she came across the river alone to have her baby."

"Lots do," Doc said. "I've delivered more babies through the years than most obstetricians."

"How many years?" Anne asked him, smiling.

"More than fifty," the old man said. "He's one of 'em."

It took a second for her to realize who he meant—not the baby she was holding, but the man still standing beside the table.

"You delivered...him?" she asked unbelievingly. Her lips moved upward slightly, reacting to the unexpected image of this dark, beautiful man as a baby, just like the one she was cradling against the warmth of her body. That was an incredible stretch of the imagination, given his size and strength.

Rio's eyes had fastened on her face, watching her reaction. "My mother wanted *me* to be born here," he said. "She made that same journey. Also alone."

There was some emotion in his voice that Anne couldn't read. Anger, maybe, but she couldn't imagine why he would be angry about that. "She wanted to be sure you'd be a U.S. citizen."

He laughed, the sound soft and without humor. It was mocking instead, like his unexpected laughter in the barn. "With all the rights and privileges thereof."

"I don't understand," Anne said, holding his eyes. They were darker than the baby's, she realized, but just as unfathomable.

"It doesn't matter," Rio said finally, the downward sweep of lashes hiding whatever emotion had been there.

"It will to some folks," Doc suggested, without looking up. "It's going to matter a whole hell of a lot to some people around here."

THEY WERE IN THE TRUCK together, heading back to the ranch in the near-dawn dimness. In the afterglow of holding the baby, of watching his birth, Anne had forgotten that she should be apprehensive about getting into this truck with a total stranger. It didn't feel as if the man Doc had introduced as Rio was a stranger, but of course, he was. She still knew nothing about him except his name.

And the fact that he had loved a horse enough to try to find him in someone else's barn, almost getting himself shot in the process. That he had chosen to help the Mexican woman rather than leave when Anne had given him the chance. That Doc had delivered him.

"What did Doc mean?" she asked, thinking about that strange conversation. She turned toward Rio, again studying the perfection of his profile, clearly limned against the lighter darkness outside the window.

He glanced at her, black eyes leaving the narrow road he was expertly negotiating. He was driving far faster than she had on the way to the clinic. It had seemed natural to let him drive since he was familiar with the country, and so she hadn't questioned when he'd politely opened the passenger door for her. She had just obediently handed him Jenny's keys and gotten into the truck.

She was beginning to realize she had done several things tonight that she shouldn't have done. Things she almost certainly wouldn't have done if she'd had more time to think about them. Things she wouldn't dare confess to Trent.

"About what?" Rio asked. His eyes had moved back to focusing on the road ahead. She watched the muscle beside his mouth move, tightening and then releasing its tension as he waited for her to answer.

"That it would be better if I forgot your name."

"Doc was just trying to warn you," he said finally.

"About what?" she asked. "About you?"

"About knowing me."

"Do I need to be warned?" she asked. "You don't seem very dangerous to me." He didn't. Not anymore. Not after she had watched him with the woman. She remembered the movement of his hand over the bulging protrusion that had been the unborn baby—remembered its slow, gentle caress.

"That's what Doc was trying to tell you. Some people

think I am. Those same people will think that you shouldn't be around me.''

It intrigued her, that both he and Doc had warned her off. The fascination of forbidden fruit, maybe. Only she still didn't know why he should be.

"You think you could be less cryptic?" she suggested. Her tone was a little amused. She couldn't imagine what this man had done that made him so totally off-limits. She waited, watching the muscle beside his mouth move again, tighten and then release, before he spoke.

"I spent the last five years in Huntsville."

Whatever she had expected him to say, it wasn't that. The quiet statement literally took her breath. No wonder Doc had said it would be better if she forgot his name.

"What did you do?" she asked.

"At least Doc had the decency to ask if I did it."

Anne remembered Doc's question. *"Did you do what they said you did?"* "Are you saying that you...weren't guilty?" she asked. "That's what you told Doc," she realized suddenly.

"It's the truth. Whether you believe it or not."

"Then how did you end up in prison?"

"Ask Chase McCullar. I'd be interested to hear what he tells you."

Jenny's brother-in-law, she realized. "He had something to do with putting you in prison?"

"It sure wouldn't have been possible without him."

"Why would he do that if you were innocent?"

Again the silence stretched before he answered, perhaps thinking about what he could tell her. "There's a lot of bad blood between us," he said finally.

"Or maybe he really thought you were guilty," Anne suggested. She had met Chase McCullar only briefly, so she had too little to go on to make that kind of judgment about his motives.

"Maybe," Rio agreed.

"Did he lie? At your trial, I mean."

"No," Rio said.

"Manufacture evidence?" she suggested.

He laughed again, the sound only a breath. "He didn't have to bother," he said. "There wasn't any."

"Juries don't convict people without evidence." She came from a family of lawyers, so she was aware that wasn't the exact truth. That was how it was supposed to work, of course, but sometimes... "I don't believe that—"

"I don't give a damn *what* you believe," Rio said, his voice suddenly harsh. "I'm telling you the truth." She saw the depth of the breath he took, and then, speaking more calmly, he added, "But they'll all tell you something different, so...I guess you'll have to make up your own mind."

"With an attitude like that, no wonder they convicted you." It was a stupid remark, and she regretted making it as soon as the words were out of her mouth. If what he said was true—and she still had no way to verify whether it was—then he had a right to be bitter.

"Maybe you're right," he agreed, his tone once again mocking.

He pulled the truck up parallel to the front of Jenny's house and turned off the ignition. They sat in the quiet darkness for a moment, listening to the small noises the engine made as it cooled. She knew she should be afraid, alone in this isolated location with a man who'd just confessed to being an ex-con, but for some reason she wasn't.... *"They'll all tell you something different...you'll have to make up your own mind."* Maybe she already had.

Finally Rio took the keys from the ignition and held them out to her. She reached to take them and in the darkness her fingers made contact with his. Surprisingly, she felt a small frisson of reaction somewhere deep inside and realized, almost with wonder, what it was.

"Where are you going now?" she asked.

He shook his head, thinking about that. There was nowhere to go. Nothing left that was home and nothing that felt like home. He didn't even have a place to spend the night. Maybe he should have asked to stay with Doc, but he had known the facilities were limited and with the woman and baby there...

"I think I may know where your horse is," Anne offered. The possibility had occurred to her during their conversation in the barn, but she had decided then not to tell him. Now it seemed right that he should know. "I think... I think it may have been Samantha McCullar who bought him instead of Jenny."

"*Samantha* McCullar?" Rio questioned, trying to place the name.

"Chase's wife."

By then he had made the connection. Sam Kincaid's daughter and Chase McCullar. Everybody had been aware that something had gone on between those two, years ago. "Samantha Kincaid?" he asked.

"Do you know her?"

"It's not likely that I'd know Samantha Kincaid. Except by reputation." Everybody in south Texas knew about the Kincaids. The old man, Sam Kincaid, owned the biggest spread in this part of the state, justifiably famous for the horses—both quarter horses and thoroughbreds—that it produced.

"Then you know that she knows something about horses."

"You think she bought mine?" He wondered if that was possible. The stallion had good lines, but he didn't know the breeding, and he couldn't imagine why someone who bred horses as valuable as the Kincaids' would be interested in acquiring a renegade with unknown bloodlines.

"She's started her own stables. If Jenny didn't buy your horse, then it just seemed a possibility that Samantha did. Only...I wouldn't go looking for him in her barn if I were you," she teased gently. "At least not tonight."

Not ever, Rio thought, not if he was smart. Not considering how Chase McCullar felt about him. And how he felt about Chase.

Getting caught in Jenny McCullar's barn tonight had made him realize what a straight-and-narrow path he was going to have to walk, especially around here, to stay out of prison. No one would cut him any slack. Hell, they'd be as eager to put him away again as they had been the first time.

"You want to sleep in the barn?" Anne asked.

He lifted his eyes to her face, surprised that she'd make that offer obvious in their darkness.

"If you don't have another place to go," she added.

Her eyes were deep blue. He had realized that with the growing light, and they met his now openly, without any of the male-female games he was familiar with. There was no invitation in their depths. No attraction. Beyond the first startled response to his face, Anne Richardson had treated him exactly as she had treated Doc Horn. With courtesy and respect and nothing else, and that wasn't the reaction he usually evoked. Especially not from women.

"I'd be grateful," he said. Again the words of thanks had been slow in coming, their usage unfamiliar.

She nodded and opened the passenger door. She climbed down from the pickup and without looking back, walked up the wooden steps and crossed the porch. It took her a moment to find the lock and insert the key.

While she was doing that, there was no sound from the truck behind her. No opening and closing of the door. She heard that distinctive sound only after she was inside, the door of the ranch house safely locked behind her.

For some reason, despite the unfamiliarity of her surroundings, she didn't have any trouble going to sleep.

THE SOUNDS THAT AWAKENED her late the following morning were also unfamiliar. She couldn't place them at first, so she lay for a moment in the unpleasant grogginess of having had too little sleep and listened, trying to identify what she was hearing. It wasn't until she heard the kind of language they were using to each other that she realized what was going on.

She jumped up and, through the window of her bedroom, she watched Rio drive his fist into his opponent's nose. The big blond man he was fighting recoiled from the blow, staggering backward a few feet before he came back at Rio again.

She didn't take time to grab a robe on the way out, but she did pick up the revolver she'd left out on the table beside the bed. Rommel was at the back door, waiting as he had last night for her to open it. But what was going on outside didn't need the big shepherd in the middle of it, she decided.

"Stay," she ordered, knowing full well that he wouldn't. She opened the door a crack and slipped out, using her knee to block the dog's exit. She slammed the door, almost catching his nose in it. She could hear his frenzied, frustrated barking behind her as she ran toward the barn.

Enough blows had already been struck that the two men were wary of each other now, more careful than they had apparently been in the first adrenaline-driven exchange. They had been on the ground at least once, judging by the dirt on their clothing. And they had both been bloodied. Now they were slowly circling, bare fists raised, their knuckles raw and eyes locked, awaiting the next opportunity to do damage.

"What are you doing?" she shouted at them as she ran. "Stop it, both of you."

The eyes of the blond, whom she had finally recognized as Chase McCullar, cut quickly away from his opponent and in her direction, but there was no other change in their watchful postures. Rio hadn't responded at all to her shout.

Even from where she was, she could see that his dark eyes were full of unthinking rage. There was a blueing lump on his cheekbone and the cut that had been opened over his left eye was seeping blood. McCullar's nose was bleeding, its normal, almost-Roman shape beginning to swell and distort.

"Stop it," she demanded again.

"Stay out of this," Rio warned. He still hadn't looked at her, his complete attention directed at his half brother.

That precaution had been wise. Rio had to duck the right Chase shot at him as he spoke to Anne. He had been expecting something like that, however, and he went in under it, delivering a short, hard jab to Chase's gut. When he heard the resulting grunt of lost breath, he smiled.

From the first blow, there had been something so intensely satisfying about knowing he was inflicting pain that it exhilarated him. Payback. Let Chase McCullar feel what it was like to be hurt.

"Stop it, damn it," Anne said. She was close enough to them now that she didn't have to yell to be heard. Close enough to see the cold hatred in their expressions. They were really trying to kill each other, she thought.

"Stay out of this," Chase ordered her. But his attention had been distracted long enough that Rio's left hook caught him off guard, rocking him with its force, so that he staggered backward again, widening the distance between them.

It wasn't much of an opportunity, but Anne took it. She ran into that opening, positioning her body like a shield in front of Rio's. She held the big gun out before her, again using both hands to keep it steady, exactly as she'd been taught.

"I said *stop* it." The words were softer now, unnecessary because there was no doubting the expertise with which she was holding the gun.

Chase McCullar hesitated, blue eyes moving unbelievingly from hers down to the weapon she held trained on his midsection. He'd been around guns all his life, so he had a healthy respect for them, for the damage they could do. He didn't move. He knew nothing about this woman, and he had no idea what might cause her to pull that trigger.

"What the hell do you think you're doing?" Rio demanded from behind her.

"Breaking this up before somebody gets hurt."

"This is none of your business," he said. "Get out of the way before that thing goes off—"

"And hurts somebody?" she jeered. "I thought that's what you were trying to do. To kill him. That's sure what it looked like from where I was standing."

"I found this bastard coming out of Jenny's barn," Chase said, taking an involuntary step closer to her, unthinking in his fury, trying to get to Rio, despite his initial intention not to do anything that might make the Richardson woman shoot him. "There's no telling what—"

The muzzle of the revolver moved slightly nearer to him, Anne's arms fully extending into the classic shooter's stance. Chase took the step back. He wasn't a coward, but he wasn't a fool, either.

"That's because I told him he could sleep in the barn," she said.

"You told him?" Chase questioned, his shock evident. "You knew he was here?"

"Yes," she said, blue eyes meeting blue. She could hear Rio breathing behind her, the sound harsh from the exertion of the fight. She was a little surprised that he hadn't tried to move her physically out of the way. Maybe because her finger was on the trigger of the .45, and he really didn't want her to gutshoot Chase McCullar.

"You don't know who this is," Chase said.

"His name is Rio," she said. "I gave him permission to use the barn because he didn't have anywhere else to sleep."

"Do you have any idea what he did?"

The man behind her made some sound, short and unpleasant. "You're not going to do any good talking to *him,*" Rio said softly.

"*He* says he didn't do anything," Anne answered Chase's question, ignoring Rio.

For the first time, Anne realized that whatever Rio had been accused of, whatever offense he'd gone to prison for, was the one thing that hadn't been discussed last night.

"He did it, all right," Chase said, his eyes moving past hers to the man standing behind her. "No matter what lies he's told you."

"Even if he did, Mr. McCullar, he's served his time. It's over. You're not going to fight with him."

"Served his time?" Chase repeated. "Do you think that matters? You think it makes any difference to me how much time he served? If he spends eternity in hell, that still won't be long enough to satisfy me. You think those five years will make any difference to Mac? Now get out of my way before you get hurt butting into something you don't know anything about."

"To Mac?" she repeated. Mac was his brother. Jenny's husband...who had been murdered. The shock of that revelation made her hands tremble. The small vibration of the gun she was holding revealed its impact.

"You *didn't* know," Chase said, apparently realizing the truth of that. "He told you something else, didn't he? Well, he lied to you, Miss Richardson, because that's what he is. A liar and a murderer. Now give me that damn gun."

Again he advanced, but he hadn't given her enough time to make up her mind about what she believed. *"You'll have to make up your own mind,"* Rio had said last night. And she remembered the quiet conviction in his voice when he'd answered Doc's question, *"Did you do what they said you did?"*

She lowered the muzzle of the revolver and squeezed the trigger, putting a bullet into the ground almost between Chase McCullar's booted feet.

"What the hell..." he yelled, but he backed up. In a hurry.

"Go home," she ordered. "Whatever the truth is, this isn't the way to handle it."

"You tried to shoot me," Chase said, as if he still couldn't believe what she'd done.

"If I had *tried* to shoot you, Mr. McCullar, you'd be shot. Go home and cool off."

"Get him off this ranch," he said. "Get him off Mc-Cullar land. Don't you realize how Jenny's going—"

"I realize," she interrupted. "And I promise you he'll leave. Just as soon as you do."

McCullar's eyes left hers to fasten on his half brother's face. They were blue flames, full of hatred and contempt. "I'm going to get you, you bastard," he said softly, "for what you did to Mac."

"I had *nothing* to do with what happened to Mac," Rio said. His voice was as quiet as Chase's had been. "I told you that. I've tried to tell you that from the beginning."

"You just knew about what was going to happen in advance?" Chase suggested sarcastically. "Somebody just told you all the details? Told you to come over here and issue that threat?"

"I overheard somebody talking."

Chase shook his head in disgust. "It won't wash. It's just more lies. I'm going to get you, Delgado. Sometime when she's not around to protect you. You can count on it."

Chase bent and scooped up his hat on his way across the yard. He got into his pickup, slamming the door. He gunned the black truck until the cloud of dust it kicked up obscured it, hiding it completely from the two people who still stood in the center of Jenny McCullar's yard.

Finally Anne lowered the gun and turned around to face Rio Delgado. She wondered if she would have remembered if she had heard the rest of his name last night. It wasn't really Rio. That was a nickname, of course, probably given to him in childhood, a mocking cruelty because of the circumstances of his birth. Roderigo Delgado was the name that had been blared across south Texas almost five years ago. Along with the details of his half brother's murder.

The cut under his eyebrow had stopped bleeding. He met her eyes. His dark gaze was straightforward and uncompromising. He had told her that he wasn't guilty, and apparently, despite Chase's accusations, his story hadn't changed.

"Why in the world would you come here?" she said. That's what she couldn't understand. Why take a chance that Jenny would be the one he'd encounter?

"I needed to find my horse," he said stubbornly, as if that explained it all.

She shook her head. She lowered the gun to her side, holding it loosely in her hand. "I think Chase is right. I think you'd just better go."

"I had nothing to do with Mac's death. I was coming to warn him. I made the mistake of telling McCullar what I'd overheard. He thought that meant I was part of what happened. That I was delivering the threat for...whoever killed him."

He still didn't know—who had really planned and executed Mac's murder—but that was nothing to him, he had decided long before he'd come back. He didn't owe the McCullars anything.

He hadn't come home to try to find Mac's murderer or even to clear his own name. He had thought he was long past caring what anybody thought. He had come home simply to settle a score. To make Chase McCullar pay for what he'd done.

Now, looking into Anne Richardson's eyes, knowing she had been sickened by what Chase had told her, he realized that wasn't true anymore. For some reason, it mattered to him what *she* thought.

Anne had hesitated, because she realized that she still wanted to believe him. She thought she could hear sincerity in his voice, but Chase had said he was a liar and a murderer. She had been mistaken about people before, she reminded herself. Badly mistaken. Surely that was a lesson she had learned.

"I'm not in a position to know which of you to believe," she said. "But I do know that you shouldn't be here. Not on Jenny's ranch. Just…go away. Please."

She began again to walk past him, but the dark hand she'd admired last night reached out, seeming to move as quickly as a rattlesnake's strike, to fasten around her wrist. She tried to jerk her arm away, but he wouldn't release her. Her eyes, wide with shock, lifted to his as she continued to struggle to free her wrist.

"Please listen to me, Miss Richardson—" he began, but suddenly she couldn't.

The panic surged upward, already beyond her control, gathering hysteria as she frantically twisted her arm, trying to pull it out of his grasp. "I just want you to—" he said.

She didn't hear the sense of the rest of it. The words roared in her head like the flow of blood that was pounding there. Its force obscured her vision, interfered with her hearing, drowned out the reality of what was happening now. Buried it in the horror of what had happened before.

She realized she was holding something in her hand, but she didn't even know what it was. It was just a *something*, maybe something she could use to make him let go, to fight him, to get free. She raised the revolver high over her head and then brought it down as hard as she could. The metal grip in her palm connected solidly with his temple.

Rio's eyes widened with shock and pain, and his long fingers unclenched, finally freeing her wrist. It didn't matter now, of course. Release had come too late. She was too far gone in the dark chasm of her own fear, irrationally reliving the past.

Anne had already pulled the gun back, striking out blindly again. Rio got his forearm up to partially block the blow, but she hit him hard enough that the force of it numbed the nerves in his arm, and he grunted in pain.

"Stop it," he said softly, still not understanding what was going on. "What the hell's the matter with you? I'm not going to hurt you. You know that."

She had already raised the gun the third time, and it was coming down once more, directed this time at his face. He turned aside, dodging the blow, so that the metal of the revolver's barrel scraped along his cheek, opening another cut, this one over the high cheekbone.

"What the hell!" he shouted, angry now. "What the hell's the matter with you?" He grabbed her arm again, the left one, and used it to shake her, trying to pull her around to make her face him.

When she did, he realized that her pupils were too widely dilated, midnight black and unseeing in an incredibly narrowed rim of blue. When she raised the gun again, Rio reached out and wrapped both muscular arms around her body in a bear hug, pinning her arms tightly to her sides. She stumbled backward, still fighting him, her body writhing frenziedly against his control.

The strength of her movements caught him off guard, and when she stumbled backward, he was pulled off-balance by her weight. He fell forward, throwing them both to the ground. He was able to brace himself by putting out his hands, but she landed hard on her back with most of his weight on top of her.

He heard the air go out of her lungs. She lay under him, and in the shock of having no air, her body had finally stilled. Her eyes were too wide, still staring almost blindly at his face. Her mouth was open, attempting frantically to get some oxygen into her lungs.

"It's all right," Rio said softly, trying to control his own anger enough to work the old magic. He made his voice low and reassuring. "I'm not going to hurt you. I'd never hurt you, Anne. It's all right. Everything's all right."

He continued to whisper to her. His fingers found the softness of her hair, blond and as fine as a child's under their caress. He moved his thumb along the column of her throat, the motion soothing as he talked to her.

Her eyes locked on his face, and she finally seemed to be listening to him. More coherent, maybe. He could feel her struggling to breathe and then the hard gasp as she was finally able to draw in some blessed air. Her breasts began to rise and fall rapidly, as she desperately pulled oxygen into her starving lungs. He could feel the small peaks of her nipples against his chest, hardened and moving against him under the covering of the thin nightshirt she wore.

With their movement, he became aware of her again as a woman. A highly desirable woman. He was suddenly conscious of their positions. Of the way she was lying under him. Just as if...

As he had in the barn, he fought to block that unwanted reaction, but it had been too long. So damn long. She took another breath, the sound she made almost a sob, exactly like the soft, grasping of a hurt child, fighting tears.

He looked down into her face and saw that her eyes had changed, the wild black of shock retreating with the growing return of the blue. He removed his hand from her throat, and put both of his flat on the ground, one on either side of her head and pushed his upper body up, away from her chest.

Except that hadn't been such a good idea, he realized suddenly, because it only increased the contact between his lower body and hers. His erection had been uncontrollable, despite the fact that he hadn't understood what was going on or why she was so furious. From the moment her breasts had begun moving under his chest, he'd been aroused. He hadn't meant for it to happen, but there wasn't a whole hell of a lot he could do about it now. He knew she could feel what had occurred, and he was embarrassed. He had a hard-on like a teenager on his first date.

He had forgotten about the gun she'd been holding when they went down—had forgotten it until he felt the cold of its muzzle pushed hard into the softness under his jaw. And then, seeing what was in her eyes, he knew, without any doubt in his mind, that she was about to pull the trigger.

Chapter Four

Rio's heart stopped while he waited. There had been other times when he'd expected to die, had been prepared for it. But this had come out of the blue. He didn't know what had set Anne Richardson off, but death was in the wide blue eyes staring up at him.

Finally he felt her take another breath. Not a gasp, but a long, slow inhalation. Her mouth was still open and despite the muzzle of the gun pressed against his throat, he fought the urge to lower his head and put his mouth over hers. Just to taste her. It would be a hell of a way to die.

And that makes me just about as crazy as she is, he thought in disgust. *Thinking about kissing her while she's trying to decide whether or not to pull that trigger.*

"Get up," she ordered softly. "Just get off me."

He pushed away from her onto his knees. As he lifted his hands off the ground, he continued their motion upward until they were raised on either side of his head, palms out, in the classic gesture of surrender.

She slithered away from him, using her left hand and her bare feet to propel herself backward. She didn't lower Mac McCullar's big gun. When she was about a dozen feet away from where he was kneeling, she stood. The movement was shaky and uncertain, awkward even, but the muzzle of the gun never wavered from its focus on his chest.

"I wasn't trying to hurt you," Rio said. "I don't hurt women."

That was the absolute truth. He didn't even like rough sex. It had never excited him. It just seemed like bronco-busting in comparison to the flawless communication between man and beast that was inherent in other forms of riding. And it simply wasn't the kind of man he was. Not even now. Not even after the brutality of the last few years.

She nodded. Her eyes were still strange, wide and darkly glittering. He couldn't decide if that was from unshed tears or anger.

"I think you'd better go," she whispered. "I think that would be best."

He pushed himself to his feet, and he staggered slightly, getting up. He was surprised to find he was a little disoriented, but he'd taken a couple of good shots to the head, between Chase's and Anne Richardson's best efforts. Despite the movies, where people got hit forty times with a baseball bat and didn't have a mark on them, those blows were probably going to have some effect, he knew. Concussion. Something.

"Are you okay?" she asked.

He glanced up, wondering if that was sarcasm. He saw that her entire body was trembling, the shimmering vibration clearly visible. She looked like somebody standing naked out in a blizzard.

He put his fingers up to where she'd split his cheek open with the barrel of the revolver. They came away covered with blood and he was aware now of the sting. He probably needed a couple of stitches in that. Maybe some in the cut Chase had opened over his eye.

"I'm just fine," he said. "But thanks for asking." There *was* sarcasm in that. Deliberate.

He turned and started back to the barn to get his pack. She'd probably sic the dog on him next. He should have left last night. It wouldn't have been the first night he'd slept out. It wouldn't have killed him. This almost had.

Knowing how close he had just come to dying made him sick to his stomach.

"I'm sorry," she said from behind him. He turned around and looked at her, his eyes narrowed in disbelief. And then he realized that she looked almost as bad as he felt.

Her dark nightshirt was splotched with dust from where he'd thrown her down on the ground. Her face was totally without color. She was still holding the gun, but it hung from her fingers now as if it were too heavy for her to manage. All the fight had gone out of her—all that courage and spirit he'd admired when she'd come into the barn last night to confront him and today when she'd stepped into the middle of the battle between him and Chase McCullar.

He didn't understand what had happened to her, what had changed her, but looking at her, he felt like he had last night when the woman in the barn had asked for his help. So he told himself the same thing he'd told himself then, knowing it was more true now than it had been then. *I've got troubles enough of my own. I don't need somebody else's.*

"Yeah," Rio said softly. He turned and went on to the barn, leaving Anne standing alone in the yard of Jenny McCullar's ranch house.

HE THOUGHT ABOUT WHAT had happened the whole time he was walking. He had probably covered three or four miles of the six-mile journey to Doc's clinic, despite the slow pace his headache demanded. And he still hadn't come any closer to figuring out what had gone wrong.

She had invited him to sleep in the barn, despite the fact that she was out there alone. She had gotten between him and Chase to protect him. There was no doubt about that. When he remembered the look on McCullar's face when she put that bullet between his toes, his mouth moved, almost into a smile, despite the way he felt.

And then... Then, all of a sudden she'd gone loco. Just

started acting like a wild woman, hitting him over the head with that damn revolver and then sticking it under his jaw. He shivered suddenly, remembering the look in her eyes as she'd held it there through those endless seconds. She had wanted to kill him. There was no doubt in his mind about that. The only question was why.

There *was* another question, he realized. Why was he dwelling on what had happened? He would never see Anne Richardson again. Whatever had happened to change her in the space of those few minutes was none of his concern. Not his problem. He had enough problems of his own. He repeated the words, trying to give them validity, but he couldn't forget her eyes. They reminded him of something, but he couldn't quite remember what it was.

He heard a truck approaching behind him. The pounding in his head that had begun before he'd left the McCullar ranch seemed to be getting worse with each step he took. That, and the knowledge of the hot miles that still stretched between him and Doc Horn's, the only place he might possibly find a friend in this county, were pretty compelling. He turned around, walking backward this time, and put up his thumb. He still had it up when he recognized the driver.

Anne Richardson stopped the pickup beside him. He could see her face clearly through the dusty window. It was strained, still drained of color, but her eyes were as they had been last night at Doc's—blue and calm, totally rational again. She reached across and opened the passenger door, but he didn't make any move toward the vehicle. He noticed that she had taken time to dress. She was wearing a T-shirt, jeans and white sneakers.

"Get in," she invited.

Rio's mouth moved then, lifting into a smile, one that contained no trace of amusement. "Thanks just the same, but I prefer to walk."

"Please," she said.

There was something in the single word that touched

him. Something that spoke of pain, and that had always been the key to reaching him.

"Why?" he asked.

"Because I'd like to talk to you."

"I don't think that would be a good idea, Miss Richardson," he said truthfully. Getting mixed up with the crazy sister of a state senator wouldn't be the smartest thing he'd ever done. Not considering the situation he was in.

"I'd…like a chance to explain," she said.

"You don't owe me an explanation. I appreciate that you gave me a place to sleep last night. I appreciate your stepping in to stop the fight. Why don't we just call it even."

He watched her take a breath, maybe as slow as the one she'd taken when she'd decided not to pull that trigger. "I listened to *your* explanation," she said. "I did what you said."

"What I said?" he repeated, trying to figure that out.

"I made up my own mind about you."

Still he hesitated. Her eyes held his, simply waiting now for him to decide. Not many people had listened to the explanations he'd tried to make five years ago, Rio realized. That Anne Richardson had was almost unprecedented. Hell, maybe he did owe her something. At least the courtesy of listening to whatever she wanted to say.

"Okay," he agreed, knowing he was a fool and that this would probably come back to haunt him. He threw his pack into the back of the pickup and climbed in beside her. He glanced at the seat between them, looking for the revolver it seemed like she'd been carrying since he'd met her.

"I left the gun at Jenny's," she said. "I locked it back up in the drawer where she keeps it."

He nodded, wondering that he was that transparent. He had thought he was pretty good at hiding what he was feeling, but it seemed she had known exactly what he was thinking.

"I…" she began and then stopped.

She took a breath, and he waited through the silence. She was the one who wanted to talk.

"It scared me that I wanted to kill you," she said finally.

"I wasn't real comfortable with the idea myself." The tone of that acknowledgment was rueful, verging on amused.

"You didn't act like you were scared," she said. The corners of her lips had arched at his confession.

"Then I guess I'm pretty good at acting."

"But you were? You knew what was going on?"

"There wasn't any doubt in my mind that you were going to pull that trigger."

She nodded. "I wanted to," she said finally.

"Why didn't you?"

"Because I realized you hadn't done anything. That it had all been me. Just…inside me."

He thought about that, but it didn't begin to explain what had happened. "I didn't do anything to deserve that."

"I know," she said. "I know you didn't. When you grabbed my arm and wouldn't let go, I guess I panicked."

"I just wanted to talk to you."

"I know. Rationally, I knew it then, but you wouldn't let me go, and I kept trying to get you to, so…I panicked."

"Why don't you tell me what this is all about."

"I thought maybe you'd figured it out," she said softly.

He didn't answer because there didn't seem to be much point. He had never been good at riddles. He waited a long time for her to say something else, but he had already put his hand on the handle of the door before she did.

"I was raped. I thought maybe you'd figured that out."

He didn't say anything, and he didn't look at her. He couldn't. He looked out the dusty windshield instead, focusing on the only tree in the desolation of the landscape, another bent, wind-gnarled cottonwood.

"He was somebody I trusted. Somebody I should have been able to trust. He wouldn't let me go when I told him to. And then…I couldn't do anything to stop him."

The words were soft and without inflection, as if she had told the story a hundred times, trying to drain it of emotion, trying to deny its ability to hurt her. He wondered if that had worked.

"Today..." she continued, the words halting now, almost whispers. "For some reason, when you grabbed my arm, it all came back. You wouldn't let go, so I hit you. And once I did, I couldn't stop hitting you. Only...it wasn't really you I was hitting." Out of the corner of his eye, he could see that she had lowered her head, and he waited. Finally she added, "I dream sometimes about hitting him, hitting him until he's dead and he can't hurt me anymore."

They sat in the unmoving truck, and the silence built around them. There were things he should say, he knew, but he couldn't think of any of them. So he said nothing.

After a long time, she asked, "Were you heading to Doc's?"

He nodded. He still hadn't looked at her. He didn't want to look at her because then she might know what he was feeling.

"I'll take you there if you want me to. I'd like to pay for the damage I did."

"Doc won't charge me," he said.

"He really likes you."

"He thought *I* should be a doctor."

He didn't know why he had told her that. He had never told anyone else about the old man's suggestion. He had just savored it through the years, knowing that someone had once thought he could amount to something.

"But you didn't want to?" she suggested.

He turned at that. Her eyes looked as if she'd been crying, an almost-burned look to the fragile skin around them.

"I guess not," he said. He couldn't explain his life to her. He suspected she wouldn't want to hear even if he tried. All she wanted was absolution for what had happened this morning. He understood that. "I don't mind walking, but thanks for offering."

"Are you sure?" she said.

"You're not afraid to go home by yourself, are you?" The thought had been sudden, and if he'd been thinking instead of just responding to her pain, he would never have voiced it.

"I'm not afraid. That's not it. I just wish you'd let me take you to Doc's. It would make me feel better about everything. I feel bad about what happened."

What the hell, he thought. That, at least, would be a pain he could do something about. And he really didn't feel like walking. He felt instead like the top of his head might come off with the next step he took. There was no one around to see them together.

"Then we're even?" he asked softly.

"Then we're even," she agreed.

"HOW THE HELL COULD HE have been paroled?" Chase asked the man behind the desk.

At the tone of the question, Sheriff Buck Elkins's hand hesitated briefly in the act of putting down the phone he'd used to solicit that information.

His eyes moved to meet those of Raymond Morales, his deputy, who had just come into the reception area from the back of the county jail, before he refocused his attention on McCullar.

"I expect that probably happened in the usual way, Chase," he said reasonably. "He had a hearing and the parole board apparently thought he deserved to be let out."

"Those brainless idiots," Chase said. "Those arrogant—"

"Why don't you try to look at it logically," the sheriff suggested, his determined calmness overriding Chase's anger. "Maybe look at it from their point of view. We both know there wasn't all that much to connect the kid with the bombing to begin with. He was sent up for his part in a murder plot that nobody else was ever convicted of. There was no physical evidence to connect Delgado to Mac's death. There was just your word against his about what he said that night. About what it meant.''

''What the hell else could it have meant?'' Chase asked angrily. ''You know as well as I do—''

''What I *know* is we were damn lucky to get a conviction in the first place. Maybe the parole board realized that. There're not many people in south Texas who don't know the details about this case. After five years maybe common sense took over in place of the emotions that were running sky-high back then.''

''Common sense?'' Chase repeated. His voice wasn't raised, but his contempt was evident.

''I said to try to look at it from their point of view.''

''So they let him out to do the same thing to somebody else. Maybe to you this time.''

''What are you trying to say, Chase?'' Morales asked.

''Buck's the law here now. Just like Mac was five years ago. Maybe the same folks might be interested in getting rid of him.''

''I'll watch my back,'' the sheriff said, but he didn't seem perturbed about the idea. Or maybe he was simply trying to stay calm because Chase McCullar had come in so riled up. ''In the meantime, you leave Delgado alone.''

''Meaning what?'' Chase asked, his eyes narrowing slightly.

''Well, unless your bride did that,'' Buck said, his head tilting toward Chase's battered face, ''I'd be willing to bet you and Rio have already tangled. Am I right?''

Chase didn't say anything, but as he remembered the interrupted fight, his lips flattened.

''You didn't kill him, did you?'' Buck asked. ''I have to tell you, I wouldn't be too happy about that. Murder makes a hell of a lot of paperwork for this office.''

''I didn't kill him.''

''Amazing,'' Buck said, shaking his head. His own lips lifted slightly, inviting Chase to lighten up.

''Don't give me too much credit,'' Chase admitted. ''It

wasn't from lack of trying. Trent Richardson's sister got in between us with a gun.''

"Gutsy, maybe, but not too bright. Course, she don't know either one of you. I'd say we were all lucky somebody didn't get killed. When did this happen?''

"Maybe ten. Maybe a little later.''

The sheriff glanced at his watch. "Took you a while to get over here. Hour, hour and a half, maybe?''

"I drove around awhile. I went home and tried to work, tried to calm down.''

"I appreciate that," Sheriff Elkins said. "Especially if you think the way you were acting when you came in here was calm.''

"Sorry I came on so strong, but I don't want him back here, Buck. He belongs behind bars. Locked up. He's a damn animal.''

"He attack you? Maybe we could run him in on assault.''

There was a small pause before Chase answered. "Hell, I attacked him. When I got there to check on Jenny's horses, they were already out in the paddock. I found Rio in the barn. I went nuts.''

"Then you better hope *he* doesn't file assault charges," Morales suggested.

Chase shook his head. "He won't go to the law. It's not his style. Why weren't we notified before that hearing? I thought that was standard policy.''

"They'd have notified Mrs. McCullar," Buck said. "Unless there was some kind of screwup, she'd have gotten a letter telling her the date of the hearing. She could have gone and spoken against his release if she'd wanted to.''

"Jenny," Chase said, his voice sharp with disgust, and then he added under his breath. "Damn it, Jenny, what's the matter with you?''

"You think she got the letter and didn't go?" the deputy asked.

"It's possible.''

"Now why would she do that?" Buck asked.

"I don't know why she'd do it. She just…might have. She wasn't sure at the time that Rio had anything to do with what happened to Mac."

"You were sure," Buck reminded him softly.

"I was *there*," Chase said. "I heard the bastard. They sent him to deliver their threat. 'Pesos or bullets.' Just like they always do. Only he timed it wrong. The son of a bitch stayed in that cantina drinking until it was too late to do any good."

"I never have figured out why they'd send him with the bomb already in place," Buck said musingly. "Never did understand that."

"Maybe his timing was off, but he was mixed up in it up to his neck," Chase said defensively. "Don't think that—"

"Mixed up in what, Chase?" Buck interrupted. "There never was any evidence that what Mac had been told about somebody running drugs here was true. I never found any evidence of anything like that going on."

"Except Mac getting blown up. Seems like that would be evidence enough." There was a challenge in Chase's eyes. He'd heard this before—that nothing had turned up to back up the theory that Mexican drug money had paid for Mac's death.

"Mac had enemies. Everybody does. Especially in this job."

"Just somebody out for a little personal revenge? Somebody Mac rubbed the wrong way? Is that what you've decided?"

"You made up your mind about what happened to Mac. I got a right to my opinion, same as you."

Chase shook his head. "At least my opinion is based on something that makes sense."

"Maybe so, but all the same, I want you to leave Delgado alone," Buck said softly. "Leave him to me. I'm warning you, Chase. Don't take the law into your own hands. I won't put up with any vigilante justice. Not in my county.''

The blue McCullar eyes were bitter as they met Elkins's calm hazel ones. The big scarred desk that separated them had been Mac's. This had once been Sheriff Mac Mc-Cullar's county. For some reason it made Chase even more angry to remember that, and to be warned off now like an outsider.

''I'll remember,'' he said curtly.

Coming here sure hadn't done any good, Chase thought, as he stepped back out into the sunshine. The law wasn't going to do anything about Rio Delgado. They wouldn't have the first time if he hadn't taken matters into his own hands. Maybe that would be what he'd have to do this time.

THERE WAS NO ONE at the tiny clinic when Rio and Anne arrived. The front door was closed, and there was a hand-printed note on it that said, Be Back at 6:00 p.m.

''Thanks for the ride,'' Rio said.

Anne had parked the truck in front, cutting off the engine this time. He had gotten out to read the note, but he'd left the passenger door open behind him. He walked back to pull his pack out of the truck bed.

''What will you do?'' she asked. They had said nothing else on the ride over.

''There's a window at the back that Doc leaves un-locked.''

''For you?''

''I'm probably not the only one who knows about it, but I've used it a couple of times.''

''You and Doc must be close.''

He thought about that. Doc was as near to a father as he'd ever had. It was Doc who had taught him that what-ever hand life dealt you, you were going to have to play. You might not like the cards, but you probably weren't going to get any others. You just had to make the best of what had been given.

"I worked for Doc when I was a kid. After my mother died. Sweeping up, washing windows, whatever he could find for me to do. I used to walk all the way up here on the chance that he'd have some kind of job. And he always did. I don't know how much he needed me, but I sure needed him. And I needed the money he paid me."

"But he couldn't do anything about..." She hesitated.

"About my conviction?"

She nodded.

"I think he tried, but Chase McCullar was obsessed. He didn't listen to anybody, not even to Doc."

"I know that Mac was his brother," she said, "but even so, it's hard to understand that he won't consider the possibility that he might just be totally..." She let the sentence trail.

"Mac was something special," Rio said softly. Her eyes had widened slightly at his comment, maybe because she had thought his hatred of Chase would automatically extend to his dead brother. "I've always understood why Chase wanted someone to have to pay for his death."

"He just picked the wrong person," she suggested.

"Not many people around here would agree with you, but...I appreciate that you believe me." He picked up his pack and began to turn away.

"What about your face?" she asked.

"What about it?" he said, turning to meet her eyes, a trace of amusement in the darkness of his.

If she hadn't told him about the rape, he would have made a joke out of her concern. Maybe asked her if she didn't like his face. He had always been good at that— turning the inevitable comments about how he looked into self-deprecating humor that women responded to. It was another form of flirtation. Simple and effective. But not here. Not with this woman.

"You probably need a couple of stitches in that cut on your cheekbone. If something isn't done within the next hour or so," she suggested, "it may be too late. You could end up with a scar."

"Can't have that, now can we?" he said dismissively, letting her hear that he didn't care. He had his pack and was standing beside the truck, the passenger door still open. And they both knew there wasn't really anything else to say.

She smiled at him, and when he didn't return it, she lowered her eyes. When she looked up again, the smile was gone, but her eyes were still quietly amused. "You just want me gone, don't you? Just want me to go away and leave you alone."

He wondered how to answer that without hurting her. She'd been hurt enough. He shook his head.

"Pretty damn awkward, isn't it?" she said. "I haven't told that many people about…what happened, but things are always different when I do. They change. What's in their eyes when they look at me changes."

"Are you sure that…" He hesitated.

"That I'm not imagining it? Maybe. You tell me."

He wondered if what he'd thought about her had changed with her story. Looking at her, he was forced to acknowledge that she was right. She was just wrong about the direction of that change, but he knew how important it was not to let her figure that out.

They heard the sound at the same time. They both looked up, watching in silence as another pickup came out of the dust, moving rapidly toward them. It slowed as it neared the clinic, the occupant probably trying to decide what was going on. It stopped next to Jenny's truck, and the driver rolled down his window and stuck his head out, propping a broad, brown forearm on the door.

"Everything okay here?" he asked. His question had been addressed to Anne, but his eyes were busy examining Rio.

"We're just waiting for Doc to get back," Anne said. "Everything's fine."

"Doc away?" the man asked.

Rio had placed the weather-beaten face by now. It belonged to a rancher named Dwight Rogers. His spread was a good twenty miles away, but given the sparseness of the area's population, everybody within a hundred miles was a neighbor. And they were neighborly. That was all Rogers was doing—just checking on a woman who seemed to be alone out here with a battered, disreputable-looking man standing next to her truck.

The rancher would be sounding a lot more concerned if he'd recognized him, Rio thought. He lowered his head, directing his gaze toward the ground, hiding his features, he hoped, without being too obvious about it. He hadn't intended to be seen with Anne Richardson. It would only make complications for them both.

"The note on the door says he'll be back soon," Anne said.

"Okay," the rancher responded, nodding. "You take care, now."

"Thanks," Anne said. She lifted her hand to wave, and the pickup pulled away. The silence was again too prolonged after the noise of the truck's engine faded. When Rio finally looked up, it was into a pair of dark blue eyes that had been focused on his downturned head.

"Thanks," he said softly. "Thanks for everything."

"What are you going to do? Are you planning to stay with Doc tonight?"

"Maybe. There's an extra bed, but I don't want to cause any trouble for him, and if the woman and the baby are still staying here—"

"You think that could be where Doc's gone? To take her home?"

"Maybe," he said. "Or to find her husband."

"If they don't find him, he may bring her back to the clinic. If he does, you won't have a place to sleep," she suggested.

"I'll find somewhere to bunk. On the floor if nothing else."

"You're welcome to sleep in the barn again."

There was a small challenge in her eyes. He couldn't imagine why she would make that offer.

"Chase McCullar's probably already called your brother," he warned.

She hadn't thought about that. He could see the surprise in the widening eyes. "Why would he do that?" she asked.

"To tell him I was there. That we've met. To warn him."

"That's none of Chase McCullar's business," she said in disbelief, but she was already thinking about Trent's reaction to such a call, picturing that damn look of concern in his eyes. "It's *nobody's* business who I associate with."

"Maybe Jenny's," Rio said. He had said it deliberately, to remind her of what he was supposed to have done.

"Even if he has called them, they won't come home tonight. Trent's accepting some award for his support of immigration. Some Hispanic group's annual dinner. He won't miss that. If they come, it won't be until tomorrow. You can be gone before they arrive. No one will ever know you were there. And maybe by tomorrow night Doc will have found a place for the woman."

"It's nothing to you if I have a place to sleep. You don't owe me anything, Miss Richardson."

"Maybe I'm not doing it for you," she said. All those hours of therapy, she thought, and the first man who had touched her, she had wanted to kill. It should have been funny, but it wasn't. It hadn't been the least bit funny.

"What does that mean?" he asked.

"No one has any faith in my judgment anymore," she said. And then, knowing he couldn't possibly understand from that how she felt, she tried to explain. "Maybe that's not really true. I suppose the truth is...*I* didn't have any faith in it anymore. I don't feel like I'm a good judge of who I should trust. I can't..." She hesitated, and he spoke into the silence.

"I'm supposed to be some kind of test?" he asked disbelievingly. "Some kind of social experiment?"

"*Could* I trust you to sleep in Jenny's barn and leave me alone?" The words were almost bitter.

"Of course."

"Then if I know that, and you know that—"

"This is crazy," he said. "What the hell are you trying to prove?"

"That I have a right to choose my own friends. That I'm still capable of doing that. Of doing a good job of that."

He held her eyes. The blue was suddenly touched with moisture, but she wouldn't let the tears come. She blinked, denying them.

"That doesn't make any sense," he argued.

"It does to me. I guess it really doesn't matter if it makes sense to anybody else. Except maybe to you."

Her chin had lifted a little, but her eyes were still dry, resolutely dry.

"I do a mean butterfly," she said.

It sounded like an offer of some kind. His first thought had been swimming, which made no sense, but then he realized she meant a butterfly bandage.

"Let me at least go inside with you and fix the damage I inflicted," she bargained. "If you wait until Doc gets back, it will be too late to do anything about your cheek. *Then* we'll be even," she promised softly.

"Look—" he began, and she quickly interrupted.

"He might have left the clinic unlocked just in case—" She stopped because she couldn't think of an "in case."

"Just in case somebody wants to steal the drugs he keeps there," Rio mocked gently.

She didn't answer. Instead she climbed out her side of the pickup and walked over to the door she'd knocked on last night. She didn't knock this time. It wasn't necessary. The knob turned under her hand, and she pushed the door open and then turned around to face Rio. She wasn't surprised that he hadn't moved.

"Just in case," she taunted, smiling at him. She stepped into the dark interior. It must be twenty degrees cooler inside the adobe building than it was out in the sun, she thought. She heard Rio come in behind her, his boot heels echoing on the quarry tile of the floor.

She led the way across the waiting area toward the examination room where they'd been last night. The empty, breathless quietness of the building was a little eerie. But it made it obvious there was no one here. Wherever Doc had gone, he had taken the woman and the baby with him.

She pushed open the swinging door. It took a second to understand what she was seeing, for her mind to comprehend what was before her. She focused first on the blood. There was a lot of it, splattered over the age-yellowed plaster walls and even in sweeping crimson arcs of droplets high up on the dingy whiteness of the ceiling.

Doc Horn was lying on his own examination table. And he was dead. Whoever had killed him hadn't been neat about it, but they'd been thorough. Before they'd left, they had cut the old man's throat.

Chapter Five

She could hear Rio's boot heels approaching behind her, despite the vacuum of horror that engulfed her. Anne turned, fighting nausea, and found him standing stock-still, trying to comprehend the unbelievable carnage of the room. As he began to push by her to get to Doc, she stepped in front of him, using her body to block the doorway.

"He's dead," she said.

He stepped to the side, trying to avoid the barrier she had made of her slender frame. "He might be—"

"He's dead, Rio," she said it again, trying to make him understand. Without any conscious decision, she wrapped her arms around his waist to stop his natural, unthinking attempt to enter that room and try to do something for the old man.

"Let me go, damn it," he said, still struggling to get by her.

He hadn't touched her. He didn't put his hands on her to lift her out of the way, and she knew that was because of what had happened before. Even now, even in this extremity, he had remembered what she'd told him.

"You *know* he's dead," she whispered, the sickness pushing upward again in her throat as she remembered the scene behind her. "He can't be alive. Not...like that."

She felt his surrender, the absolute, suddenly unmoving capitulation, caused by his recognition of that painful truth.

Finally she leaned against him, still holding him, because she needed to. Her knees felt too weak to support her. "You can't do Doc any good by going in there, but you can do yourself a lot of harm."

"Harm?" he repeated.

She knew then that he hadn't realized all the potential for disaster their presence here, last night and today, offered. "Doc wouldn't want you to be blamed for this."

His body had been rigid, absolutely motionless. The muscles of his chest lifted suddenly. She could feel that jerk of motion against her breasts. The breath he took was deep and shuddering. If it had been devastating to her, finding the old man slaughtered like an animal, she could only imagine what Rio, who had loved him, must feel.

"Why would anybody want to hurt Doc?" he questioned softly. Rhetorical, but at least it indicated that he was beginning to think again. To be rational.

She shook her head, her hair brushing against his shirt-front. His right hand came up to touch lightly between her shoulder blades. His thumb caressed slowly up and down her spine, gentle and unthinking. Like the movement of his strong, dark fingers over the belly of the woman they had brought here, she understood that this touch was asexual.

She laid her cheek against his shoulder, and they stood for a moment without speaking, simply holding each other. Human contact. Shared grief. Relief that there was someone else here who cared about what had happened to the old man.

"Come on," she said finally.

He released her at once, his hand no longer on her back, but for some reason she found herself reluctant to move away from the solid, protective warmth of his body. Finally, she made herself step back. She took his arm, turning him from the examination room. Together they moved out of the doorway and into the waiting room. Knowing it wouldn't change anything, she pulled the swinging door closed, hiding what they had found.

"What about the woman?" Rio asked.

"Oh, my God," Anne whispered. She had held the baby last night, and now… "There was no one else in that room," she said. She forced herself to think about her first shocked survey of its perimeter, at the same time fighting the mental picture of the mother and baby, slaughtered like Doc had been. "I'm sure of it."

"I'm going to look in the windows around back," Rio said. "Maybe they're in Doc's rooms."

They both knew the unlikelihood of someone doing what they had done to Doc and leaving a witness around to report to the authorities. If they were there, then in all probability they, too, were dead.

"Don't touch anything," Anne remembered to warn him, just before Rio disappeared through the outer door they had left open. It took an eternity for him to return. Anne stood in what had, only minutes before, seemed the cool, pleasant dimness of the waiting room, and prayed for the mother and for the baby she had held last night. She looked up when Rio's body blocked the light from the doorway, her heart pounding in her throat.

He shook his head. "There's no one there. The curtains were open, and I could see into both rooms. There's nobody else here. They're gone."

THERE WAS NO DISCUSSION about whether or not to call the sheriff, despite Rio's situation. The fact that Dwight Rogers had seen them outside this clinic not fifteen minutes ago had assured the inevitability of that.

The other was not so easy. It would become complicated when they tried to explain why Rio had been in Jenny's barn last night. That trespass was a violation of his parole that the authorities here would probably be eager to pursue. Yet they were both reluctant not to mention the woman and child, and the trip they had made to bring them to the clinic last night. It was possible the woman had seen or heard something that might help the authorities find out who had killed Doc.

At least, that was the argument Anne made.

"Even if she knows something, she won't come forward," Rio said. "Why should she? It would only endanger herself and the baby. She's already lost her husband."

"The birth certificate," Anne remembered. "Her name will be will be on the certificate Doc filled out."

"If he had time to fill it out. We can't look for it. Not in there."

"The authorities can."

Rio nodded.

"Maybe they can find her," Anne continued. "Question her about what happened. Do you think... Is it possible the killer took them with him?" she questioned, thinking out loud.

"He kills Doc and then kidnaps the woman and her baby?" Rio said. "Why would he do that? Why not kill them all?"

"Then where is she?"

"Back home, probably. Only we don't know where that is, either. I didn't ask any questions last night. It didn't seem important."

"She couldn't have gotten back home. She just had a baby, a difficult birth."

"Doc took her this morning, maybe. He might have done that if he knew she had someone to look after her there. Anything's possible."

"Even...that she killed Doc?" she questioned softly.

He took time to think about it. It had seemed ridiculous to suggest it, but as he had said, anything was possible. They couldn't know what had happened.

"No," he said finally. "I don't believe that."

"Neither do I," she agreed. "The woman and baby left—or Doc took them somewhere—and when he returned..."

"He surprised someone who was already here?"

"Maybe stealing the drugs you said he kept?"

"Drugs are too easy to get without having to kill for them. Especially that way."

"That way?"

His lips tightened. "It looked like they worked at it awhile."

"What does that mean?"

"They wanted something. Doc didn't give it to them. At least not for a while."

"Oh, God," Anne whispered, thinking about the old man. About the way he'd cared for the baby and for the mother. "Dear God."

"We have to tell them everything," Rio said. "There may be some evidence in that room that we were here last night. I may have touched something. We may have left fingerprints."

Reluctantly, she nodded. Maybe with a murder this vicious to work on, the sheriff's office wouldn't be too concerned about trespassing. Rio was right. They really didn't have any choice. They had to tell the truth. All of it.

ANNE MADE THE CALL from the phone in Doc's waiting room. While she listened to the three rings it took before somebody picked up, she studied Rio's face.

He had loved the old man. That had been evident in every aspect of their interaction last night. Even today, Rio's respect for Doc had been clear. More telling, this small clinic had been where Rio had headed after the events at the ranch this morning. He was coming here because this was where he would be assured of welcome. Where he had been believed.

Now there was nothing left of what Doc had given him, and his dark features, hard-set as if they'd been carved from stone, reflected the enormity of his loss. The muscle beside his mouth twitched occasionally with the control he was exerting over his emotions.

"Sheriff's office." The voice that answered her call was

casual and bored, verging on indifferent. Probably too accustomed to answering complaints that didn't amount to a hill of beans to anticipate the seriousness of this one.

"This is Anne Richardson," she said, and then she wondered if she should identify herself further. She had never traded on Trent's position or her relationship to him, but she found herself thinking that she should if it would offer some protection to the man who stood silently beside her, his eyes focused unseeingly on the closed door that hid what was in the small examination room.

"Ms. Richardson," the voice said. It had suddenly been filled with interest. It was obvious that whoever had answered the phone knew exactly who she was. "What can we do for you today?"

The words she said were in her head, put there by a hundred movies and TV shows through the years, and so, because using them prevented her from having to formulate any others, she said them. "I want to report a murder."

"A murder?" There was an element of disbelief in that. Despite its proximity to the sometimes-violent border, there were probably not that many homicides in this small county. After all, there were no major cities, and not even many minor ones, located within its rural boundaries.

"Someone's killed Doc Horn," she said.

"Doc Horn?" There was a long pause. "Are you sure, ma'am?"

She thought about what she had seen. Briefly seen, maybe, but there was no doubt in her mind. There hadn't been from the beginning.

"I'm sure," she confirmed softly.

"Where are you, ma'am?"

"We're at Doc's clinic."

She had no choice but to make that plural, she reassured herself. It was too late for Rio to leave. It had been too late when Dwight Rogers had seen them here together. They had both agreed on that.

Rio glanced at her, and then his eyes went back to their

concentration on that closed door. She wondered what he was thinking. He knew the implications of their discovery better than she possibly could. His was a knowledge based on experience. He had already spent almost five years in prison for a murder he didn't commit.

"You stay right there, ma'am," the voice on the phone ordered. That voice, which represented the law establishment that had unjustly convicted Rio Delgado the first time, was speaking briskly now, the previous indifference wiped away. "We'll be there just as soon as we can."

"NOW LET'S GO THROUGH what you told me one more time, Ms. Richardson, if you don't mind," Sheriff Elkins suggested. He had just come back into the room where they'd taken her after they'd arrived at the sheriff's office more than an hour ago.

She didn't know where Rio was, and she had gotten no response when she'd asked. At least no response that gave her any information. So she had told her story, in detail, because she assumed that would be the quickest way to get Rio released and get them out of here. After she and Sheriff Elkins had gone over it a couple of times, someone had called him out. He'd been gone maybe fifteen minutes before he'd come back to make that polite request.

He'd been polite to her from the beginning, of course. Even when she'd protested their putting handcuffs on Rio back at the clinic.

"It's just standard procedure, ma'am," he had explained. "Just because Mr. Delgado is on parole. It doesn't mean anything's going to happen to him. Don't you worry about that. We just need both of you to come into the office. You'll be willing to do that, won't you, ma'am? Help us get to the bottom of what happened to Doc? Help us catch whoever did this terrible thing?"

The patronizing tone had made her skin crawl. It made her feel as if he thought he was talking to a not-very-bright child, but maybe that was just the way he talked to women.

She'd run into a couple of other policemen who had used that tone.

"I don't mind going with you," she had said finally. "We'll follow you in Jenny's truck," she offered.

She could see him consider that, could almost watch him weighing the implications, the thoughts moving behind his hazel eyes. He didn't want to offend her. To offend Trent, she amended, but he was also investigating a homicide.

"*You're* welcome to follow me in the pickup," he had said finally, "but I guess Delgado better ride in with me. Deputy Morales can stay here and wait for the Maverick County coroner."

"Maverick County?"

"Doc was ours. Never had too much to do with stuff like murder, but in normal circumstances he would have been the one we'd have called. As it is, it may take their coroner a while to get over here, but we don't have to wait, ma'am. The quicker we talk, the quicker you can get on back to Mrs. McCullar's."

She had agreed because she hadn't felt she had any choice. Rio had made no protest, but his eyes had met hers as Sheriff Elkins had helped him into the patrol car, his hand on the top of Rio's head to keep him from bumping it.

There were too many emotions in the dark depths of Rio's eyes for her to identify them all. There had been anger, certainly, but he'd kept that controlled. Humiliation over the cuffs, maybe, or over knowing she was watching the awkwardness they caused. Most frightening of all was the cold resignation. This had all happened to him before, and she knew he had to be remembering the last time he'd been led away in handcuffs.

They had been deliberately separated after they'd arrived at the sheriff's office, and she hadn't seen Rio during the time she had spent telling her story to Buck Elkins. And now he was asking her to tell part of it again. She knew that leaving her here to wait alone, wondering what he was doing, had been deliberate.

"What else do you want to know?" she asked. Her narrative had seemed pretty straightforward, and she thought she had explained it well, considering. She had told him about the trip to the clinic last night, about Rio's fight with Chase McCullar late this morning, and about taking Rio to the clinic to get stitches. About how they had found Doc's body. She had even mentioned the rancher who had stopped to check on why they were there, although she hadn't known his name.

"Well…" Sheriff Elkins said, looking at the ceiling as if he were trying to get everything straight in his mind. Then his eyes cut down to her, and he studied her face a few seconds before he spoke. "It looked to us like Doc put up a pretty good fight for a man his age. Judging by his hands. The condition of the room. That kind of thing."

She waited for him to go on. She couldn't possibly have any information about Doc's last minutes. She didn't even want to think about them, and she couldn't imagine what the sheriff expected her to say.

"Yes?" she asked finally.

"So it seems to me whoever killed him would be…marked up, maybe. Show some evidence of that struggle."

"I told you about the fight this morning," she said, understanding now where this was going. "I'm sure Mr. McCullar will verify what I said."

"Well, you see, ma'am, I asked Chase to come over and do just that."

Again she waited, but he didn't go on. She realized that what he was doing was a very effective method of interrogation. It encouraged the person being questioned to talk because the sheriff wasn't. Not many people would be comfortable with a prolonged silence in this kind of situation. Elkins probably solicited a lot of information just by throwing out a supposition and then keeping his mouth shut.

"And Chase McCullar denied the fight?" she asked finally. It was hard to believe anyone would lie in a situation like this, but Rio had blamed McCullar for what had happened to him before.

"No, ma'am, he didn't deny it. As a matter of fact, Chase had already reported that altercation before your call came in."

"Then...I don't understand the problem."

"The problem is Chase don't remember causing some of the injuries Delgado's got. I just thought maybe there was something else you'd like to tell me."

She wondered if that was the truth. Maybe Rio had told whoever was questioning him about what had happened between them. She couldn't blame him, considering what was at stake, but it felt somehow like a betrayal. She hadn't thought he would say anything about that.

But then she also hadn't thought that Chase, in his fury, would remember each separate blow he'd struck. Maybe she hadn't thought about those possibilities because she hadn't wanted to face what she'd done. Now she had no choice.

"I caused the rest of Mr. Delgado's injuries," she admitted softly.

The hazel eyes reacted to that. The pupils widened, but the sheriff's voice was still carefully controlled when he asked, "*You* caused them?"

"Yes," she agreed.

"You want to tell me what Delgado did to make you hit him, Ms. Richardson?"

"It wasn't like that," she said.

"What was it like?"

She lowered her eyes, momentarily escaping from the penetrating hazel assessment. She knew she was going to have to tell it all, and although she recognized the necessity, she dreaded dredging it up. Twice in one day seemed like overkill.

"I was raped. About...seven months ago." As always,

the rest of it came out in spurts, lacking much coherence or continuity, she imagined, and probably including information not pertinent to this investigation. Talking about what had happened was still hard for her, despite the number of times she had honestly tried to talk it all out. "He was someone I knew. Someone I trusted. And he raped me."

There was no response for a long time, but she kept her eyes directed downward because she didn't want to see whatever was in his.

"This morning," the sheriff suggested cautiously, "Mr. Delgado tried something that—"

"No," she denied sharply. She looked up then, her eyes widened in indignation. "It wasn't anything like that. He didn't do anything except touch my arm, but...for some reason I panicked."

"And?" the sheriff prompted.

"I had Mac McCullar's gun in my hand. I had carried it out with me to break up the fight. I hit him with it. Several times."

"Why don't you tell me exactly where you hit him?"

She should have been expecting the question, should have been preparing to answer it, but she'd been too concerned about the other. She knew how important this was, that what she said corresponded to what Chase McCullar had claimed.

She closed her eyes, trying to think, to recreate the scene this morning. So much of what had happened was hidden in the fog of her unthinking panic. She wondered if Chase McCullar's memory had been better than hers.

"On the cheekbone," she said. She knew that was right. That cut hadn't been on Rio's face after the fight. "And on his head. The left side of his head. His temple." As she said it, she could see that bruise in her mind's eye, part of it extending under the raven's-wing blackness of his hair. She knew suddenly that that was right, too, and she spoke with more confidence. "I know it was on his left temple because I'm right-handed." Then she hit a blank wall. "I'm not exactly sure…"

Her voice faltered while she tried desperately to remember, to picture Rio's face. She couldn't remember him facing her in the pickup. He had looked out the windshield, avoiding her eyes. She couldn't remember any other marks, other than the ones that had been there after the fight with Chase. "Maybe there was another blow or two, but…" She shook her head, slowly, still trying to think. "I'm not sure. I was pretty upset."

"Uh-huh," Elkins said, jotting down something on his notepad. "That's all?"

"I'm not sure that's all. It's all that I can remember."

"Okay," he said. He hadn't looked up from his notes. "Does that fit?"

"Ma'am?" he said, hazel eyes lifting again to her face.

"Does what I said fit the injuries Chase claimed he didn't cause?"

"I'll have to double-check that. I guess that's all we need from you. For the time being anyway."

"I can go?"

"Yes, ma'am. You want me to call your brother for you?"

She was already standing, fumbling in the pocket of her jeans for Jenny's keys when he said it. "Call my brother?" she repeated. "Why would you think I'd want you to call my brother, Sheriff Elkins?"

He lifted both hands, palms up. "Just thought you might want to let him know what's happened. Must have been a shock and all, finding Doc." Again the hazel eyes were assessing her reaction.

"Of course, it was a shock, but my brother's in Austin on business. I don't think this is something to call him back here for."

"What if he finds out about all this from someone else? How's he going to feel about that?"

"All *this?*" she asked. She knew what he meant, but she

didn't intend to give him the satisfaction of thinking he was scaring her. "I don't believe Trent knew Doc Horn all that well. I don't know why you think he'll be so…disturbed."

"I wasn't talking about Doc."

There was silence for a couple of heartbeats. "Well, maybe you should be," she suggested softly, "instead of whatever you *are* talking about. After all, it's your job to find out who killed him. Maybe you and your deputy should be out looking for his murderer right now instead of worrying about calling my brother. If I decide my brother needs to be called, I assure you I'm fully capable of doing it."

She turned and walked out of the office and through the short hallway that led out to the reception area. When she got there, Chase McCullar was standing near the outer door, leaning against the wall. It was obvious he was waiting. He straightened when he saw her.

"I thought I'd follow you back to Jenny's. Check things out for you," he said. His nose was more swollen than it had been this morning and the area on either side, under his eyes, was turning blue-black.

"Where's Rio?" she asked.

There was a momentary hesitation, but he told her. "They're going to hold him."

"For what?" she asked.

"As a suspect in Doc's murder," he said.

"He couldn't be a suspect. He was with me, maybe even with you, when Doc was killed."

"We can't know exactly when that was until the coroner gets through," Buck Elkins said from behind her.

She turned around to find him standing in the doorway to the hall, watching them. "The blood in that room wasn't dry. Not just the pool…" She hesitated, fighting the images. "A lot of the rest of it was still wet. You *know* that. Rio was with one or both of us," she said, indicating Chase with a quick slant of her head, "from about ten o'clock on. There was no way he could have had anything to do with

Doc's death, and you know it. Both of you know it," she said, glancing again at McCullar.

The sheriff's eyes connected briefly with Chase's and then came back to hers. "Time of death's a hard thing to determine, Ms. Richardson. I've seen cases where—"

"Where blood drops stayed moist in this climate? For several hours?" she asked. "I don't think so, Sheriff Elkins. I don't think you think so either. And I want you both to know that this isn't going to work again."

"Again?" Chase repeated.

"Framing Rio Delgado for murder. Don't let success go to your head."

"Framing?" Chase's voice had risen sharply.

"You know. That's where someone is convicted for a crime he didn't commit. Only this time, you'll have me to contend with. *And* my brother." The last she had directed at the sheriff. "Trent's a pretty good lawyer. He always has been, and I have to tell you that I think it would probably be a very big mistake to hold a man when you have no physical evidence to tie him to a crime. *And* more importantly, when you have a reliable witness to provide him with an alibi. Maybe even two witnesses."

She deliberately locked her gaze on McCullar's when she said that. She could tell he was thinking about it. She just needed to scare them enough that they would at least think twice about trying to railroad Rio again.

"What makes you think we've got no physical evidence?" Elkins asked.

"Do you?" she challenged, and, although her heart rate had accelerated because she knew they both had been in the examination room last night, she waited, outwardly calm, through his silence. "I didn't think so," she said finally. "All you've got to tie Rio to Doc's murder is that we were the ones who found the body. Shouldn't that make me a suspect, too?"

"Except you're not a convicted murderer," Chase reminded her.

"Maybe that's because I wasn't around when Mac was killed. Just lucky, I guess."

"That's not fair," Chase said, but he wasn't backing away from this confrontation, and there was no embarrassment in the strong features.

"Neither is railroading somebody because you need revenge for your brother's death."

"What makes you think Rio was railroaded? How the hell can you be so sure he didn't do what an impartial jury found him guilty of? You just met him. You don't know anything about what went on here five years ago or about Delgado."

"I know what he told me. That he didn't have anything to do with Mac's death. I believe him. More importantly, *Doc* believed him. *Doc* knew what went on five years ago. He knew Rio a lot better than I do. Apparently a lot better than you do, Mr. McCullar."

"He's got to have somewhere to go before I can release him, Ms. Richardson," the sheriff said, deliberately interrupting the increasingly heated exchange. "He's got to have some place to live. That's a condition of his parole." He shrugged his shoulders as if to imply that he had no other choice than to keep Rio locked up.

"Then he'll be staying with me," she said, burning her bridges with a vengeance. She could imagine Trent's reaction to that. And Jenny's. "We'll be at Jenny McCullar's ranch. You can reach us there if you have further questions."

"At Jenny's?" Chase asked incredulously. "You think you're going to take that bastard back to Jenny's?"

"For the time being. It doesn't seem there's anyone else in this place who understands the concept of 'innocent until proven guilty.' I think Jenny will."

"I don't give a damn who your brother is, you're not going to take Mac's killer there," Chase retorted. "Not to Mac's house."

"I'm not planning on it," Anne said. "I'm planning on

taking Rio Delgado there. You're welcome to call Jenny and tell her all about it. Meanwhile, Sheriff, if you'd get Mr. Delgado, please?"

SHE HAD THOUGHT IT WAS worth a try, but she had never in her wildest dreams believed it would work. She didn't know whether it was invoking Trent's name or not, and she didn't really give a damn. She'd deal with Trent when he showed up. And he would. Probably just as soon as Chase McCullar could get to a phone.

"How did you manage this?" Rio asked softly when they were in the truck.

McCullar and Buck Elkins were standing outside the sheriff's office watching them. "I have no idea," she said honestly. "Bluff. Name-dropping. Reminding them of the Constitution."

"You mean they've heard of it?" Rio asked.

"All the rights and privileges thereof," she suggested softly. She had put enough distance between them and the watching men that she felt free to glance over at him. "You okay?" she asked. He didn't look okay. He looked like hell.

"I'm fine," he said succinctly, his voice denying the concern in hers. "I'm just sorry you got mixed up in all this."

"What do you think would have happened if I *hadn't* been mixed up in it?"

"I'd still be in Buck's jail."

"Then you probably shouldn't be too sorry," she advised. This time she smiled at him before she directed her eyes back to the road.

Chapter Six

"I think that's about all I can do," Anne said, stepping back to survey her handiwork. "But I'm not sure it's going to do any good now."

They were in Jenny's kitchen. Rio was sitting in one of the ladder-back chairs they had pulled from under the table. Anne had positioned it near the windows over the sink to give her enough natural light to work. Rommel was spread out on the coolness of the tile floor, his nose resting on top of Rio's boot. The dog made an occasional snoring noise, and his legs twitched periodically. He was obviously dreaming about chasing jackrabbits or maybe about protecting pregnant illegals.

Anne hadn't been surprised when the shepherd had welcomed Rio as if he were a long-lost friend. Or maybe his master, she thought with amusement. Rom had greeted her politely, of course, pushing his nose into her hand, but it had been the man who had received the lion's share of his adoring attention.

Rio's fingers touched the neat row of tape butterflies with which she'd tried to reconnect the split skin over his cheekbone. "It doesn't matter," he said. "Thanks for trying."

"For somebody who looks like you..." she began, and his eyes came up quickly. There was something in them that made her hesitate and then amend what she'd been about to say, "Vanity doesn't seem to be a vice," she finished.

"I've got plenty of others to make up for it."

"I haven't noticed that many," she denied, smiling at him. She hadn't. So far only some pretty admirable qualities had been revealed. She had found nothing that might cause the bad blood he'd claimed was behind Chase McCullar's long-standing enmity.

"You just haven't known me long enough," he suggested.

She stopped to figure. Less than twenty-four hours? It didn't seem possible it had been that few, but a lot had happened to them in that short time. "A heap of living," her grandmother would have said. And they'd done most of it together.

She didn't know why she had no doubts about her assessment of Rio Delgado. There was no logical reason for her to be so certain he hadn't been involved in what a jury had sent him to prison for. It just didn't feel right. Nothing she had learned about this man made her believe there was any truth to that accusation.

"Why does Chase McCullar hate you? I mean… obviously he hated you even before Mac was killed. If he framed you."

Rio didn't answer for a long time, trying to find the right words. Their relationship wasn't easy to explain. He'd never tried to explain it to anyone. He was probably the only person in the world who understood Chase McCullar's feelings. He even shared some of them. He understood all that, but telling it to an outsider…

"It can't be any worse than what I told you," she said softly.

Again, she had seemed to read his mind. It was uncanny that there was this connection between them. He was good at that kind of thing. It had something to do, maybe, with what he could do with animals, that ability to read past their pain and fear. But he'd never known another person who had been able to read him so clearly.

Doc, maybe, he thought, and then he remembered the room where they'd found the old man, the image suddenly there, unforgivingly clear and unwanted. That was something he'd been pushing out of his head all afternoon.

"We had the same father," he said, pulling his mind away from the loss of Doc. He watched her think about what he'd said.

"You're…"

"Chase McCullar's half brother."

"And Mac's," she breathed.

He nodded. "And Mac's."

"Mac was something special," he had told her. "Then how could Chase think…" She shook her head. "How could he possibly believe you had anything to do with Mac's death?"

"Mac's murder," he corrected. "Another murder."

"You believe they're…connected?"

"I wouldn't think so, not with five years between. But who knows?" he said, shrugging. "Nobody knows what happened to Mac, even after all this time. Maybe…" He stopped the words, reaching down to run his fingers through Rom's thick coat.

"You're afraid they won't find whoever killed Doc."

"Let's just say I'm not impressed with Buck Elkins's track record. I'm still their likeliest candidate. You know they're not going to give up trying to blame it on me. It's not going to be as easy as it was this afternoon."

"I know," she said. "You need a lawyer. A good one."

"Yeah," he agreed. His small smile was almost twisted. "Always did."

"Maybe… Maybe if I asked Trent, he'd be willing to do something."

"Miss Richardson, I think the only thing your brother's going to be willing to do is to throw me out of here. Just about as fast as he can manage it."

She knew he was right. Trent would not be pleased about their relationship. The word surprised her. It usually wasn't used in a context that encompassed whatever it was that they shared. Friendship? she wondered. Even that didn't seem to fit. Whatever she chose to call what was between them, she knew it was not something her brother would approve of.

"And Jenny," she said aloud, realizing Trent wasn't the only one she should be worrying about. "What's Jenny going to think about me bringing you back here?"

"You want me to leave?"

She thought about it. It would make things easier. Except for him, of course. Buck Elkins would have him back in a cell in a second. She had heard too many stories about things that happened in the jails of small, isolated communities like this to be comfortable with Rio going back there.

Besides, it simply wasn't fair. She knew Rio had had nothing to do with Doc's death. It wasn't fair that he was being blamed for something that wasn't his fault. That injustice had been echoing in her mind since she'd watched them put the cuffs on him this afternoon. Since she'd seen what had been in his eyes.

She found herself remembering her own struggle with being unjustly accused, even if that accusation had been given voice only in her own mind. *It was not my fault.* But even there, in her head, the words were damaging, her counselor had told her. The idea that she should have to deny—even to herself—that she had in any way, shape, or form been responsible for what had happened to her was damaging.

"I don't want you to leave," she said, looking up into his eyes. They were soft and dark, but they weren't pitying. They weren't doubting her ability to get on with her life. They never had. "You shouldn't have to explain that you didn't have anything to do with Doc's death. It's obvious. It's not fair that they doubt you."

"Somebody tell you life's fair?" Rio asked. Then he smiled at her, for the first time without mockery or sarcasm. It was a real smile, devastatingly beautiful despite his battered features.

In response, something moved inside her, shifting hotly, deep within her body. The feeling was unfamiliar, almost forgotten, but despite that unfamiliarity, she knew, as she had when she had touched his fingers last night, exactly what it was. And she didn't want to think about it. She couldn't afford to think about it.

"I guess whoever did was wrong," she admitted. She took a breath. It was a little uneven because the sensation was still fluttering somewhere within her lower body. "Where would you go if you left here?"

"That's not your problem."

"It might be. If you just disappear, I think Sheriff Elkins might hold me responsible. If you ran, maybe he'd decide *I* had something to do with Doc's death."

She could tell he hadn't thought about that possibility, and as she had hoped it would, it made him pause and rethink leaving the ranch.

"Why didn't you do that before?" she asked. "Why didn't you go back over the border and disappear?"

He laughed. "I didn't know what they thought when they asked me to come in. I was at Doc's. Elkins came out there and said he had some questions about what I'd overheard that night. About the threat against Mac. I thought maybe I could help them find whoever had killed him. I thought they wanted my help."

"Instead they arrested you."

"I was pretty young at the time and incredibly naive."

"If I weren't mixed up in this," she asked, "is that what you'd do now? Just...disappear?" She wouldn't blame him. As he'd said, Elkins's track record at catching murderers wasn't comforting.

"If I did, it would be an admission of guilt, I guess. At least to them."

"You don't want to give them that satisfaction?"

"Not unless I have to. But the offer's still good. I can go back to Elkins's jail."

"After that great bluff I ran? You want to let that all go to waste?"

He laughed.

"And besides," she said, "you're the only one in this county I know for sure *didn't* do it."

The question was in his eyes, wondering, she supposed, about that segue.

"You're the only one I know for *sure* didn't kill Doc Horn. Whoever did is still out there, running around loose while Elkins and his deputy try to pin it on you."

"You think…" He paused, and she knew it was because he didn't want to frighten her.

"I think that other than the woman we took to the clinic last night, we're the last people to see Doc alive. The last ones to talk to him. And a lot of people probably know that by now. Frankly, it scares me. So…no matter what my brother and Jenny will have to say about it when they get home, I really *don't* want you to leave."

He thought about that. "Somebody else talked to Doc after we did," he reminded her.

"Whoever killed him," Anne said, nodding agreement. "Trying to get information from him. Believe me," she added, and she shivered despite the heat, "believe me, I hadn't forgotten."

"WHAT DO YOU MEAN, you let him go?" Dwight Rogers demanded angrily.

Word about Doc's death had spread like wildfire. The old man had been loved, and everyone in the county had depended on the little clinic. They were pretty far from any kind of emergency care out here, and despite his age, Doc had been more than capable of dealing with the injuries that sometimes resulted from trying to make a living from this unforgiving land. Almost everybody within this county had been to visit Doc at one time or another.

"I didn't have any grounds to hold him," Buck Elkins explained patiently.

It was an explanation the sheriff or his deputy had made both over the phone and in person all afternoon. The sheriff's office hadn't provided any details about the nature of Doc's death, but that hadn't prevented word from leaking out.

"Delgado was right there. Standing outside Doc's clinic, bold as brass. I didn't recognize him right away, but then later, when I heard that he'd been involved in Doc's death, I knew that's who it was. It was him, all right. For heaven's sake, Buck, what other kind of evidence do you need?"

"The kind that'll stand up in court, for starters. You said Ms. Richardson was there, too. You think she helped him kill Doc?"

"I don't know *what* she helped him do. Finding that out is your job, but it don't seem like you're inclined to do it."

"Don't you tell me how to do my job, Dwight, and I won't tell you how to raise sheep." There was anger in the sheriff's voice now. He'd been patient with their questions, but he wasn't known for being a patient man and this questioning of his authority and his judgment had been going on for quite a while now.

"Delgado ain't been back more'n forty-eight hours and already we got another murder," Ben Pirkle said. "Wished I'd 'a drove my truck off a cliff somewhere while that bastard was in it. I *knew* I should have recognized that face. Kept trying to think where I'd seen him before. He got out maybe five miles as the crow flies from the McCullar spread. I didn't put that together then, 'cause I didn't recognize him, but I reckon he was aiming to meet up with that Richardson woman soon as he arrived."

"This is Senator Richardson's sister we're talking about, here," Deputy Morales reminded them. "It's not likely she knew Delgado before he showed up there yesterday."

"Then what's she doing out running around with him?" Rogers asked. "*And* providing him with an alibi. You think she'd do that for somebody she just met? That doesn't make any sense, Ray, and you know it."

"Maybe she's providing that alibi because she's just telling the truth," Chase interjected, feeling for some reason that he ought to defend his sister-in-law's guest. It somehow seemed disloyal to Jenny not to. "Maybe it happened just like she said. Rio came to Jenny's to find his horse, and it went on from there."

"And you believe they carried some pregnant Mexican to Doc's like they said, too?" Bobby Thompson mocked. "The very night before he was killed? Then they show up at the clinic the next day just in time to find the body? Sounds mighty convenient to me."

"Convenient how?" Chase asked. He was leaning again against the wall near the door, listening to his neighbors' heated reactions to Doc's death.

"May be a way to explain it if they'd left any fingerprints or bloody footprints or some such."

"You been watching too much TV, Bobby," Sheriff Elkins said in disgust. "If they'd left bloody footprints, being there the night before sure as hell wouldn't explain 'em away. All this speculating is getting us nowhere. Unless you all got something to tell me about Doc's death—something concrete—then you need to get on out of here. Go home, so me and Ray can do our jobs. You're just getting in the way. We'll get a hell of a lot more accomplished without you all in here."

The crowd of hard-bitten ranchers milled around awhile after that, still complaining, still mourning the loss of Doc, but eventually they complied. There was nothing they could do here besides let the county know they weren't happy with the situation, weren't happy at all that Rio Delgado was back and on the loose.

When they were gone, Chase studied the sheriff's darkly tanned face for a moment. "Watch your back, Buck," he advised softly before he opened the outer door. "I'm telling you he needs to be locked up. If he hurts Trent Richardson's sister, there's going to be hell to pay."

"What else is new?" Buck said. "There's always some kind of hell to pay in this job. You ought to remember enough about it, Chase, to realize that."

ANNE DIDN'T KNOW WHAT she had expected when she brought Rio home to Jenny's, but certainly not the ordinariness of the evening. After she'd taken care of the cut on his face, she had heated one of the casseroles Jenny had left in the refrigerator and cut squares from the congealed fruit salad she'd found there as well.

They had eaten at the small kitchen table, and there hadn't been much conversation. She had a feeling that Rio didn't talk very much anyway, and after today...

Too much had happened for them to pretend to make light, dinnertime conversation. She could probably still have managed that, having served as Trent's hostess on numerous occasions, entertaining people she barely knew and had little in common with. But to have pushed Rio to talk would have struck the wrong note, intruding on his very private grief. Despite the fact that he hadn't said anything else about the old man—not since they'd left Doc's clinic, anyway—she knew very well that Rio was grieving.

After their simple meal was over, he'd carried his plate to the sink and had even offered to help her wash up.

"Two plates and a couple of forks?" she said, smiling at him. "I think I can handle it. And before you offer, I don't dry. I just put them in the drain tray and leave them. Go watch the news or something."

She was standing by the sink, letting the water run over her hand to gauge when it got hot enough that she could put the stopper in.

"You think Mrs. McCullar would mind if I took a shower?" he asked.

The image formed quickly, clear as a snapshot in her

head. Water streaming in hot rivulets over the dark skin of his chest. She wondered if there was a mat of hair there that matched the midnight blackness of his brows and lashes. Or a thin, dark line of it tracing downward between the muscles of his flat stomach. She forced her mind away from that thought and became aware that the water running over her outstretched hand was getting hot. Too hot for comfort.

She put the stopper into the stained porcelain sink and squirted in the detergent before she answered him, trying to keep her voice steady. "If Jenny were here, we'd ask her. Since she's not, I don't see why you can't. There are clean towels on the shelf above the john, soap and shampoo in the shower enclosure."

"You want me to wait until you've finished the dishes?" he asked.

"I'll be through with them before you can get undressed." The word echoed in her head. Undressed. Naked. She took a breath, again fighting the images.

"If this is going to make you uncomfortable, then I—"

"Don't," she ordered, turning around to face him. "Don't do that. That's one thing I really liked about you. You don't treat me like…" She took another breath, feeling her control beginning to unravel.

"Okay," he said, and then more softly, holding her gaze, "It's okay." The tone was the same reassuring one he had used in the barn. And at Doc's.

She looked down again into the swirling bubbles of the dishwater and listened to his footsteps fade away down the hall, moving past the overblown roses and toward the small, old-fashioned bathroom.

She had made too big a thing of his question, she knew. She closed her eyes, thinking that it was so hard to walk that line. Hard to figure out how a normal person would act.

Normal? She rejected the word, furious with herself. *I am normal. I can say whatever I feel like saying. There's nothing wrong with what I said. Anybody else would have said the same thing.*

She slipped the two plates they'd used into the hot, soapy water and enjoyed washing them. Enjoyed making them clean again with her trembling fingers. That was so damn easy. It was just a shame that everything in life was not as easy to wash away. Not nearly as easy to make clean again.

"YOU REALLY THINK HE had something to do with Doc's death?" Samantha McCullar asked her husband.

"It's a pretty big coincidence," Chase said. His long fingers finished unbuttoning his shirt. He shrugged out of it and threw it over the foot of the iron bed. "He's home maybe forty-eight hours and somebody else ends up dead."

"Why would Rio kill Doc? I thought Doc looked after him after his mother died. As much as anyone did."

Samantha was sitting cross-legged in the center of the big bed, her nightgown bunched up around her thighs. She had been brushing her hair when Chase had come in. She held the forgotten hairbrush in her hand, her eyes on her husband. She knew how much Chase had loved the old man.

"Who knows what that bastard will do? I thought he…" He hesitated, his lips tightening over the words as if to prevent them from slipping out.

"You thought he cared about Mac, too," Samantha said softly.

Chase nodded. "That was one thing that made what he did so hard to take. Mac had been good to him. Protected him when he got into trouble. I knew Rio was trash, pure border trash, but Mac never saw that."

"Maybe Mac saw something else," she suggested.

"Like what?" Chase asked.

He had thought about what Trent Richardson's sister had said all evening. About the blood not being dry. About how maybe there were *two* witnesses who could verify that Rio wasn't the one who had killed Doc. It had bothered him because he knew what the dryness of the desert air would have done to that blood as well as she did. And it made him wonder.

"Maybe Mac just saw his brother," Samantha said. "Another little brother he needed to love and take care of."

"I don't need to hear that tonight," Chase said angrily. "Especially not from you."

His blue eyes were hard and his mouth had tightened. Samantha smiled at him because she loved him, even when he was stubborn and angry and so very McCullar. "What *do* you need?" she asked softly. "From me, I mean."

"I thought you'd never get around to asking."

His fingers moved to the metal buttons of his fly. Samantha leaned back, her elbow on the mattress. Her fingers found the switch on the bedside light. She clicked it off, plunging the room into forgiving darkness.

ANNE WAS PRETENDING to read the same book she had been pretending to read last night, when she heard Rio come into the den. Rommel got up from where he'd been lying beside the couch and padded across the floor to say hello.

She watched Rio bend to greet the dog. His long, dark fingers caressed behind the shepherd's ears, and the dog sat down, eyes raised to the man's in soulful canine worship. Rio's mouth curved slightly in an unconscious response to that look.

His hair was still wet from the shower, gleaming blue-black in the lamplight. He had put on the same clothes he'd been wearing. Wearing for at least a couple of days now, Anne realized belatedly.

"I should have thought. There are probably some things of Mac's around. You could have had a change of clothes, too."

He looked up at her, eyes unfathomable. "These are fine. I don't think..." He paused. Even his fingers seemed uncertain for the first time since she'd known him, hesitating just above the dog's thick fur.

"You wouldn't want to wear something that belonged to your brother," she realized. "I understand that."

"It's not that. I'm not sure they'd *want* me to wear Mac's things, but thanks for...thinking about it."

"Jenny and Chase?" she asked.

He smiled—the small, almost-twisted one instead of the one he had given her this afternoon. "I guess when I said 'they,' I was thinking about Mac and Chase. That doesn't make much sense, does it? Mac sure wouldn't care anymore who wore his clothes. Not even if it was me."

"You said that Mac was...special." She had thought about that a lot since she'd found out what he'd been sent to prison for. Thought about the difference in what the jury had believed when they'd convicted Rio Delgado and the soft admiration in his voice when he'd talked about his dead brother. "What did you mean by that?"

"I don't know. Just that he was...a good man, maybe. Everybody in the county felt that way. As for me..." He took a breath before he finished that thought. "I guess I thought he was special because it didn't seem to matter to Mac that I was just a bastard."

He squatted down in front of Rom, balancing on his bare toes. His feet were narrow and well made. Just like the rest of him, she thought, and then her mind flinched away from that unwelcome realization and back to what he'd said.

"He...treated you like a brother?" she asked.

"Not really. But that wasn't Mac's fault. I knew I wasn't his brother. Just his father's bastard."

"With an attitude like that..." she said softly. The admonition was deliberate this time, and gently mocking. Not mocking him, but her own lack of understanding the first time she'd said it to him. He looked up at her, amusement in the dark eyes.

"I know. Even if Mac had wanted to...acknowledge our relationship, I would have rejected any attempt he made. I was prickly as cholla and convinced they both hated me as much as I hated them."

"Why did you hate them?"

His gaze dropped back down to the dog. He lowered his head, and Rom obligingly licked his face. Rio grinned at the wet kiss, and watching them together, Anne felt her own lips tilt in response.

"Because I thought they had it all. Everything I didn't have."

"A father?" she asked.

"I didn't realize until years later that they didn't really have one, either. Drew McCullar was pretty much an all-around son of a bitch. Mean as a copperhead snake and drunk half the time. Mac and Chase worked the ranch, and he—" The words were cut off, and she waited for a long time in the silence.

"He what?" she asked finally.

"Rode over the river and made love to my mother."

"And you resented that."

"Hell, I resented the air back then." He didn't say anything else for a while, and when he did, his voice was calm and controlled again. "I resented that he didn't even know my name. Maybe he did, but he never called me anything. He'd flip me a quarter when he got there and tell me to get out. There was never anywhere to go. I used to sit outside listening to them, even in the winter, just waiting for him to leave. Sometimes he didn't."

"And you'd sit there all night," she whispered.

His eyes came up, and he smiled at her again.

"It was a long time ago. I was a little boy. I didn't know what it was like between a man and a woman. I didn't know much of anything."

You knew you were outside, she thought. *Always outside in the cold. And you thought everybody else was inside, safe and warm and protected.*

"That still doesn't explain why Chase would hate you," she said instead of voicing that realization.

"McCullar's wife had bone cancer. She died slow and hard. I knew that because Doc made a point of telling me.

Maybe to help me understand. A lot of that time, while she was dying, McCullar spent with my mother. Chase knew it. Hell, everybody knew it. There are no secrets here.''

"Chase blamed *you* for that?'' There was condemnation in her voice. She knew whose side she was on. That decision had been made very quickly after she'd met Rio, and nothing she had learned since had made her change her mind.

"When you're a kid watching your mother die by slow and painful inches, you have to blame somebody. I guess my mother and I were natural targets for his hatred.''

"You sound like you think that makes sense,'' she said.

"My mother died of pneumonia when I was eleven. I blamed Drew McCullar. How much sense does that make?''

She shook her head, knowing those hurts were probably too old and too deeply embedded to do anything about now.

"Where do you want me to sleep?'' he asked.

He stood, black eyes meeting hers without any apology for or awkwardness about his question. He had taken her at her word. *Don't walk around me on tiptoe. Don't examine every word you say to see if it might remind me.* And again she was grateful for his sensitivity.

"I'm sleeping in Chase's old room. You can have the master bedroom where Jenny sleeps or Mac's room.''

It wasn't much of a choice, she supposed. The bed Mac and Jenny had shared during their marriage or the one Mac had slept in those nights his father hadn't come home from across the river.

"I'll take Mac's, I guess,'' he said. The knowledge that he knew exactly what she'd been thinking was in his eyes.

"First door on the right,'' she directed.

"You get Mac's gun back out and put it on the table beside your bed,'' he ordered.

"Why?'' she asked, wondering if he thought she was afraid of him.

"Just do it. I'll feel better knowing it's there.''

"Because you're here?" she asked unbelievingly. "Because—"

"Because whoever killed Doc is still out there. I don't mean to scare you, but you said it yourself. We need to be careful."

"Then put the gun beside *your* bed. I'll feel better that way. Safer. I'm not sure how I'd react in an emergency."

She was surprised when he laughed.

"Judging from the way I've seen you react in the past day or so, I'd say you'd do just fine in an emergency. Any emergency."

She was a little embarrassed because she'd pulled the gun on him *and* on Chase, but still, she was pleased by the compliment. Apparently he thought that she'd handled herself well during the events of the last couple of days. And that made her feel...normal, she thought. The woman she had always been. Whole. And well.

"I'll go get you the gun," she said, fighting not to reveal her emotion in her voice. She got up and walked across the room. He had squatted down again in response to Rom's paw batting demandingly against his thigh. When she reached the door to the hall, she turned back, watching them together.

"Rio," she said. He pivoted on his toes, not getting up. His eyes were questioning; one hand was still on the big dog. "Thank you," she said softly. "Thank you for saying that. I guess...I guess I just needed to hear it. I don't know how you knew that, but... Anyway, I want you to know that I'm grateful." She turned and disappeared into the dark hallway.

The man she had left behind lowered his face and rubbed his forehead slowly against the dog's. His dark fingers still moved restlessly in the soft, silver fur.

Chapter Seven

The dreams were unclear. The images shifted even as she fought them, fought to pull herself from their dark power. Doc's body and the blood-splattered examination room. The ever-present memory of the assault. Her assailant's handsome face. Her hand, holding the revolver, striking at that hated visage again and again until somehow it metamorphosed into Rio's dark beauty. The fight between the half brothers, their expressions revealing all the old hatreds. The hollow thud of their blows, echoing in her head as they hit each other. Over and over again. And the revolver in her hand, rising and falling.

It was near dawn before, exhausted, Anne finally slipped into the first real sleep she had found during the long hours of darkness. When a hand closed over her wrist, it didn't seem she had been dreaming of anything. There were no dream images to fit that unmistakable sensation. She came awake instantly, fully aware that someone was touching her, holding her arm. Someone real. She knew before she opened her eyes that it was not a figment from her dreams.

Instinctively, her legs pushed away, scrambling backward, across the bed, trying to escape the touch of that hand. It didn't release her, however, and panic began to claw at her chest. She recognized the voice that whispered out of the darkness. Again there was no doubt in her mind who was talking to her.

"Anne," Rio whispered. "It's all right. It's me."

All their warnings about him rushed into her brain. Along with the fears she had not realized were hiding there. *He's just what they said he was,* she thought. *And he'll hurt me. He'll hurt me again.* Except that hadn't been Rio. That was someone else, and she knew that.

"There's someone outside," he said. "Listen to me." The hand that was fastened over her wrist shook her slightly, trying to wake her, to bring her back to face the reality of what he had just told her.

Someone outside? Outside Jenny's, she realized, finally remembering where she was. Maybe someone who would… Maybe the same someone who had done that to Doc. The arc of dark droplets that had been thrown high on the ceiling above Doc's head was suddenly in hers again, clear and terrifying.

"Come on," Rio whispered. "Stay right behind me so I know where you are."

She scrambled across the bed toward him, moving awkwardly on her knees. He hadn't released her arm, and she was grateful now for the strength of his supporting hand. Even in the dimness, she could see that he held the revolver she had given him in his other one. He handled the gun as if he knew how to use it, and she found herself praying that he did.

He released her arm, and she stood beside him, breathlessly listening. In the quietness, she could hear the small noises from outside, whatever had awakened him. Somewhere a car door was closed, not slammed, but closed with deliberate softness. Then, at last, there was the unmistakable sound of someone walking up the steps to cross the wooden porch, coming toward the front door.

"Stay behind me," Rio warned again before he started forward.

Together they moved silently down the shadowed hall. The roses were barely visible, dark blobs against the paler cream of the background. They were almost to the end of it when Anne recognized the next sound. Someone was fitting a key into the lock of the front door, turning it.

She reached for Rio's shoulder, but he was too far ahead for her fingers to make contact. As the door swung inward, Rio raised Mac's revolver, focusing it steadily toward the opening that widened as they watched.

Jenny McCullar's small form moved into the den first, followed by the taller shape that Anne recognized immediately as her brother. Not whoever had killed Doc, she thought with relief. That person had not come to find them. It was only Trent and Jenny. She knew she shouldn't be surprised. Someone had probably called Austin. People had been threatening to call her brother since this had started.

"Anne?" Trent asked. His voice was rich with disbelief, and she could imagine what he was thinking.

She was standing in back of Rio, wearing her nightshirt. Rio had pulled on only his jeans, and she knew they would be able to see his half-clothed body better than hers, almost hidden in the shadows behind him. They could probably see the muzzle of the .45 best of all, pointing straight at them out of the darkness.

"Yes," she answered. "It's my brother," she said softly, for Rio's benefit.

She moved around him and into the den at the same time Jenny's small, competent fingers flicked the light switch by the front door. The room was suddenly flooded with artificial light, which revealed Rommel, sitting beside the front door, tail gently moving in welcome. Apparently he had recognized the sound of Trent's car, which was why he'd given them no warning that someone was outside.

"What the hell's going on here?" Trent asked. His eyes were wide and dark, blinking to adjust to the sudden brightness. They were focused on the man who was now standing behind Anne. "Who the hell is that?" he asked.

"His name is Rio," Jenny said softly. "You can put away Mac's gun," she suggested. "I don't think he would want you to shoot me with it."

"I'm sorry, Mrs. McCullar," Rio said. "We thought you might be…"

"Might be who?" Trent demanded when Rio hesitated.

"Whoever killed Doc Horn," Anne explained.

"Why would you think—" Trent stopped, shaking his head. "Just what the hell's going on around here?"

"You think whoever murdered Tom might come here? Come after you?" Jenny asked.

Anne was surprised that Jenny seemed to be addressing the question to Rio. And surprised when he answered it.

"We were probably the last people to see him alive."

"That doesn't mean that…" Jenny paused, apparently trying to follow the logic of that. "Why would that make you think they'd come after you? That's…"

"Paranoid?" Rio suggested. At what was in his tone, the quiet mockery, Anne turned to look at him, and wished that she hadn't.

Rio hadn't taken time to button his jeans. He had simply pulled them on, and despite the flatness of his stomach, the Levi's gaped slightly at the waist, revealing that he was wearing nothing under them. And revealing that the narrow line of dark hair she had envisioned was reality.

She tore her eyes away, but not before they had acquired an image of the smooth darkness of the skin that covered his chest, the small brown nubs of his nipples centering the bulge of muscle on each side. She made herself look at Jenny. At Trent. At anything but that. Anything but Rio.

She watched Jenny shake her head, a small negative movement.

"Maybe not. Not in your case," Jenny said.

"But that doesn't explain what he's doing here." Trent apparently felt that things weren't proceeding as well as they might if he were in charge. He always took charge. It was his nature.

"I asked Rio to stay with me," Anne said. "I was afraid that… I guess I just didn't want to be out here alone."

"I *knew* that would happen," Trent said. "I tried to tell

you that you needed to come with us. I knew that it would all—''

"*Not* because of that," Anne interrupted. "This is…something entirely different. Someone was murdered, Trent."

"You found the body. The sheriff told me."

"He's the one who called you?"

"Of course, he called me. He was worried about you. Justifiably worried. The only thing I don't understand is why *you* didn't call."

"It didn't seem there was anything you could do," she offered. It sounded unconvincing, even to her.

"But there was something you thought *he* could do?" Trent asked, his eyes focused again on Rio. "Pull a gun on us, maybe?"

"We didn't know who you were. It's the middle of the night. Why didn't *you* call and let me know you were coming home tonight?"

There was silence for a moment, and then Trent asked, his voice holding an emotion she didn't immediately identify, "Are we…interrupting something? Is that the problem here?"

"Trent," Jenny said.

In her voice was caution or admonition. Anne couldn't quite decide which, and it didn't really matter—not given what her brother had just suggested.

"You're *not* interrupting anything," Anne said. There was bitterness underlying the words because she finally understood what he was thinking.

"I see," Trent said.

"I don't think you do. Rio's here because I asked him to stay with me. I was with him when Doc Horn was killed. He's the one person in this county I knew couldn't have had anything to do with the murder."

"Maybe not with *that* murder," Jenny said.

"Or with any other," Anne denied. Despite her certainty about Rio's innocence and her desire to help him, this was the last thing she had intended—to hurt Jenny. "He told me that he didn't…" Somehow, she couldn't bring herself to say it.

"Didn't help someone kill Mac?" Jenny finished for her. "Is that true?" she asked, and Anne realized that Jenny was again addressing the man behind her, the man who had been convicted of conspiring to murder her husband.

"Mac was my brother, Mrs. McCullar," Rio said. "Half brother. I swear to you I had nothing to do with what happened to him."

"A lot of people in this county don't believe that," Jenny said.

"Then a lot of people are wrong."

"Why should I believe you?"

He said nothing for a moment. Anne finally turned and looked at him again. His dark eyes were locked on Jenny's. "No reason, I guess. No reason you should believe me instead of Chase. Or the others. But I swear to you it's true. I had nothing to do with what happened to Mac. He was my brother," he said again.

"Would somebody tell me please what's going on here?" Trent demanded. "Who the hell *are* you?"

"His name is Rio Delgado. Chase thinks he had some…part in Mac's murder. He was sent to prison because of that." Jenny's tone was almost dispassionate, as if she were speaking about the death of a stranger.

"To prison?" Trent repeated. His face had reddened. "They warned us about this," he said. The comment made no sense in the context of the conversation that preceded it. "Damn it, I *knew* something like this would happen."

Even Jenny looked at him then, pulled her eyes away from the remarkable face of the man who had been accused and convicted of helping bring about her husband's death.

"Something like what?" she asked, puzzled.

"Risk taking. They all said it. Sexual risk taking. It happens with a lot of women who are…assaulted. You told me yourself, Anne, that your therapist—"

"Don't," Anne ordered. She could feel the rush of heated blood moving into her neck and cheeks. "That's not true, Trent. *Nothing* like that is going on. There's been nothing like what you're suggesting. How can you even think that I would—"

"What else *can* I think? We come home and find you…" He faltered, searching for words. "With some ex-con murderer. Not just that. That's bad enough, but with someone who… Do you realize that you've brought the man who killed Jenny's husband into her home? We walk in and you're both half-naked. You're here together. Spending the night here alone. What the hell do you expect me to think, Anne?"

"Not that," Rio said. His voice was soft, but there was something chilling under the quietness. And compelling. Not as it had been when he had whispered reassurance to the woman in labor or when he had talked to Rommel. It was commanding. That was what she heard in his tone, Anne realized. A deliberate command.

One that even her domineering, self-assured brother had sense enough to recognize. Trent's mouth closed suddenly, shutting off the insulting suggestions he had been in the process of making.

"There's nothing like that going on here," Rio said. "Miss Richardson was kind enough to speak up for me today. She assured the sheriff that I couldn't have had anything to do with Doc's murder. She knew that because I had been with her—and with Chase McCullar—when Doc was killed. When the sheriff planned to hold me because I had nowhere to go, she offered to let me come here. That's all that happened. I think you owe your sister an apology."

And you, Anne thought. *But don't hold your breath expecting one.* Trent always had a hard time admitting when he'd been wrong.

"It just looked as if…" Trent began, his tone more reasonable. "I mean we walk in here tonight, worried to death about you, and find a stranger holding a gun on us. What were we supposed to think?'' he asked.

''That maybe I knew what I was doing,'' she suggested.

Her brother said nothing for a moment. She watched his mouth tighten, and she knew that he still didn't believe that. He hadn't believed it for a long time. No matter that she knew his doubts about her actions were the result of his love for her, it hurt. Rio, who knew nothing about her, had more confidence in her.

Sexual risk taking. The words echoed in her head, reverberating with the horror that had been in her brother's voice when he had said them. She had been told that was often a side effect of having been raped, and Rio could certainly be considered to be a prime candidate if she *were* engaging in that behavior, but that was not, of course, what was going on between them.

Again she was surprised by what she had just thought. *Going on between them.* Nothing was going on between them. Nothing that wasn't—

''I don't think you can stay here,'' Jenny said. She was still watching Rio's face. He had lowered the gun and finally, at her words, he laid it down on the table beside the door.

''I understand,'' he said. ''I'm sorry for what happened tonight.''

''There's nowhere else for him to go,'' Anne protested. ''Except back to jail. Trent, you know what small-town jails can be like. There's no telling what might happen to him there.''

''Maybe—'' Trent began.

''There's a line shack,'' Jenny interrupted before Trent could voice whatever suggestion he'd intended to make. ''It's not been used in years, but there are beds. The place is pretty primitive, but at least it's somewhere to sleep. You can stay there until…'' She paused, obviously reluctant to make any promises, and finally she continued, ''At least until this is resolved.''

Anne wondered what that meant. Until the authorities had captured Doc's killer? Or until Jenny could think about Rio's claim not to have had anything to do with Mac's death?

"I'd be grateful," Rio said softly.

Anne had expected him to refuse. She turned to look at him, but his gaze was still focused intently on Jenny, maybe still trying to convince her that he had told her the truth.

"I'll give you directions if you need them," Jenny said. "You can leave as soon as it's light. I'll give you some things from the kitchen. There's a woodstove out there. You can cook."

"Thank you, ma'am," Rio said. "I appreciate it."

"And you can take Mac's gun," she added. "Just in case." Jenny turned and went outside, back into the pre-dawn darkness.

Trent looked as if he were no longer sure which of the women needed him the most. He stood for a moment, an unfamiliar uncertainty reflected in his handsome features.

"I'm all right," Anne said. "I promise you, Trent, I really am all right."

Her brother nodded, and then he followed the woman he loved outside. When Anne turned around, the dark hallway behind her was empty.

"I JUST THOUGHT I OUGHT to let you know what we've found out," Buck Elkins said. It was the morning of the day after Doc's body had been found. "I thought if anyone deserved to be kept up-to-date on the investigation, you did. I really appreciate your restraint about Delgado, Chase. No matter what the bastard's done, we don't need anyone going off half-cocked."

"And knowing me, you didn't expect that restraint."

"In all honesty, no. Especially not after the way you came in here yesterday."

"Well..." Chase said slowly, "I guess that's okay. I'm

not sure I expected it, either. I thought I'd still want to kill the bastard every time I saw him.''

"What changed?" the sheriff asked. There was a trace of amusement in the question. They both knew that the law probably wouldn't have been able to do much to prevent him if Chase had been determined to pursue that course.

"Maybe what she said," Chase admitted.

"The Richardson woman?"

"Yeah," Chase acknowledged. "What she said about there being two witnesses. She was right, Buck. I was with Delgado during the crucial part of yesterday. Just like she was.''

"We won't know what part of the day was really crucial until we get the coroner's report."

"Was that blood still wet like she said?"

"Hell, I don't know. I promise you I didn't go around checking that out. I liked Doc. I *didn't* like seeing what had happened to him. Maybe she thought it was wet. Or maybe she was lying about that also."

"Also?" Chase questioned.

"She must have been lying about the woman and the baby. About what had happened at the clinic the night before. There are no records of any kind to indicate anyone had been there that night. You know Doc was pretty meticulous about his record keeping. Everything else's there. Notes jotted down on charts about everything from the size of Dwight Roger's kid's tonsils to Jenny's birth weight. But there's no mention of a birth that night. No birth certificate. No chart."

"Maybe whoever killed Doc took them."

"Maybe," the sheriff admitted. "Or maybe they never existed. Somehow to me, one of those possibilities makes a lot more sense than the other, but I guess you'll have to make up your own mind. I just thought you might want to know what we found. I know how you felt about Doc."

"Not much different from the way everybody around here felt, I guess," Chase said.

"He's gonna be missed," Buck said softly. "There's no doubt about that. We all depended on Doc."

The silence stretched across the line. There didn't seem to be anything else they could say about the old man. For a county this spread out and isolated, that said it all.

"Thanks," Chase said finally. "I appreciate you letting me know what's going on. If there's anything I can do to help…"

Chase let the suggestion fade. He was an ex-lawman, both here as Mac's deputy a lot of years ago, and then later with the DEA. It was possible he had some expertise that the sheriff's office could use, but he also knew that law-enforcement officers usually guarded their jurisdictions with jealousy. They seldom welcomed outside help from someone they thought might try to come in and tell them how to solve a case.

"Well," Buck said hesitantly, "I don't know what that might be right now, but I appreciate the offer. And I'll keep it in mind. I don't mind telling you that folks are pretty hot. You might warn Ms. Richardson. Since Delgado's staying out there. I'd hate for things to get out of hand. I'd hate for somebody to get hurt."

"You hear something?"

Again the sheriff hesitated. "Ray says there's a lot of talk. Course, there's always a lot of people blowing off steam when something like this happens. You remember what it was like when Mac was killed. Folks want a case solved and somebody convicted before the corpse is cold." Then, apparently realizing how that sounded in relation to the sentence that had preceded it, he added, "Sorry, Chase. I guess I'm just not thinking too clearly right now. I didn't mean to remind you…."

"It's okay," Chase said. "Let me know if you find anything else. I appreciate the information, Buck. I'll call over at Jenny's and pass along the warning. And *you* take care."

"That's one thing you can count on. Whoever did that to Doc… I know you didn't see the body, but I have to tell you, it wasn't pretty. In all my years in this business, I've never seen anything like it.''

"They wanted something," Chase said.

"And Doc didn't give it to them. At least not at first."

"You think he did eventually?"

"I would," Buck said. "I'd have told them anything they wanted to know. I just wish I knew what that was."

RIO LOOKED AROUND the line shack as the sound of Trent Richardson's car faded in the distance. It wasn't that far in miles from the main houses and had probably been more of a bunkhouse than anything else. It was exactly as Jenny McCullar had warned him it would be—primitive. Not much different in that respect from the house where he'd grown up, he thought.

Rio threw his pack onto one of the beds and watched the dust billow upward in a small cloud. Jenny had tried to give him clean sheets, and he probably should have taken them. But it had been hard enough to agree to stay here. Hard to take something from the woman whose husband he'd supposedly helped murder.

Although he'd had nothing to do with that, everyone had always been convinced of his guilt. Everyone, it seemed, except Anne Richardson. And she was the reason, of course, that he was still here, and not miles deep into Mexico and still running.

He took a breath, thinking about the scene last night. About what her brother had said. *"Sexual risk taking."* He wondered if that had anything to do with what had happened between them. Had she spoken up for him because it was dangerous? Or because it seemed he was? Because for some reason she needed that risk?

He didn't know much about the aftereffects of rape, but somehow that didn't fit with what he did know about her, which was little enough. He knew that she had believed him when almost no one else ever had. And that there was nothing sexual about the way she looked at him. She wasn't interested in him that way. He would have known if that had been the case. He had always known.

So her brother was wrong, but that wouldn't stop him from taking Anne back to San Antonio as quickly as he could. *If* the sheriff agreed to her leaving, and there was no reason for him not to.

It was over. He'd never see Anne Richardson again. He fought down the sudden despair at that realization. He didn't need any complications, he told himself. Not that kind. He had enough troubles. He was still Buck Elkins's prime suspect. Soon there would be no one around to protest when they framed him for this murder. Just as there had been no one to speak up for him almost five years ago.

ANNE WAS SITTING in the den, again holding the book she'd been trying to read since she had arrived at the ranch. She had acknowledged by now that it wasn't ever going to get read, and it probably didn't deserve to be, but still it was a pretty good prop. Its presence had prevented the questions she had seen in Jenny's worried eyes, or at least put them off for a while.

Trent wasn't as sensitive, or maybe that was just big-brother prerogative. She had been aware for several seconds that he was standing in the doorway, watching her. Finally she gave in and looked up at him. She might as well get this over with. She had only been delaying the inevitable.

"I just wanted to say that I'm sorry for what I suggested last night." He moved farther into the room since her raised eyes had given him permission to interrupt her solitude.

"I know," she said. "I know you were just worried."

"Still…it doesn't make any sense, Anne. Even Jenny says that—"

"I'd really appreciate it if you wouldn't talk about me with Jenny," she said softly. "I know you love her, but…what happened to me really isn't any of Jenny's concern."

"It is if it has implications for her life."

"Implications?"

"Your bringing Delgado here. You knew what he'd done. I can't understand why you'd bring him here. To Jenny's house."

"I explained all that. I know Rio had nothing to do with Mac's death. Chase McCullar railroaded him. When he and I found Doc's body, I knew he had nothing to do with that murder, either. I was afraid they were going to do it again. They got away with it once, but I don't intend for them to get away with it again."

She could tell that her surety about Rio's innocence wasn't having any impact on Trent's discomfort over their relationship, so she reminded him of something else that she believed was important to them both. She hadn't followed Trent and her father into law, but the principles by which they had been raised were the same. "I was only doing what you taught me. You and Dad."

"Maybe we taught you too well. How can you be *so* sure—"

"Because I am. Because I...know him."

"After...what? It can't be much more than twenty-four hours?"

"He didn't do it, Trent. It doesn't matter how many hours are involved, I *know* he didn't do it."

"But surely you can see why we're concerned about you?"

"We?" Anne asked quietly.

"I'm sorry, but Jenny and I talked. I just think it would be best if you come back with me. I can take you home and then go on to Austin. I still have some business there I have to complete. There's no way I can put it off, but I don't think you ought to stay here."

"Are you saying Jenny doesn't want me here? Because I brought Rio to her house?"

"Jenny said nothing like that. In fact, I think she's been remarkably understanding. Considering. She hasn't mentioned your leaving. I'm the one who feels that would be best.''

''I don't think the sheriff is going to be eager to have me leave, not in the middle of a homicide investigation. I think I'm what you'd call a material witness.''

''I'll talk to him. I'm sure I can make him see that you don't really need this right now. When I've explained the situation to him—''

''The situation?'' she questioned, but she knew what he meant, what he intended to tell the sheriff.

The color rose slowly into Trent's fair cheeks. ''You know what I mean,'' he said.

She laughed, recognizing the same bitter quality in her own laughter that she had heard in Rio's. ''I know *exactly* what you mean. I'm not going home, Trent. Not now, at least. I'm going to stay right here, if Jenny will let me. If she won't, I'll find a room somewhere nearby. But I'm not going to run away. You might as well get that idea out of your head.''

''Anne—'' he began to protest, but again she cut him off.

''I thought you might do something for Rio.''

''For Rio?''

''I told him you're the best lawyer I know.'' A little flattery couldn't hurt, she thought, and besides, she knew Trent was a damn fine attorney, even if this wasn't exactly his specialty. ''I told him you might agree to represent him.''

Her brother stood there for a few long heartbeats without saying anything, and then finally he shook his head.

''You shouldn't have suggested that to him,'' he said. ''You had no right to do that.''

''You think I'm wrong about him. You think he's guilty. Of Mac's murder and maybe even of Doc's.''

''I don't know enough about either to form an opinion, but Delgado's not my client, and he's not going to be. I think that my taking him would be a slap in the face to Jenny. It's bad enough—'' He stopped the words abruptly.

''Bad enough that I'm involved with him?'' she suggested.

He nodded.

''You think that's an insult to Jenny?''

''Let's say that it at least seems…ungrateful. Maybe just unthinking. Neither of those is like you. You've never been insensitive to people's feelings.''

''I'm sorry you feel that way, but I'm afraid I have to do what I think is right.'' She smiled at him before she added. ''It's the way I was raised. Believing you *can* fight city hall. That people can make things right if they stand up and fight injustice. I guess it's too late to change that now.''

''I don't like leaving you here.''

''I know you don't, but it is *my* life, Trent, and you can't live it for me. Even if I make mistakes, they're my mistakes. And I'm entitled to make them.''

''The trial's in a few weeks,'' he reminded her gently. ''You're going to need every bit of strength you have to get through that. I just hate for you to be involved in all this right now.''

She thought about the man who had left at daybreak. A man who had always been outside, alone in the cold darkness. She remembered his hand closing around her wrist last night. Supporting her. Protecting her.

''But I am involved,'' she admitted softly. ''And I guess there's really nothing either one of us can do about that now.''

Chapter Eight

He had forgotten how good the sun felt beating against the bare skin of his shoulders. Forgotten how it felt to breathe in the hot, dry desert air while he worked. Forgotten how his hands felt doing something that had purpose.

Rio straightened, feeling a spasm in the tired muscles of his lower back. He put his gloved hand there and pressed down into the ache. He knew he'd pay a price for this tomorrow, but it was one he was more than willing to pay.

There wasn't much point in what he was doing, repairing fence on a ranch that didn't run stock. But the line had needed fixing and the tools to do the job had been in the shack. More importantly, he had had nothing else to do. Nothing besides thinking, and he had found that wasn't any more worthwhile an activity than mending fence around an empty range.

He took off the battered straw hat he'd found in the shack, lying on a shelf beside the leather gloves he was now wearing, and wiped the sweat from his brow with the back of his arm.

He heard the sound of a vehicle approaching from behind him. He turned around, and his eyes followed the line of dust the truck was raising across the horizon. He had seen that black pickup only once before, but he didn't have any trouble recognizing it. He remembered the revolver Jenny

McCullar had given him. He had almost refused to take the gun; now he was grateful that he hadn't.

His eyes tracked to where the big .45 was lying. It was a pretty good distance away, loosely covered by the shirt he'd discarded only a couple of hours after he'd started to work this morning. He thought about moving toward the revolver and then decided that would be asking for trouble. Just because Chase McCullar showed up out here didn't mean he needed a gun to deal with him. Not yet, at least. Not until he knew what his half brother intended.

He watched as the truck came to a stop near where he was working. Chase climbed out, hatless, his eyes narrowed against the glare of the afternoon sun. Jenny McCullar might have told him he could bunk in the shack, but Rio suspected that permission didn't sit too well with the other half owner of the McCullar land.

"Jenny said you were out here," Chase said. His nose looked a lot worse than it had yesterday, as did the bruising under his eyes. Rio could see the scrapes on his knuckles, and he wondered if Chase's hands had been as sore and swollen as his had been when he'd started work this morning.

McCullar's jeans were certainly as old and worn as his. His boots were just as scuffed. They were working clothes, and they'd obviously seen their share of the kind of backbreaking labor Rio had been doing for the past few hours. For the first time in his life, Rio realized that there didn't seem to be quite as much distance between himself and his half brother as he'd always believed there was.

Except I'm mending fence on somebody else's land, he reminded himself, *and Chase McCullar owns his own.*

"Unless you're trying to trap coyotes, you're wasting your time," Chase said. His narrowed blue eyes had traced along the long line of new fencing before he'd said it.

"That's okay," Rio said. "I've got lots of time."

"Jenny doesn't run any stock. Not anymore."

"She told me."

McCullar lowered his eyes, maybe examining the gloves his half brother was wearing, maybe just thinking about what to say next. Rio couldn't really tell, but Chase wasn't meeting his gaze, so he guessed it was time to move past the pleasantries—if that was what that conversation was supposed to have been—and get around to whatever had really brought him out here in the heat of the day.

"Mac used to run a few head," Chase said softly. There were memories caught in the deep timbre of his voice. "Just to keep his hand in. Always said he didn't have enough time to baby-sit cows *and* this county."

Rio wasn't comfortable listening to Chase's memories. Not since he knew McCullar still blamed him for what had happened to Mac, since he still was convinced Rio had played a part in Mac's murder.

"They say sheep are even dumber than cows, but that's pretty hard to believe," Chase said. His voice was low, almost as if he were talking to himself. When Rio said nothing in response, Chase's eyes finally came back up. They were blue and clear, just like Mac's had always been, Rio remembered.

He had never thought the brothers looked that much alike, but it was there, the McCullar heritage, stamped on Chase's strong features as it had been on Mac's. On their father's. And apparently on his. *"Looking at you,"* Mac had said, *"there's not much doubt—"*

"I came to tell you that the sheriff can't find any record of the woman and the baby you claim to have taken to Doc's. There are no notes. No birth certificate. Nothing."

"Hell, Elkins couldn't find his ass if he used both hands," Rio said disgustedly. "So you think I lied about the woman? You think I made that up?"

"I don't know. I can't figure out why you would. Unless you were trying to cover something up. Maybe the fact that you'd been to the clinic the night before. Been there for some other reason."

"You think she lied, too?" Rio asked. The question was soft, but the dark eyes were cold.

"I think maybe…" Chase's mouth moved, the lips tightening and then releasing enough to say, "Maybe." Reflectively. Thinking about that possibility.

"You got some explanation for why she'd do that?"

"They always said you had a…gift."

It was just another euphemism for what her brother had suggested. Maybe it was worded a little more kindly, but it was obvious what Chase was getting at. Sexual risk taking. Rio had thought a lot about the phrase Trent Richardson had used this morning.

"Not that kind of gift," he denied, controlling his anger. "She's not that kind of woman."

"What kind of woman *is* she?" Chase's question seemed edged with derision, maybe mocking Rio's defense of Anne Richardson, mocking her involvement with a man she didn't even know.

"The kind who doesn't need you suggesting things like that about her." Rio's tone was the same one he'd used in the hallway to Senator Richardson. His voice was still soft and yet somehow menacing.

"It's what a lot of people around here are suggesting."

"Then a lot of people around here are just as wrong as you are."

"Everybody's always wrong but you," Chase said. "Everybody else is always lying, but never you."

"I don't know why you came out here," Rio said. "You've already got it all figured out. I came back here to seduce Anne Richardson just so we could get together and kill Doc. I needed some kind of alibi for killing the only person in this godforsaken county who's ever—" Rio's voice had risen with his growing anger, and when he cut off the words, the silence was too sudden, still filled with the pain that had been evident in that last statement.

The only person in this godforsaken county who's ever given a damn whether I lived or died, he had started to say.

But that wasn't the kind of self-pitying confession he'd ever make to Chase McCullar.

"I didn't kill Doc," he said instead. "Anne Richardson didn't lie. From what I've seen of her, I don't think she knows how. She sure isn't going to start because of the likes of me. You can get that idea out of your head."

"Then you tell me what happened to those records. You know Doc would have written everything down, recorded whatever treatment he'd given. You know how Doc operated as well as I do."

Rio thought about what Chase was suggesting, still working to keep his anger tamped down. "Somebody took them," he said finally. "It's the only thing that makes sense."

"Why? Why would somebody take those two records?"

"To keep people from finding out that woman was there. Or from finding out who she was. From asking her what she saw."

"That's what I think," Chase said.

"What you think?" There was disbelief in Rio's voice at his half brother's agreement.

"I don't think Anne Richardson is a liar, either."

"Well, I guess that's something," Rio said softly. It was. Considering.

"Is there anything else that happened that night you didn't tell Buck about?" Chase asked.

Rio shook his head, even as he tried to remember. The only thing he hadn't told Elkins about was the incident between him and Anne Richardson. That had happened the next morning, and it was no more Chase McCullar's business than it had been the sheriff's.

"The woman didn't give you a clue about where she lived?"

"It didn't come up. I figured she'd tell Doc after we left. It didn't seem important."

"There's got to be something," Chase said. His frustration was growing. There had always been questions about

Mac's death, and now it seemed that the same thing would happen all over again.

"Doc said he'd heard it all before."

"What?"

"When I told Anne what the woman had said about her husband disappearing after promising to send for her, Doc said he'd heard that before."

"What about her husband?"

"He came north because somebody had promised him a job. Offered good wages. He was supposed to send for her as soon as he got settled. But it had been more than five months, and she hadn't heard from him, so when it was time for the baby to be born, she came across alone."

"That's all she said?"

Rio went back over it in his head. He couldn't remember anything else, so he nodded.

"You think Doc meant that literally?"

"Literally?"

"That he'd heard the story before? You think someone else came to the clinic and told the same story about somebody disappearing?"

"I thought he was talking about men leaving their families, deserting their responsibilities, but I guess..." Rio shrugged. "I guess it's a possibility." It didn't seem to make much difference one way or another. It didn't seem to help them figure out what had happened to Doc.

"Then I need to see Doc's records," Chase said. "Buck suggested they were all there at the clinic, all but those two. If someone else *did* tell Doc that story, then whoever did will be in those records. They'll have a chart if Doc treated them."

"Along with everybody else in the county and a few thousand illegals. Doc wouldn't have written anything about disappearing husbands on a medical chart."

"It's a place to start."

"*If* Buck'll agree to letting you look through the records."

"If not, there's a window in the back I can always get through," Chase said.

Again there were memories in his voice. And Rio found he didn't want to hear those, either. Memories of the old man they had both loved.

"Doc never did get around to getting the lock fixed," Chase continued. "Probably didn't get around to it on purpose. I slept on Doc's spare bed a few nights through the years."

"I'm surprised you found a night when it was empty," Rio said softly. He'd spent more than a couple of nights coming in that same window, sleeping in that same narrow, uncomfortable bed.

"I guess a lot of people knew about Doc's hospitality."

"Maybe one too many," Rio said, thinking how vulnerable Doc had been. That potential danger had never stopped the old man from offering sanctuary to whoever had needed it most. Some nights it had been him, and some nights, surprisingly, it had been Chase McCullar.

"We all owe a lot to Doc around here. Folks are pretty riled up about his death," Chase said.

"I don't blame them."

"Most of them are convinced you had something to do with it."

"You gave them good reason, I guess."

"*I* gave them reason?" Chase asked.

"Five years ago. When you convinced them I was capable of helping kill somebody else who had been good to me. I guess they're just remembering that."

"I haven't made any accusations against you," Chase denied. "Not about Doc."

"You think I should be grateful for that?" Rio asked. There was disdain in the quiet question.

"Maybe," Chase said.

"I'd be grateful if you'd just tell the truth for a change."

"Are you calling me a liar?"

"Did you tell those folks who were riled up that I was with *you* when Doc was killed?"

"I don't know that for a fact. There's been no report on the time of death."

"Judging by the state of the blood in that room, I'd say Doc couldn't have been killed more than an hour before we got there. I could be wrong, but I don't think I'm off by much. I'm willing to wait around and see what the coroner's report says."

"I'm not sure anybody else is willing to wait," Chase warned. "I'm not sure they're going to give you that much time."

"Is that supposed to be a threat?" Rio asked, and the mockery was back in his voice, hard and cutting.

"It was supposed to be a warning, but you can take it however the hell you want to. I really don't give a damn what you think it was."

Chase turned and began walking back to the pickup.

"You'd better be glad nobody else heard that, Mc-Cullar," Rio called after him. "Especially if something happens to me."

Chase turned. "What the hell is that supposed to mean?"

"Trying to *warn* somebody can be dangerous. Somebody who heard what you just said might misinterpret it as a threat."

Chase stood for a moment, holding his half brother's gaze, shocked into having to think about that. He turned away, angry now, trying to dismiss from his consciousness the suggestion Rio had made. But after he climbed into the pickup, he sat without moving, his hand on the key, remembering the horror of that night.

Even now, after all this time, he never turned the key in an ignition that he *didn't* remember. This time, the memory of Rio's words came along with the nightmare image of the exploding truck. Not the words he'd just said, but those he had said that night. Chase played them over and over in his head, trying to remember how they had sounded. Trying to recreate their exact tone. And wondering again, as he had been after Anne Richardson's accusation, if he could possibly have been wrong.

Finally, one-handed, Chase lifted the rifle from the gun rack behind him. He climbed out again and walked near enough to his half brother to toss the Winchester across the short distance that separated them. Rio caught the gun in midair. His dark eyes were wary.

"Watch yourself," Chase said softly. "You're a long way from any help out here. If somebody wants you…" He stopped, and the muscle in his jaw knotted before he spoke again. "That's just a warning, Delgado," he said. "*Not* a threat. Not from me."

He turned and retraced his steps to the pickup. This time he didn't hesitate in starting the truck. Rio watched until even the dust trail behind the vehicle had disappeared, and then he went back to work repairing a fence that would keep nothing in. And would keep nobody out.

"I WANT TO THANK YOU for letting me stay," Anne said. "I know that what happened last night was hard for you to understand."

"You think he's telling the truth?" Jenny asked.

Her hands were dealing with the supper dishes, scraping the plates and bowls with quick efficiency and then slipping them into the water in the sink. Her small fingers hadn't hesitated in that task, even when Anne broached the subject that had lain uncomfortably between them all afternoon.

"Yes. I know that I've only known Rio a little while, but he's not the kind of person who would have anything to do with hurting someone."

When she looked up, Jenny's brown eyes were watching her, maybe trying to determine the truth of that.

"And he loved Doc," Anne added. "Doc was good to him when he had no one else to look after him."

Jenny nodded. "That's the one thing that would make it hard to believe Rio would do anything to hurt Tom Horn.

He was more of a father to him than Drew McCullar ever was."

"And he admired Mac. I know...." Anne hesitated. Jenny's eyes had fallen to the dishes in the sink, but her dark, gamine-cut hair was too short to hide the quick color that came into her cheeks. "I'm sorry," Anne continued, watching that flush, "but I can't believe Rio would have been involved in Mac's death. No matter what Chase says."

"Maybe Chase was looking for someone to blame. Rio just gave him the opportunity to put the blame on him."

"Are you saying that *you* think it's possible Chase was wrong?"

"I've always thought it was...possible."

"Then...if you knew that—"

"I didn't *know* anything. Except that Chase was sure he was right. And that a jury agreed with him."

"Is that why you told Rio he could use the line shack?"

"Mac's dead. Putting Rio back in jail isn't going to bring him back. If you're right, and Chase is wrong..." Jenny shook her head.

"Then Rio Delgado spent nearly five years in prison for something he didn't do."

"And that didn't bring Mac back, either," Jenny said softly. Then, surprisingly, she said, "Poor Chase. I think it would kill him to find out he'd been wrong."

Anne thought about the fight between the two brothers. She couldn't credit the Chase McCullar she had seen with that kind of sensitivity, but of course, Jenny knew him far better than she did. Maybe she was right. Maybe it had been an honest mistake, compounded by grief and the need to punish whoever was responsible for his brother's death.

"*When you're a kid watching your mother die by slow and painful inches, you have to blame somebody,*" Rio had said, revealing his own sensitivity. Maybe that same need to blame someone for Mac's death had driven Chase to take out his mistaken revenge on his half brother.

She couldn't hope to understand the reasons for what he had done. All she knew was that Chase *had* been mistaken. There was still no doubt in her mind about that.

RIO DIDN'T WANT TO light the stove. Not with the heat that had built inside the line shack during the course of the long, hot day. To build a fire in here would make it feel like he was trying to sleep inside an oven.

He hadn't bothered to put his shirt back on when he'd quit for the day. Instead, before he'd come inside, he had poured part of the bottled water he'd brought out from the ranch over his head and shoulders and then had used his shirt to wipe it off, hoping to take some of the covering of dust he'd acquired off with it.

He sure wasn't clean, but there wasn't much more he could do, given the primitive conditions. He remembered the shower he'd taken at Jenny McCullar's house last night. The unfamiliar luxury of it. He had had privacy. And enough hot water. Clean towels. The slight scent of lavender had clung to them, and the memory of that fragrance evoked the unwanted image of the slender woman who had stood by the sink, hands trembling under the cascade of hot water from its old-fashioned faucet.

Trembling because some bastard had raped her. Some bastard had hurt her so that maybe forever there would be an element of pain and distrust in her dealings with men. The pain had been clear in her voice when she'd told him about what had happened.

And distrust? For some reason, he realized, she had trusted him from the beginning. At least from the aftermath of the fight he and Chase had had. The fight she'd broken up by putting her body in front of his. Just as she'd protected him from making a fatal error in judgment at the clinic. And she had stood up for him against both Chase and Buck Elkins.

Unconsciously he shook his head, wondering why she had bothered. Because she felt guilty that she'd hit him?

Would that be enough to explain all she had done for him? Somehow, that didn't seem enough, but he couldn't think of any other reason why someone like Anne Richardson would go to all that trouble for him.

If she had been any other woman, he found himself thinking—and then he banished that incredible possibility as he had before. There had been nothing to suggest that she was even aware of him in that way. Aware of him as a man. And considering her background, that shouldn't be surprising. Not even given the supposed ''gift'' Chase had mocked.

He found he was standing in the middle of the shack, holding his damp shirt in one hand and staring unseeingly at the toes of his boots. He had still found no answer for what she had done. Maybe just kindness. Maybe she was like Doc.

He threw the shirt over the back of the chair that someone had situated in front of the stove. This place wouldn't be too bad in the winter, he thought. He'd slept in worse. A lot worse.

When he had cooled off a little, he finally opened a couple of the cans he'd brought out from the ranch house. The first was baked beans, which he ate cold, standing in the open door. And then he ate the peaches.

They were cool and sweet against his tongue, a pleasure almost forgotten, like the honeyed taste of a woman's mouth. Something else it didn't do him any good to think about.

There was an oil lamp in the shack, but he hadn't bothered to light it, and as night fell, he stood in the doorway and watched the stars slowly dot the darkness overhead.

When the air had cooled a little, he stretched out on the bunk nearest the door. His body was sore and tired, but it felt good to have worked that hard on something of his own choosing. And besides, he had known that exhaustion was the only hope he had that he would sleep tonight.

There was too little out here to take his mind off what

had happened to Doc. Too little to intrude between his memories of Anne Richardson. Neither of those were things he could afford to think about. He focused instead on the largest of the stars that he could see through the open doorway and forced everything else out of his head.

That control was an art he'd perfected through the last five years. He supposed he should be grateful that he hadn't forgotten how it was done.

HE HAD BEEN SLEEPING too deeply to be aware of their approach. His body had been almost drugged by the long day's exertions, so that they were around him before he woke. He jerked awake suddenly, briefly disoriented. His first thought was that someone was coming into his cell.

It wouldn't be the guards, he knew. Their steps were so well-known in the night that they went unheard. Their familiar pattern didn't disturb his sleep. This was something else. Someone else. In prison that could mean only a couple of things, and neither of those was good.

So the adrenaline had already been pumping into his bloodstream even before he was fully awake. Gradually he became aware of where he was. And that reality was no better than the prison nightmare.

Someone was walking around outside the line shack. More than one person. He lay for a few seconds in the darkness, trying to figure out exactly where each of them was. Trying to think what to do.

He reached down, and his fingers made contact with the rifle Chase had tossed him this afternoon. He had spent part of the remainder of the hours he had worked trying to figure out why his half brother had done that. He still hadn't decided, but the gun Chase had given him had been loaded, and he had laid it beside his cot when he'd gone to bed. He hadn't really expected anyone to show up out here tonight, despite Chase's warning, but he'd known it was a possibility, so he'd prepared for it.

His hand closed around the gun. He lifted it, and held it

one-handed, the stock between his upper arm and his side. He positioned the long barrel so that it was trained on the open door, even as he sat up. The bunk protested his careful movement. Too much noise, he thought. And the bed would probably be even more noisy as he crawled out. There wasn't much he could do about that, and maybe it would even give whoever was out there pause—knowing he was awake and expecting them.

He stood, the bed creaking in protest, just as he'd expected. He was barefoot, but he had slept in his jeans. It had somehow just seemed like a good idea. He had left Mac McCullar's revolver lying on the chair by the stove, and it would be a better weapon at close quarters. He had already begun to tiptoe across the wooden floor toward the gun when the smell stopped him. It was the sharp, unmistakable scent of gasoline.

Images flickered with the fleeting brilliance of summer lightning through his head, reflections of the primitive, instinctual fear of fire. One of them was of Mac McCullar's burning body being thrown from the disintegrating truck. Of Chase's hands, trying desperately to beat out the flames. Another was the remembrance of a pitifully scarred child, who had not been much older than he when the tragedy had happened. The little girl had somehow survived the fire that had killed the rest of her family, a fire started by a new heater, bought through careful scrimping of their meager resources, bought to provide some warmth for their shack. He visualized those flames leaping into the night sky as the men of the village fought uselessly to contain them. And fought to rescue the screaming children.

So instead of continuing to move toward the .45, instinctively he turned toward the open door. Enough gas thrown on these wooden walls and this place would go up just like that tar-papered house, the sparks drifting upward into the night as the fire crackled and the screams echoed. This building would quickly become that same kind of inescapable inferno.

Except he wouldn't be in it, he had decided instantly. He'd rather take his chances on whoever was outside. He'd far rather be shot than burn to death. Besides, he had the rifle Chase had given him, and he was a pretty good shot.

He had two choices, he realized. Move out slowly and carefully or rush them while they weren't expecting him. Shoot at whatever moved out there. He wouldn't care if he took a few of them with him. There was something so cowardly about that damn gasoline. He wouldn't have expected that from the people of this county, but Chase had told him they were stirred up. It was ironic that he was going to be made to pay for Doc's death. That was the last thing Doc would have wanted, he thought.

By then he had reached the door, and it was decision time. It probably didn't make a whole lot of difference which way he went, but he was pretty keyed up, and the smell here was even stronger. He glanced down and realized that the dark stream spreading outside the open door was gasoline. Enough that it hadn't completely soaked into the dry dirt. And as soon as they dropped a match—

Not slow then, or careful, he decided. There wasn't time for that. He burst through the open doorway, his finger on the trigger of the rifle Chase had given him.

He hadn't counted on the rope. Or that they had been banking on him making the decision he'd made. That they had been trying to scare him out into the open. As soon as they had, the loop of the lasso had dropped down around his shoulders. Whoever threw it was good, but then that skill level wasn't surprising in this country.

A hard yank on the other end pulled him off-balance, making him stumble sideways. His upper arms were pinned to his sides, but he still had the rifle and his finger was on the trigger. He tried to regain his balance, bare feet flinching from contact with the rock-strewn ground and his body fighting against the continuing pull of the rope.

Dark shapes appeared out of the night. They seemed to be all around him. More of them than he'd realized from the soft noises he'd heard. But he didn't regret coming out. Even out here, in the openness of the desert night, the smell of gasoline was strong and frightening.

He tried to raise the barrel of the gun so he'd at least hit one of them. He wasn't going to be able to stop whatever was about to happen, but maybe he could still take a couple with him. But before he could pull the trigger, something hit him. A shovel, maybe. He heard metal clang against the barrel of the rifle, knocking it away from its alignment.

His finger had completed the motion it had already begun, however, squeezing the trigger. The shot rang out into the night, but he didn't think he'd hit anything. He didn't have much time to come to that realization. The next time the shape of the shovel appeared in his peripheral vision, it connected with his elbow, almost numbing his lower arm. He got off another round, but he heard that bullet strike uselessly into the hard, rocky ground.

By that time, they were all around him. He was conscious of the next blow of the shovel, against the side of his head, but as a result of it, he was almost unaware when someone jerked the rifle from his suddenly paralyzed fingers.

And unaware, thankfully, of some of the rest of it. It would have been over a lot quicker if they'd continued to use the shovel. They decided instead that their boots were more democratic. That gave everybody a chance.

Despite the restraint of the rope and the blow to the head, he tried to fight them. They had taught him that when he had first gone to prison. You had to fight, even if you knew you were going to lose. Even if it was a sure thing. It would only be worse the next time if you didn't fight. Rio Delgado's entire life, it seemed, had taught him that, if it had taught him nothing else.

But after a while, he couldn't fight them anymore. Then he just prayed for it to be over. Just prayed for the pain to stop.

Chapter Nine

Chase McCullar came awake suddenly. His mouth was dry and his heart rate elevated, despite the peacefulness of the surrounding night. This had once been a familiar feeling, this helpless, nighttime panic. But the frequency of the nightmares had faded with the passing years, and this hadn't happened in a long time now—dreaming about what they had done to Mac.

He lay in the quiet darkness thinking about what might have triggered the old dream. Doc's death, certainly. The unexpected return of Rio Delgado. Maybe even what his half brother had said today.

"Somebody who heard what you just said might misinterpret it as a threat."

As he lay there remembering, he gradually realized that what had awakened him hadn't been the familiar nightmare. Its horrors were not lingering in his consciousness. Something else had intruded into his sleep, but not enough to leave any clear impression. A sound, maybe, half heard through the veil of sleep, and so not clearly identifiable?

He could hear now only what was known and familiar. Samantha's breathing beside him. The ticking of the clock on the mantel in the den. The background hum of the air conditioner. He even heard the refrigerator kick on. There was nothing else. Nothing disturbed the peaceful night.

He closed his eyes, preparing to go back to sleep. Despite

the fact that his pulse rate had slowed to something that approached normal, eventually the blue eyes opened again. There was something wrong, damn it. He knew it.

He sat up, pushing the sheet off his legs. He and Mac used to joke about this unexplainable uneasiness. A prickling on the back of your neck. A sudden cold stirring in your gut. *Lawman's instinct,* Mac had called it, and it was something Chase McCullar never ignored. It had saved his hide too many times to deny its existence.

"What is it?" Samantha asked. "What's wrong?"

He looked down and found her green eyes, watching him in the dark. He shook his head, but the feeling was still strong, almost frightening in its intensity.

"I don't know," he said softly. "Something..." He waited, trying to decide what to do. "I'm going to check on Mandy and then take a look outside. Call Jenny for me. Make sure they're all right."

"Jenny?" his wife questioned. "Why would you think—"

"Just do it, sweetheart," he ordered. "Just call her. See if they're okay."

SAMANTHA MET HIM AT the bedroom door when he returned from their daughter's room. He had found nothing out of place there. Mandy had been sleeping peacefully, blond curls spread over her pillow and her thumb almost to her mouth. Close enough for comfort, Chase thought, smiling as he tucked the sheet around her again. In the quiet yard, the same shadows were cast by the old cottonwood that had always been cast. Nothing was moving outside, either.

"Jenny said they're fine. She sounded like she thought I'd lost my mind. But...she did say to ask you about Rio."

"Rio? She thinks Rio might come here?"

"She wondered if he's all right."

Suddenly, Chase knew what was going on. He had told

Delgado himself. ''Folks around here are pretty stirred up,''
Chase had warned.

''Because you gave them reason…''

''Get the shotgun out of the case. I'm going out there,''
Chase said. He brushed by her and had already begun pulling on his jeans when she spoke.

''You think…'' Samantha hesitated.

''I think I might need that gun,'' he said, smiling at her.
''I can go without it, if you want me to, but I'd sure feel
a hell of a lot better taking it along.''

She moved at that, despite the humor he'd tried to inject
into his request because he knew he was scaring her. By
the time she'd returned with the shotgun and a box of
shells, he had managed his jeans and shirt and was pulling
on his boots.

''I'm going with you,'' Samantha said.

''I'll be fine. Probably a wild-goose chase.''

''You don't believe that.''

''What I don't believe is that I'm running out of bed in
the middle of the night to make sure somebody hasn't put
a hole through Delgado.''

''Is that what woke you? Did you hear a shot?''

And thinking about it, Chase McCullar finally nodded.
''Yeah. I think…maybe I did.''

''You be careful, Chase McCullar. You hear me?''

She was talking to the darkness. Chase was already gone.
Her words echoed softly in the empty bedroom. She didn't
want him to go, but Chase had already lost one brother.
Maybe he didn't feel he could afford to lose another.

THE FEELING THAT HAD awakened Chase grew stronger
with each minute that passed. It wasn't that far out to the
line shack, not in miles, but the journey tonight seemed
endless.

Then he was near enough to see the shack, a dark little
box silhouetted against the horizon. It got bigger by the

second, as the speeding truck approached. And a split second later he could see the shapes moving around it.

He thought about dousing the headlights, but that wasn't what this was about. He wasn't trying to sneak up on whoever was out there. This was about stopping whatever was going on, and the unexpected arrival of an unidentified vehicle was probably the quickest way to do that, even if whoever was out here disappeared without a trace into the surrounding desert.

Even as he thought that, they began to scatter. He watched them run as the pickup barreled across the open range. He was driving way too fast. He had left the dirt road and headed cross-country. And he knew now that he hadn't been wrong about what he had expected to find out here.

By the time he stopped the truck, there was no one left. He hit the ground running, despite the fact that it was black as night in hell. He couldn't see two feet in front of him, but the smell was all around him. Gasoline. Apparently they'd been throwing it around real generously.

He stumbled over Delgado and almost fell. He wondered briefly if he'd hurt him, and then, as he knelt beside the still figure, he realized that his half brother hadn't been aware that he'd hit him. He touched Rio's face, and the pale crescent moon, which had found the only cloud in the desert dryness to hide behind, slipped out, imperfectly illuminating what they had done.

Chase felt the bile rise in his throat. His hand cupped his brother's jaw. It was slick with blood. There was so damn much blood.

I've got to get him to Doc, Chase thought before he remembered. Doc was gone. Somebody had already killed Doc. They had cut his throat and left him to bleed to death like an animal.

They weren't going to get away with it, he found himself thinking. *Or with this. Not again. Nobody was going to get away with this again.*

THEY HADN'T GONE BACK to bed after Samantha's phone call. Too much had happened in the last few days to find sleep again that easily. When Jenny had suggested coffee, Anne had been so grateful she had felt the burn of tears at the back of her eyes.

She hadn't thought she would be able to go back to her room. She would have, of course. She would have pretended everything was fine—she had had a lot of practice at that these last months—but still, she was infinitely grateful when Jenny's own unease gave her permission not to have to. And permission to feel that it was normal not to want to be alone in the dark tonight.

It had probably not been fifteen minutes after Samantha's call that they heard the truck. Rommel heard it first, of course, and he reacted, scrambling across the kitchen tile to the back door. He had begun barking almost before they had time to put their mugs down on the table.

Jenny got up to look out the window above the sink.

"It's Chase," she said, her relief obvious. She hurried to the back door and threw it open, allowing the shepherd to disappear into the night, followed closely by Jenny herself.

Anne stood, but she didn't rush to greet Chase McCullar. She still wasn't sure of her feelings about Jenny's brother-in-law, and she couldn't imagine what he was doing here in the middle of the night. Something must have happened, given the phone call and his arrival, and she was afraid that he would again find a way to blame Rio for whatever it was.

Nothing had prepared her. She didn't even know who Chase was supporting when Jenny preceded them back into the kitchen. It was just a man, dark head drooping almost to his chest, face hidden. One of his arms was over Chase's shoulder, but McCullar was having to hold it in place. Chase's other arm was around the man's narrow waist. Chase was almost carrying the staggering, barefoot figure, supporting most of the other man's weight.

Chase's blue eyes made quick contact with hers. In them was regret. Or apology. And by the time she had read those emotions, Anne had realized that the burden Chase McCullar staggered under was his half brother's body. Her mind shied away from the word.

It was Rio, and he was hurt, but he was alive. She stood paralyzed, desperately holding on to that thought while Jenny followed Chase down the narrow hall. To Mac's room, she realized, watching them.

"Get some clean towels," Jenny called, breaking the spell that held her immobile. "Second drawer. And the scissors from the top drawer."

Anne's hands were trembling, but she obeyed. She had used these same scissors to try to fix the cut on his cheekbone, carefully putting her little bits of tape over the split skin, but that bloodied head and torso wouldn't be fixed with bits and pieces of tape, she thought.

Then, along with the fear that had been there from the first, anger blossomed. Fury that they had done this to him. Maybe the same mindless, shapeless "they" who had already brought such horror to this community.

When she carried the things Jenny had asked for into the bedroom, Jenny was sitting on the edge of the bed where Rio lay, his skin dark against Jenny's sun-whitened sheet. Only now did Anne begin to realize the true extent of the damage. Someone had beaten him. The evidence was there on his body. And on his face. That once-beautiful face.

She wanted to turn away, to hide from the knowledge of how much he'd been hurt, but his dark gaze had already found her. One of his eyes was closed, already swollen shut, the abused skin around it reddish purple. The aquiline nose was misshapen, almost certainly broken. There was a lot of blood, most of it from a cut on his head, and that was probably masking other injuries.

Jenny was looking at his ears. Then she gently opened the eye that had swollen closed, comparing the size of the dark pupils.

"We have to get him to a hospital," Anne said. They couldn't treat this here, and with Doc gone...

"No," Rio said. His voice was hoarse, ragged with pain or with the effort to find the breath needed to voice that single syllable, to give it strength.

"Why not?" Jenny said, her hands still gently examining his face. "I think that's a very good idea."

"No money," Rio said. "No money for a doctor."

"Hell," Chase said. "If you think—"

"No," Rio said again. "Please, Mrs. McCullar. No hospital. Just do whatever you can."

"That's ridiculous," Anne argued. "You can't—"

"Ribs are the worst," Rio said. His words were still hesitant. He was being careful not to increase the agony by breathing too deeply.

"Don't talk," Jenny ordered. "I'll see what I can do. Maybe..." Her voice faded, and she held the dark, pleading eye of the man on the bed. "Maybe it's not as bad as it looks."

"I've had a lot worse," he said. The simple confession had the unmistakable ring of truth.

Jenny took a breath, deep and hard, forced to think about that. He meant in prison, she supposed, where he had been sent for a murder he claimed he had had no part in. Mac's murder. The murder of his half brother. She could still hear Rio's voice from the dark hallway last night, his denial of guilt. And the unarguable reason he had given her. *"Mac was my brother."*

They were the same words Mac had used to explain his anonymous protection of the Mexican kid who seemed destined to go bad. *"Hell, Jenny,"* Mac would say in that deep Texas drawl she loved, *"I have to take care of him. He's my brother. He doesn't have anyone else."*

Unconsciously, Jenny McCullar's hand found Rio's, and she squeezed it, but he gasped with the shock of her touch, with the unexpected pain. Gasped loudly enough that they all heard it.

"This is crazy, Jenny," Chase said. "We have to get him to a hospital."

"I put my hands over my head. To keep it protected," Rio whispered. "Most of the rest is just bruises. And the ribs. It's just a little hard to breathe."

"I can strap ribs," Jenny said. She was still touching his hand, but she was no longer putting pressure on it. "Let's get you cleaned up a little and maybe I can tell more about what's wrong."

Rio nodded carefully, still holding her gaze.

"But if I think you need to go to the hospital," Jenny said sternly, "then that's what we'll do. I believe the three of us can scrape up enough to pay for whatever's needed."

"Mrs. McCullar—" Rio began.

"And that's final," Jenny interrupted his protest. "I don't need another stubborn man around here. You're going to do exactly what you're told," she ordered, but her voice was surprisingly gentle. "*I'll* be the one to make that decision when the time comes."

"I THINK HE'S ASLEEP," Jenny said. She had come out of Mac's room to find Anne waiting in the dark, rose-covered hallway.

"Is he...?" Anne didn't know what she needed to ask. She knew it was probably too early to know if Rio was really going to be all right.

"I think his assessment was pretty accurate." *"I've had a lot worse,"* ran fleetingly through her head, but Jenny found she couldn't think about that tonight, about all Rio Delgado had been through. Or about her own role in that. So she went on, keeping her voice clinically objective.

"The worst does seem to be his ribs. I'm a little concerned about his right hand. It probably should be X-rayed, but the important thing is he's coherent and his pupils are reactive and normal. I'm certain he's concussed, but we'll watch him."

"Where did you learn all that?" Anne asked. "What to look for."

"There are always injuries on a ranch. Some of it I just picked up, but…at one time, a long time ago, I planned to be a nurse. I was almost through training when I decided I was in love with Mac McCullar. Too much in love to even finish school. Too much in love to wait. I thought about going back to it after he died, but somehow…" Smiling, she shook her head. "Maybe I will someday."

"Trent will be disappointed if you do."

"Poor Trent," Jenny said softly, and at her tone Anne wondered again about her brother's hopes. "Somehow I just can't see myself as a politician's wife. It's not something that…" The soft voice hesitated. "Not something I ever imagined I'd be doing at this stage of my life."

"What *did* you imagine?" Anne asked, smiling. And only when Jenny's eyes fell, did she realize the cruelty of that question.

"Having babies," Jenny said. Her voice was filled, not with pain, but with memories. And with tenderness. "Loving Mac. Just…being his wife." Her dark eyes lifted, and they were smiling. "That's not very feminist, I guess."

"I don't know. I thought that's what it really was all about. Being allowed to decide what we want to do and nobody thinking it's wrong."

"What do you want to do?" Jenny asked, smiling again.

What did she really want for her life right now? It was almost too complicated, too hard to think about. "Just to be safe," she admitted softly. "To feel safe again, I guess. And to feel normal. To trust. To be able to let someone love me."

Once she had started, all of it had rushed out. All the fears and doubts she had never told anyone else. She had asked her brother not to discuss her with this woman, and yet here she was, laying open her soul for Jenny McCullar's inspection.

Jenny nodded, and surprisingly her dark eyes had filled

with tears. She blinked them away and asked, "You want to sit with him? I think somebody should."

"I won't know what to look for."

"Just wake him up every couple of hours. Make him talk to you. I hate to do that. He needs sleep to heal as much as he needs anything, but it's the safest way. And I really believe he's okay. If I didn't, I would have made him go to a hospital, no matter what he said. It's just a matter of whether or not you want to sit with him."

"I'd like to," Anne confessed. "If you're sure I can do it."

"You'll do fine. You can call me if you need me."

JENNY HAD BEEN RIGHT. Rio was sleeping. He looked better, if only because they had cleaned off most of the blood. His ribs were bound, the bandage starkly white over the dark skin of his torso, hiding a lot of the welts and bruises. His right hand rested on top of the sheet that covered his lower body. The limp fingers were swollen and discolored.

Anne fought the urge to touch them, just for reassurance. For the first time since she had known him, Rio looked vulnerable. Even when she had held the muzzle of Mac's revolver against his throat, she hadn't thought of him as vulnerable. He had never seemed to need anything from anybody. And then tonight...

Chase had left them the shotgun, but he'd gone home to check on his family. If anyone who had been out at the line shack had recognized his truck, they might come there looking for Rio in order to finish the job. Chase couldn't take a chance on that happening, even though they had all recognized the unlikelihood of it. The men who had done what had been done to Rio were the kind who worked in darkness. They wouldn't want to chance being recognized.

Anne glanced at her watch and was surprised to find that it was three-forty. It would be daylight in a couple of hours. She would welcome the end to this night. She shivered, knowing too well what would have happened if Chase hadn't frightened those men away. They would have finished what they had begun.

She watched her trembling fingers brush the black hair off Rio's forehead, wondering at the same time how her hand had gotten there. There was a smear of blood and dirt that Jenny had missed across his brow. It was visible even in the dimness. She thought about the day he and Chase had fought. It had been an equal battle then. They had both been marked.

Her hand slipped to the side of Rio's dark head, her fingers moving in the gleaming midnight strands, her thumb tracing gently over the healing cut under his eyebrow that Chase McCullar had inflicted. She smiled slightly, thinking about the neat, careful line of tape butterflies she'd put over the cut on his cheek. Most of them had disappeared. The bruise she'd made on his temple wasn't visible in the darkness, maybe hidden by one of the newer injuries or his disordered hair.

"What are you doing here?" Rio asked.

When she glanced down, she realized that his eye, the one that was still functional, was open. She couldn't be sure how long he had been watching her.

She thought about what she should say, but finally she told him the truth, even though she had quickly removed her hand. As quickly if she had been caught doing something wrong. And for her, she supposed, touching him was forbidden. Off-limits. Just as he had warned her.

"Making sure you're all right."

"I'm all right. You need to go back to bed," he suggested softly. "Get some sleep." But his dark gaze held hers.

He wasn't closing her out as she had sometimes felt he would like to. She wanted to be here with him. To make sure he was really all right. Jenny had said she needed to make him talk and since he was awake anyway...

"Who was it?" she asked.

His head moved slightly on the pillow, side to side. "Too dark."

"Did you recognize...anything? Size or shape? A voice?"

"They weren't there to talk," Rio said.

They had been there for one thing. They both knew that.

"You think it was whoever killed Doc?" she whispered.

"*I* think it was the good citizens of this county."

"Trying to...frighten you away?" she asked, hoping that might be what this had all been about.

"Maybe. Maybe just out to punish me for what they think I did."

"For killing Doc."

"And Mac."

She took a breath, thinking about the implications of that. She had been thinking about those since Chase had brought him home. "Then somebody stirred them up," she suggested. "Somebody organized that attack."

He didn't respond. That was obvious. But he couldn't identify that person or any of the others who had appeared out of the darkness tonight.

"Chase?" she questioned, finally voicing the persistent thought. "Could Chase have had anything to do with what happened tonight?"

Rio remembered the rifle he'd been given and Chase's arrival tonight at the line shack. If his half brother hadn't shown up when he had, things would probably have turned out very differently. He couldn't be sure those men had set out to kill him, but if that hadn't been their intent, they had done a pretty damn good imitation of it.

Given the damage they'd already inflicted, even if they had called a halt to the beating, he might have bled to death out there alone. If he hadn't regained consciousness before it was too late. He had known that to have happened before. But not this time. And the only reason it hadn't was McCullar's unexpected arrival.

The bruised lips moved, but Rio was forced to swallow

against the unaccustomed thickness in his throat before he answered.

"Not this time," he said softly. "That's the one thing I *do* know about tonight. This time it isn't Chase McCullar who's out for my blood."

WHEN RIO OPENED HIS EYES the next morning, it wasn't Anne who was sitting in the chair she had pulled next to his bed. Chase McCullar was asleep there, blond head back and mouth slightly open, his breath sighing in and out in a low, regular rhythm. Almost a snore. Rommel was asleep at his feet, and the audible breathing of the big shepherd formed a syncopation with Chase's. Rio's lips tilted, but even that small movement was painful and quickly controlled.

He lay in the late-morning sunshine that was streaming into the bedroom and thought about last night. About all the surprising things that had happened. About Chase showing up out at the line shack, riding that pickup to his rescue like the cavalry in a Western. About the sensation of Anne Richardson's fingers moving in his hair. About Jenny's kindness. Again his throat closed, and he felt the sting of emotion behind his eyes.

Rio couldn't even remember the last time he had cried. When his mother had died? He didn't think he'd cried even then. That was another lesson he had learned early and learned hard. Nothing was accomplished by showing emotion. Nothing changed except someone was more likely to jeer and to mock. The iron control that had served him so well in prison had already been deeply embedded before he had gotten there.

"I went to Doc's," Chase said.

Rio turned his eyes toward his half brother and found that the blue eyes were alert now and focused on his face. The bruising under them was beginning to fade to a dark olive. Rio directed his gaze back to the ceiling, wondering what the bad news was now. That it was bad had been evident in Chase's voice.

"AMPEX mean anything to you?" Chase asked.

Rio tried to think if he'd ever heard the word. If Doc had mentioned it to him. It sounded like a word formed from initials. And if so, maybe they represented some government agency.

"I don't think so," he admitted finally. "Should it?"

"I don't know. Doc had written it in the top right-hand corner of four of the records I pulled. All of them for people whose names I didn't recognize. Hispanic names. Folks who don't live in the county."

"That's all you found?"

"I went through the last six or seven years of Doc's stuff. That would have been a hell of a lot easier if he'd used a computer to keep his records."

"How could you possibly tell which ones—"

Chase's short laugh interrupted. "I was real scientific. I picked out the folders that *looked* new. I didn't have much else to go on, not unless I wanted to read through fifty years of measles and constipation."

"What do *you* think it means? That notation?" Rio asked carefully.

"Maybe nothing. I just thought you should know what I found. Or maybe what I didn't find. I guess you should also know that I went by the sheriff's office this morning and reported what happened last night."

Rio didn't respond for a moment, thinking about what that might mean. "I wish you hadn't done that," he said finally.

"Yeah, I figured you'd feel that way. Maybe nothing will come of Buck knowing, but…" Chase paused, and his lips tightened. "Maybe if everyone realizes the sheriff's office is looking into the attack, it will offer you some protection, at least for a little while, anyway."

"I don't want to put Mrs. McCullar or Miss Richardson in any danger."

"Jenny?" Chase repeated, his voice full of amusement. "Hell, if Jenny had been there with a shotgun, we'd have never lost the Alamo. Don't worry about Jenny. Besides..." Again the deep voice hesitated, maybe thinking about how to phrase the next. "If the folks who attacked you were riled up about Doc and Mac, then being here with Jenny is probably the best thing you've got going for you."

The best thing you've got going for you. Rio couldn't deny the truth of that. Not to himself, anyway. Considering how the McCullars had treated him last night, there was no doubt of that. It was something he'd never expected. Had no right to expect. And it was all the more reason not to stay.

"I can't hide behind Mrs. McCullar," he said softly.

Chase pushed himself up out of the chair and stood for a moment, looking down on the man in the bed.

"Nobody thinks you're hiding," he said.

The blue eyes didn't waver from their focus on his face, but for the first time, they weren't cold. Or judgmental. Rio wasn't sure what had brought about that change, but it was there. He was sure of that. Finally Chase broke the contact that had flared briefly between them and walked to the door. He turned when he reached it.

"By the way, Buck said he wants to talk to you. I told him not to bother you today. Jenny would have had my hide. But I guess you should expect him or Morales to show up out here tomorrow."

Rio nodded. Still Chase didn't leave.

"Why would you try to warn Mac?" he asked finally.

This was why his brother had come here today, Rio realized. Not to tell him all the things he'd talked about. Chase had come just to ask that one thing. And Rio thought about what that question revealed about the man who had had to ask it.

The reason he had ridden to warn Mac had been so obvious to Rio that he had never considered the possibility that Chase McCullar didn't understand. But after all, it had been to him that Mac had explained it all. A long time ago.

"Blood's thicker than water," Rio said softly. "Even river water."

He saw the depth of the breath his half brother took, the strong muscles of his chest moving under the tan shirt. Then Chase turned and disappeared into the hallway where his mother's beloved roses still bloomed.

RIO SLEPT MOST OF the day, drifting in and out of troubled dreams that he didn't fully remember. Jenny had given him some kind of painkiller, big white caplets that he'd washed down with the water she kept waking him up to get him to drink. At least she brought a flexible straw, so he hadn't had to move any more than was absolutely necessary.

As the pain grew and expanded during the long, hot afternoon, he thought about asking for another couple of those pills, but if she realized how much pain he was in, he was afraid Jenny would insist on taking him to a hospital. So he lay there with his eyes closed, riding it out. Listening to Rommel's breathing. Trying to think about anything else besides the pain.

The only problem with that was that the images of Anne Richardson somehow kept intruding. No matter how determined he was not to think about her, especially not about those slender fingers moving through his hair last night, the more often those thoughts surfaced.

Just as they were now.

He opened his eyes to find Anne standing in the doorway to his room. She didn't say anything, but her lips moved slightly, almost smiling at him as soon as she realized he was awake. She looked as if she hadn't gotten enough sleep, and he knew that was his fault. She had sat up with him most of the night. He wondered what she was thinking. She had never indicated that she had been physically attracted to him, but still he was uncomfortable to find her examining his face.

Sometime after she'd left his room this morning, he'd gotten up and made his slow, painful way to the bathroom. He had put it off for as long as possible, and the journey had been every bit as bad as he'd anticipated. At least he hadn't fainted. That had been the one thing he'd really been afraid of.

But while he was there, he had caught a glimpse of his face in the mirror over the sink. After the initial shock, he'd kept his eyes carefully directed downward.

When he made it back to the bed, he had lain there trembling with pain and weakness. There had been a lot of blood in his urine, and he tried not to think about that. It was normal after what had happened. He knew that. As he had told them last night, he'd had worse beatings.

He wondered what Anne Richardson had thought about that confession, about the sordidness of his past. And what she had been thinking as her eyes scanned his face. It shouldn't matter that he looked like something out of a horror movie. He wasn't vain. She had been right about that. But still, he was uncomfortable with her seeing him like this.

And it wasn't hard to figure out why. He'd figured it out sitting in Jenny's truck on the way to Doc's office that day. The day after he'd met Anne Richardson. Only…that wasn't anything that was ever going to happen. For a lot of very good reasons.

"You okay?" he asked softly.

"Am I okay?" she repeated. And then she did smile. "I think maybe *you're* the one who should be answering that."

"Nothing else is going to happen," he said, trying to let her hear reassurance in his voice, trying to work the old magic. "You don't have to be frightened. The more I think about it, the more I'm convinced last night didn't have anything to do with the people who killed Doc."

"You think I'm afraid of them?" she asked.

He tried to smile at her, but his mouth hurt, so the movement was distorted. Probably just grotesque. "I think you'd be smart to be. I just don't think that's who came after me."

"So...I don't need to worry about them coming after me. Is that what you're saying?"

"I just thought you might be uneasy."

"I'm not uneasy. What I am is mad. Angry that they can get away with that," she said quietly. Her eyes traced over his features again.

"Buck'll get 'em," he said. He allowed the undamaged lid to drop slowly over his good eye. He had intended to wink at her, but he realized that, like the smile, it was only going to look ridiculous, given the fact that his other eye was already swollen closed.

She laughed, however, just as he'd intended. They both knew how much confidence he had in Buck Elkins's detection skills.

"He's probably already got them all rounded up," he added. He felt better watching her laugh, relieved that she was all right. He didn't like seeing her down. The way she had looked last night was too reminiscent of the day she had told him she'd been raped.

"You don't believe that," she said, but she was still smiling. "Not any more than I do."

He shook his head, moving it carefully, trying not to set off the pounding agony at the back of his skull.

"I know it hurts to talk," she said.

And to think. Or breathe, he thought.

"But Jenny sent me to find out if you could eat something."

He probably should make the effort, he knew, but he wasn't hungry. The thought of food was almost nauseating. And someone would probably have to feed him.

"I'm not hungry," he said. "Tell Mrs. McCullar I'm fine."

"I don't ever lie to Jenny," Anne said, "but I'll leave

you alone. Let you get back to sleep. Sorry I disturbed you.''

''You didn't disturb me,'' he said.

And then Anne, too, disappeared into the hallway, again leaving him alone, with nothing to do but think.

''You didn't disturb me,'' he had told her. And it was the truth. Only not all of it.

No more than you always have, he should have said. *No more than you did the first time I saw you, standing in the door of Mac McCullar's barn. No more than you have during the rest of the hours I've known you. And no more than I know you will for the rest of my life.*

Chapter Ten

The following morning Jenny was up early, fixing a breakfast that she hoped would tempt Rio to eat. The enticing smell of bacon filled the house, along with the aroma of the good, strong coffee that was gently perking in the metal pot on the back of the stove. Mac had taught her how to make coffee in that pot—just like his mother had made it, and now it seemed to Jenny to be the only coffee fit to drink.

She was aware suddenly of an "eyes-on-the-back-of-my-neck" feeling. She glanced toward the door to the hall, expecting Anne. Instead, Rio Delgado stood in the doorway, wearing Mac's shirt she had laid out for him and his own jeans, which she'd laundered yesterday. His hands were fastened to the frame on either side, and he was holding on tightly enough that the fingers of his uninjured left hand had whitened at the tips.

"Why don't you sit down at the table," Jenny suggested. She turned back to the strips of bacon sizzling in the pan. "Before you fall down," she added under her breath.

Deliberately, she didn't watch Rio negotiate his way across the room. When she heard the soft grunt of effort that indicated he'd lowered himself into one of the kitchen chairs, she reached above her head and took a mug out of the cabinet. She filled it with coffee and walked over to the table to set it down in front of him.

"Cream and sugar?"

"A little cream," he said. It would help to cool the steaming coffee, maybe enough that he could drink it, he hoped. His mouth was pretty bad.

"Think you can eat?" Jenny asked.

He had wrapped his left hand around warmth of the mug. The right one he left in his lap.

"I…" He paused, thinking about that. "Just the coffee will be fine," he said finally, despite the emptiness of his stomach.

"You could probably manage the eggs. They're scrambled."

"I'm fine, Mrs. McCullar."

"Jenny," she corrected. "My name is Jenny. Nobody ever calls me Mrs. McCullar."

"Yes, ma'am," he said.

"Or ma'am. I have to tell you that reminding a woman she's older than you isn't a very good idea."

She took the milk out of the refrigerator as she talked and poured a generous amount into his mug, stirring it with a spoon she had put beside his plate.

"Any blood in your urine this morning?" she asked matter-of-factly.

Despite the bruising and the normal darkness of his skin, she could see the blush spreading along his high cheekbones.

"Now *that* I haven't seen in a long time," she said, her voice filled with amusement. "I didn't know McCullar men were even capable of blushing."

McCullar men. The words hit him hard, somewhere around his gut, almost like one of those booted kicks.

"Well?" she asked.

"No, ma'am," he said softly.

"Liar," Jenny said succinctly, but she turned and went back to the stove, leaving him alone with his coffee.

ANNE JOINED THEM BEFORE Rio had managed to finish the eggs. Using his left hand was awkward, and his mouth hurt like hell, but he forced himself to eat. The quicker he could get back some strength, the quicker he could get out of here and quit putting these women in danger.

He was aware that Anne was playing with Jenny's well-cooked breakfast more than she was eating it. He glanced up and found her eyes on his face. He waited too long before he broke the contact, but he hadn't been able to force his eyes away. And what was in hers didn't help.

He wondered if she could possibly know what he'd been thinking last night, if that almost-telepathic connection that had been between them from the beginning was still there. And if so, he knew he'd have to be more careful. He was too close to the edge, far too close to revealing how he felt about her.

Suddenly Rommel barked, sharp and demanding. Seconds later they heard the vehicle the shepherd had apparently already identified as friendly, judging by the movement of his tail. Rom was standing impatiently by the kitchen door, and Jenny obligingly opened it for him.

"It's Chase," she said over her shoulder as she again followed the big shepherd outside.

Jenny reentered the kitchen only a few minutes later. She found the two of them still sitting at the table. Rio's back was to the door, and he didn't make the effort to turn around, given the state of his ribs.

Anne Richardson's eyes had lifted automatically, but when Jenny first opened the door, they had still been focused on Rio Delgado's face. And having once loved a man exactly that much, Jenny had had no trouble recognizing what had been in their blue depths.

She remembered the whispered conversation in the hallway yesterday morning, the simple things Anne Richardson had said she wanted. *"To trust. To be able to let someone love me."* It appeared she had already decided who that someone should be.

Poor Trent, Jenny thought again, knowing how far from

his intentions for Anne such a relationship would be. Even though she understood all the logical reasons he might have for objecting to what was obviously happening between his sister and Rio, she found herself hoping that he would be wise enough not to.

"There's something outside I think you need to see," she said softly.

"Me?" Anne asked, her eyes widening in surprise.

"Rio," Jenny corrected. "Think you can make it?"

Something about Doc's death? Rio wondered. If it was, he had no choice but to make it. He put his good hand against the wooden table and used it to push himself upright.

Standing was almost worse than getting down had been, but he needed to move, needed to walk. That was why he'd forced himself out of bed this morning. And he knew that if he didn't force himself to *keep* moving, his body would stiffen up even more, and getting his strength back would only be harder. Harder to get out of here before something happened. He didn't even clarify in his own mind which "something" he was more worried about.

He had already started toward the door when Anne moved alongside him. Smiling at him, she lifted his left arm and put it carefully across her shoulders. He met her eyes, dark blue and filled with concern.

Concern for him, he realized. That was almost unprecedented in his life, just as her unquestioning belief in his innocence had been. He forced his eyes away again, but he didn't refuse her help. He found that he couldn't, and that was not the result of any physical weakness.

Her bones felt slight, fragile under the weight of his arm. And he could smell her. He didn't think the subtle aroma was perfume, although it was undeniably feminine. Soap, maybe. Her shampoo. He didn't know, but the scent was too near and too evocative.

He fought the hardening of his groin, fought his automatic reaction to the impossible wonder of Anne Richardson's body moving against his. It took a moment before he could take another step, but Anne didn't hurry him.

She didn't look strong enough to bear even a part of his weight, but he had always known that her apparent fragility was deceptive. She was tough. She had been tempered with fire, and the result was the tensile, unbreakable strength of steel, down at the very core of her being. Where it mattered.

When they finally reached the door, Anne moved back to allow him to go through it alone. He put his good hand on its frame as he had at the hallway door. He needed that support when he finally realized what Jenny McCullar had brought him out here to see.

It was Diablo.

He didn't recognize the slender redhead who was leading the stallion out of the horse trailer that had been hooked to the familiar black pickup. But it didn't take him long to figure out that this must be Samantha Kincaid. Except now she was Samantha McCullar, Chase McCullar's wife, who certainly knew something about horses. And with her was Chase's daughter, the McCullar heritage obvious not only in the blond ponytails, but even in the delicate features.

The big black was surprisingly docile, but Samantha was near enough to the stallion to make Rio's heart turn over. Diablo was sweating and nervous, but it was obvious that he trusted the woman who held his lead. That she trusted the black was also obvious, despite his nervousness.

The place he had once held in the stallion's heart had apparently been taken by his new owner. An owner who, Rio acknowledged, could certainly provide for the horse far better than he could. Better than he had ever been able to provide. The glistening sleekness of the coat that sheathed the stallion's well-conditioned muscles should only give him comfort, but somewhere inside Rio's soul he knew there was and always would be an emptiness that owning this animal had once filled.

He still hadn't moved out of the doorway, but again it wasn't a physical weakness that prevented him from approaching the black. Too damn much had happened in the last week to destroy his control. First there had been Doc's death. Then the realization of how he felt about Anne Richardson and acknowledging the bitter impossibility of ever doing anything about it. And Chase McCullar's unexpected behavior. Now he was forced to face the loss of the stallion. That was something else he had been pushing to the back of his mind.

"He's yours," Samantha said softly, maybe in response to what was in Rio's eyes. "He's always been yours. I was just keeping him safe for you, I suppose."

Rio's gaze moved from the horse to focus on her face. He took a breath, not daring to believe what she had just said. And then another, because he knew there was no way that could come true. Not now.

It should be enough to know that the stallion was being taken care of. It would *have* to be enough, he thought grimly, and only he would ever know that it was not. He shook his head.

"I can't pay you for him," he said.

"I didn't expect you to. It doesn't matter. He didn't cost me much. They didn't have any idea what he's worth."

"Why would you…" he began, and then unexpectedly, he felt his throat close. The black had moved his head, pushing his nose into the slim shoulder of Samantha McCullar. Smiling, she turned to put her gloved hand comfortingly on the expanse of shining darkness between the stallion's ears and ran it down his long, patrician nose before those remarkable emerald eyes came back to meet Rio's.

"I *know* what he's worth," she said, smiling at him. "I should. I was there when he was born."

"He's…Kincaid?" Rio asked unbelievingly. That would explain the stallion's exceptional looks and abilities, but it didn't explain how the horse had ended up at the Mexican auction where he'd bought him, where if he hadn't bought him, the black's next stop would likely have been a pet-food processor.

"When you're in the business of breeding horses to sell, you can't always guarantee where they'll end up," Samantha said. She turned again to look at the black. "You always try, but sometimes…" She paused, and her eyes came back to Rio's. "They weren't horse people. Maybe that explains some of what happened. Sam—my father—always says that when someone pays that much for an animal, you have to believe they'll take care of it. And trust me, they paid a hell of a lot of money for this one."

"What happened?" Rio questioned. His gaze was on the black, and he wasn't aware of the hunger in his eyes.

"By the time we heard he'd gone bad, he'd been sold. Several times. And then he just…seemed to disappear. Sam didn't stop looking, of course. Eventually someone told him about your black. He went to watch you ride, some little rodeo near Laredo. After watching you, watching the two of you work together, he knew the horse was in good hands."

"He didn't try to buy him back," Rio said.

"Would you have sold him?" She didn't wait for the answer they both understood. "Sam's no fool. The black was yours. He was with someone who was good to him. That's all my father wanted to know, all he cared about."

"He's worth a lot of money."

Samantha nodded. "Want to sell him?" she asked, but she was smiling again.

Slowly Rio shook his head. "He's still yours, Mrs. McCullar. You bought him. And more importantly…" He hesitated before he made himself finish it. "You're in a position to take care of him. I'm *not* in any position to buy him back, and even if I were, I couldn't afford to keep him. He's better off with you."

"Except for the fact that he's not *my* horse. No amount of money changing hands makes him mine. You know that as well as I do. Besides, I've already gotten my money's worth. He's serviced a couple of my mares. I'll make plenty from those foals.'' She waited, but the dark eyes of the man in the doorway hadn't moved from their contemplation of the stallion.

"How can you and your father be so sure this is the same horse?'' he asked.

"Sam knew as soon as he saw him.''

Rio's dark head moved, questioning.

"We *are* horse people,'' Samantha said softly. It wasn't a boast. It was simply the truth. "I can put him in Jenny's barn until you decide where you're going. She's got plenty of room. Or I can keep him at our place until you have time to make some arrangements.''

Mouth tight, Rio shook his head.

Samantha Kincaid's lips pursed slightly, an unintended imitation of her famous father. "Then you should at least say goodbye,'' she suggested. "You owe him that, I think.''

She began to lead the horse toward the foot of the steps that led up to the narrow porch where Rio was standing, still gripping the doorway. He released the frame slowly and stepped across the wooden boards. The horse struggled briefly against Samantha's control, more a matter of form, Rio recognized, than any serious protest. He knew all the black's tricks.

"You are all bluff, my heart,'' Rio said in Spanish. His voice had fallen, softened, and the syllables slipped off his tongue like water cascading in a fountain. The stallion's ears flickered.

Rio used the railing to help himself down the steps, still crooning the familiar endearments. The black listened, and when the man reached the bottom step, the stallion was there.

Neither of them was aware when Samantha McCullar released the lead. Somehow it ended up in Rio's undamaged left hand. Exactly where they all knew it belonged.

"I THOUGHT I MIGHT FIND you out here," Anne said softly.

The sun was going down, and the heat of the long afternoon had settled over the ranch like a blanket, even inside the house. Jenny had suggested she offer Rio something to drink, but he hadn't been on the bed in Mac's bedroom, where Jenny had sent him to rest. Or anywhere else in the house.

Rio looked up at the sound of her voice. The barn was deeply shadowed. The fading light filtered in through the cracks between its weathered boards, but in the dimness, his dark eyes were shining, even the one that was still little more than a slit between the swollen, discolored skin that surrounded it.

He held a brush in his left hand, and he had been moving it in slow, even strokes across the stallion's flank. That motion stopped at the sound of her voice.

"It just seems..." He shook his head.

"Too good to be true?" she asked.

"Maybe," he acknowledged. The brush drifted across the gleaming flank again.

"I think maybe you deserve a little good for a change."

"I guess I'm just...not accustomed to it."

She nodded. "I know the feeling."

She hadn't meant for that to slip out. She had fought self-pity from the start, fought against the destructive "Why me's." *Why anyone?* she amended.

"You still okay?" he asked, as softly as he had when he'd asked it before, and she smiled at his tone.

"I'm fine. Just..." She hesitated, thinking about it. She put her hands on their opposite shoulders, running them slowly down her upper arms. "I expected to spend two weeks in peace and quiet, and instead..."

"You want us all to leave?" he asked.

"Umm," she said, pretending to consider the offer. At least his tone had changed from concern to amusement. "Maybe I should be the one to leave. Since I'm the one who doesn't belong. The rest of you—"

His laugh interrupted, the sound soft and deep in his throat. "*I* don't belong here. I never have, and I never will. Maybe he does," he said, running his hand down the stallion's nose. "At least he's got the right bloodlines."

"It's a funny thing about blood," she said. She walked across the dark space between them. "It always shows. When you think about someone like Sam Kincaid out searching for a horse he had sold years before..." She shook her head.

"And someone like me ending up with him?" he suggested.

"I wasn't thinking that."

They didn't say anything else for a moment, but the silence was comfortable, unstrained, as they stood together beside the black. At least they were friends, she thought. At least she would have that when it was all over.

"You think he'd let me touch him?" she asked, her eyes on the stallion.

When Rio didn't answer, she turned to find that he was looking at her. The dimness softened a little what they had done to his face. It was no longer the same as when its beauty had almost startled her the night she had met him. It might never be that again. But the underlying strength and courage and honesty were still there. They would always be there. As recognizable to her as the bloodlines of the stallion had been to Sam Kincaid.

Rio nodded, and she put her hand lightly on the warm skin of the horse. It felt like satin under the slow glide of her fingers, and watching their movement, unconsciously she smiled. It was an almost-sensual pleasure. Dark, smooth skin covering the underlying strength of muscle. Then, suddenly, the forbidden images were as clear in her head as they had been in Jenny's small kitchen that first night.

"It'll be dark soon," Rio said, interrupting the wonder of those. "We should probably go in."

"Do you think they'll come here?" She caressed the horse again, aware this time of the comparison her senses had just suggested. Aware and uninhibited. It was quiet and safe in the barn. She was safe with Rio. She had always known that. Despite what he'd just suggested, she didn't feel threatened. Not by anything.

"They won't come here," he said. "They won't bother what was Mac's. Not his wife or his ranch."

"Or his brother?" she asked.

"I don't think many people remember that."

"Jenny does. *And* Chase. At least now."

He nodded.

Anne removed her hand from the horse, but she didn't want to go inside. Jenny would be there, and the quiet intimacy that was between them here would be lost. And she didn't want it to be.

Again she saw her fingers move, almost, it seemed, without her conscious direction. By their own volition. She watched as they touched lightly against Rio's lean cheek.

He hadn't shaved. That was probably still too painful. His whiskers were dark against the bronze of his skin, and their rough texture was as sensuous under her fingertips as the sliding smoothness of the stallion's coat had been.

She looked up from the place where her hand made contact with his face to find that he was still watching her, his eyes very dark, almost black now, the pupils distended with the dimness. Or with emotion. His mouth had tightened, the damaged lips compressed into a hard line. She could see the muscle beside them tic.

Her thumb found that small pulse, found and smoothed across its involuntary movement. It was such a short distance from there to the curve of his mouth. Her thumb moved, its motion caressing. The compression of his lips lessened fractionally, and the small breath he expelled touched the pad of her thumb as it brushed across them. That seemed as involuntary as her own action had been. As unthinking. As unplanned. But undeniable.

It was permission, somehow. And she recognized that. Her palm cupped under the strong line of his jaw and she stood on tiptoe, her body reaching upward toward his. She held his eyes as she moved inexorably nearer. His mouth would be sore. Still too tender, she knew, from what they had done to him.

Her lips touched his. Then they softened and opened slightly, her breath mingling with his. Inviting.

His head tilted, and his mouth opened under the caress of hers. His tongue slid against her lips, and she knew that she wanted it there. She moved her head to fit her mouth to his.

The contact was slowly made, lingering, and remarkably gentle. She wasn't sure if that was due to his situation or hers. It didn't matter. What was important was that he was touching her, kissing her, and she wanted him to. She knew that it was right. *Someone to trust. Someone to love me.*

He hadn't touched her in any other way. Their bodies were not together, nothing but the slow, heated contact of their mouths and their tongues.

There was no demand and nothing controlling about what he was doing. Yet there was no doubt in her mind that he *was* in charge, and that he knew exactly what he was doing. Exactly what he was doing to her.

Eventually she was the one who broke the contact, simply by stepping back, no longer on tiptoe. No longer reaching for his lips.

His eyes were still on her face. They were calm and dark, no longer glittering, but almost luminous in the growing shadows.

"Thank you," she said softly and watched his slow smile. It was one-sided, moving carefully against the pain of his injuries.

"For what?" he asked. His tone was as quiet as hers had been. As intimate.

"For making that what it should always be."

"Mutual?" he asked. The small smile had widened minutely, and the darkness in his eyes lightened with amusement.

"Pleasurable," she corrected. "A pleasure. A very great pleasure."

He nodded. "Then I guess I should thank you. Because I assure you, that pleasure was all mine."

She smiled, feeling her heart lift. Feeling something move and soar that she had not even realized had been weighted down for months under her unacknowledged fear and uncertainty. And despite her smile, she also felt her eyes fill with tears. Past her control, beyond it, one traced downward. She could feel the warmth of it against her skin.

His eyes followed, tracing its downward journey. When it reached the corner of her mouth and hesitated, he brushed it off with the pad of his thumb, and then his eyes came back, questioning.

Embarrassed, she simply shook her head. She couldn't have told him why she was crying. Not now, anyway. Not after the quiet joy of what had just happened.

"Why are you crying, my heart?" he asked softly in Spanish, the same caress in his voice that had been there when he had whispered endearments to the stallion, who had been beaten and abused by those he should have been able to trust.

And it was only then that Rio realized what her eyes had reminded him of that day. The day she had told him what had happened to her.

His arms enfolded her, pulling her gently against the warm, solid safety of his body. He gave her time to resist, to refuse. But instead she almost melted against him. Her head fit against his shoulder. As if she had been made to fit there. As if she belonged.

But even as Rio held her slender body against his own, he acknowledged that she didn't belong there. Anne Richardson could never belong to him, and he had known that from the first.

But for now, he thought, moving the palm of his hand slowly down the fragile curve of her spine, *just for now, I will hold you, my dearest heart. I will protect you and keep you safe.*

Chapter Eleven

Rio tried not to think about anything else, tried not to even be aware of the passage of time, of the precious minutes drifting by as the darkness gathered around them. Finally he had been allowed to hold Anne Richardson as he had wanted to almost from the beginning. Allowed to shelter her, maybe. Allowed to assuage some of the pain that had been in her eyes since he'd known her.

In spite of his undeniable desire for so much more, he knew this was far beyond what he'd ever expected. More than he'd ever believed *could* happen between them. She had given him the precious gift of her trust. He knew without any doubt that he was the first man she had kissed since she'd been raped.

Although he didn't understand why this had happened tonight, he knew that, whatever her reasons, he didn't want it to end. And he understood that as soon as they left the barn, that other world would intrude. The world where they should still be strangers. The world where they should never have met. The world of violence and betrayal that had touched and marked them both.

So he didn't move, even when he became aware of the sound of a vehicle pulling into the yard. But he knew by the sudden tenseness of her body that Anne had heard it, too. When the car door slammed, she lifted her head from his shoulder.

Was that Trent? Anne wondered. Had he made the trip from Austin again? If he had, she suspected it was as much to check on her as to see Jenny. And she knew that he wouldn't like again finding her with Rio.

Even as she thought it, Rio's arms released her, and he eased his body away from its contact with hers. She realized only then that what had happened the day in the yard when he'd fallen on top of her hadn't happened tonight. He wasn't aroused.

Asexual, she thought, feeling a disappointment she didn't fully understand, one she shouldn't feel. He had held her like a brother. Or a friend. Maybe what she thought had been happening between them had been something else. Maybe he had responded to her overture tonight out of that same sense of compassion he'd shown the woman they'd found hiding in the barn.

She looked up into Rio's eyes, trying to read what was there. His face was too shadowed for her to be sure. The play of fading light emphasized only the hard planes, the underlying beauty of bone structure that the beating had not, and could not, destroy.

"That may be Trent," she said softly, trying to control her own emotions. Trying not to give away how much it had meant to her to be held, to finally feel his arms around her.

"Or Elkins. Chase asked him to come by today."

"About Doc?"

"About the men at the shack. Did Jenny know you were coming out here?"

"I don't think so. She did send me to find you, so I guess when she realizes that we're both gone…"

She smiled at him, trying to let him know that she didn't care if Jenny figured out they were together. There was no answering relaxation of his expression.

"Go around the back of the barn. You can go in the kitchen door. No one will know you've been out here."

"I don't care if they know," she protested. She was surprised that he didn't understand that—how little she cared who knew. What had just happened was something she had been afraid would never happen again. And now...

"*I* care," he said softly. "Go on. You can think of something to tell Jenny. Make up a story about something that distracted you, kept you from looking for me."

"Why would you—"

"Go on," he ordered again. "Our being found out here together is just going to make everything harder. Not only for you," he added. This time he put his left hand on her shoulder, turning her and pushing her gently toward the double doors.

She refused to move, holding his eyes. There was nothing of what had been in them before, when her mouth had lifted to his. They were shuttered. Black and cold. And they seemed to give her no choice.

Harder for *him?* she thought, trying to decide why he was so determined no one should know she'd been out here. If he believed the car that had just pulled into the yard belonged to Elkins, she realized, and if she was his alibi for Doc's murder, then the authorities would be far less likely to believe her if they thought they were...involved.

Finally she nodded, agreeing to the unspoken logic of his demand. When she slipped out the barn doors, she could see the sheriff's car parked between the two structures. Rio had been right. Elkins and not her brother.

She was surprised at how strong her sense of relief was. Trent was her brother, and she loved him, but she hadn't really wanted to try to explain her feelings about Rio tonight. They were still new enough to defy articulation.

She had almost reached the end of the far side of the barn when she heard Jenny call Rio's name. And heard his response from inside the building she'd just left. It appeared he had been right about that, as well. The sheriff had come out to talk to him about the attack, just as Chase had said he would. And Rio had also been right about the other, she admitted. Elkins shouldn't find her anywhere near the barn, anywhere near Rio.

She edged toward the corner, thinking that they would probably all be out in the open yard. This would be the trickiest part, cutting across from the back of the barn to the kitchen door while they stood in front talking together.

From where she stood, still hidden by the barn, she could hear their voices, the masculine tones carrying more clearly through the clear air. Her eyes began to trace the path she would take, mentally measuring the distance to the steps and narrow back porch that led to Jenny's kitchen door.

Her heart stopped. The woman they had carried to Doc's clinic that night—the night before he had been killed—was huddled in the shadows of the porch, as well-hidden as she was from the group standing in the front yard.

Their eyes made contact. In the dark ones, clearly, was a plea. A silent entreaty. Slowly the woman lifted one hand from the bundle she cradled against her body. The baby, Anne realized, still wrapped in the same towel that had come from Doc's clinic. She watched as the woman put the tips of three fingers over her lips and shook her head.

The command was unmistakable. She was asking for Anne's silence. Wordlessly, Anne shook her head, trying desperately to communicate that there was no need for her to be afraid, that no one would hurt her. But she couldn't think of any gesture that would instantly convey that meaning. So she smiled instead, hoping that, too, was part of a universal language.

The woman began easing backward, still maintaining her crouching position. Still holding the baby against her chest. Desperately, Anne raised both hands and moved her fingers toward herself, encouraging her to stay.

The woman shook her head vehemently. Her backward movement seemed to become more hurried, almost frantic, moving farther away from the protecting shadows of the house.

Anne could still hear the voices from the front. She eased

closer to the corner and peeked around it. She jerked away, quickly leaning her head back against the rough boards of the barn. The two men were standing directly between the barn and the ranch house. And that meant there was little hope she could cross that expanse toward the woman without attracting their attention.

Despite what Rio had said, despite the undeniable logic of it, she thought it would surely be more important to stop the Mexican woman from leaving, as she obviously intended to do. Except it had also been obvious that that was the last thing the woman wanted—to let anyone know she was here.

Because she was afraid she'd be sent back? Afraid of the authorities? Or because she had seen something at the clinic that day and was terrified that if she came forward, whoever had killed Doc would kill her? Had she been making her way back here, hiding these last three days? Hiding from the killer or from the authorities? Anne remembered Rio's warning. He had said the woman would never come forward voluntarily.

She heard the screen door slam, and then the sound of Jenny's voice, distinctive because of its lighter tone. Had Jenny been inside looking for her? Anne wondered. Had Jenny been searching the house for her as she stood here, silently trying to convince the woman who knew something about Doc's murder not to run?

She eased nearer to the corner to take another quick look, again taking pains to reveal as little of her body as possible. The three of them were standing in the yard. Both men were listening to Jenny. She gestured toward the house with her hand.

Anne strained to catch the words, but she couldn't hear enough to make sense of any of them. She couldn't get Rio's attention or Jenny's without letting Buck Elkins know she was here.

It seemed then that the best option was simply to openly cross the short distance and join them. Tell them about the woman and let the sheriff take it from there. Maybe he wouldn't connect her with the barn and with Rio. Maybe he'd think she'd come out the back door of the house and around the side.

And as far as the woman's fear was concerned, this had gone beyond worrying about an illegal border crossing. That happened every day. Anne didn't know exactly what the penalties were, but she had a feeling they were not that severe.

If the woman had been hiding from the people who had killed Doc, Elkins would protect her. But if the sheriff wasn't allowed to question the woman about what she might have seen, then they might lose valuable information.

Anne glanced back toward the shadows of the porch. There was nothing there. Her eyes frantically scanned the area behind Jenny's house, which was open and relatively free of any other hiding place.

There was nothing there but darkness. There were scattered pools of deeper shadows and then the expanse of night-shrouded desert beyond. A small area of the yard was dimly illuminated by the lights Jenny had turned on in the kitchen before she'd gone outside to talk to Rio and the sheriff. But nowhere was there any sign of the woman and the baby. They had disappeared, just as completely as they had vanished once before.

Even as she was trying to decide what to do, she heard the sound of a car door closing. And then the engine starting. She waited, still indecisive, as she listened to the noise of the car fade away down the dirt road that connected the two McCullar ranches.

As she hesitated, her eyes traced again over the shadowed yard, hoping she'd been wrong. Hoping that she had just missed what she had been seeking in that first panicked response to the woman's apparent disappearance.

The front screen slammed again, and its sound seemed to release her. Anne stepped out from behind the barn. Only Rio stood in the front now, still looking in the direction the

sheriff's car had taken. She ran across the space that separated them, yelling to him.

"She was here. The woman and the baby were here."

"Here? How do you know?" Rio asked.

"I saw her. She was here. Just now. At the back. She
asked me not to say anything. I guess she was afraid, and
then while I was trying to decide what to do, she disappeared."

Rio had begun moving before she'd finished. "Why
didn't you tell us?" he asked. "Why the hell didn't you
just tell us she was here?"

"I don't know. She asked me not to. By the time I'd
figured out that I had to tell someone, she'd just vanished.
I swear, Rio, she just disappeared. One minute she was
here, and then the next…"

He was right. She knew that even as she tried to explain.
She had made the wrong decision. Talk about a material
witness. If she herself could be considered one, then the
woman who might have been there when Doc was killed
was certainly material to any case the sheriff might try to
make against his killer. And she had let her go. Let her
leave because she had hated to betray her to the authorities.
Or to betray Rio, maybe. But she knew now that had been
the wrong choice.

"Show me," Rio said. He wouldn't admonish her again
for the mistake. She knew him better by now, certainly well
enough to know that he wouldn't try to make her feel any
worse than she already did.

She led him around to the spot where she'd first seen the
woman. She bent down in the shadows cast by the porch
to see if there was any sign that she'd been there, anything
to show him. There was nothing. She pivoted on the toes
of her tennis shoes, looking up at Rio to shake her head.

"She was right here."

"And you're sure it was the same woman?"

Could she have been mistaken about the woman's identity? she wondered. She turned to look at the place at the

back of the barn where she had been standing, again trying to gauge the distance between them. No wonder their eyes had made contact, she thought. It would have been almost impossible to miss one another, considering their relative positions. And suddenly she remembered why she had been so sure it was the same woman.

"We thought Doc might have taken her back home, but he didn't, Rio. The towel that came from the clinic was still around the baby, so she's been here all along."

Her eyes moved toward the front of the house. From this angle, from the place where the woman had been crouching when she had first seen her, none of the people who had been standing in the yard would have been visible.

The woman couldn't have known Rio was there, she realized. Not unless she had heard his voice, but the distance was great enough that Anne had had trouble distinguishing their voices. Maybe the woman wouldn't have disappeared if she had seen Rio. She had trusted him, and he had been able to communicate with her.

But by the same token, Anne realized suddenly, the woman couldn't have seen Buck Elkins, either. There was no way that from this position she could have identified the people who were talking.

"She couldn't have known," Anne said, thinking aloud.

"Couldn't have known what?" Rio asked. He wasn't looking at her. His eyes were tracing across the same barren and seemingly deserted terrain that hers had searched so desperately minutes before.

"That the sheriff was here. I thought she was afraid because she thought he'd send her back, but she couldn't have known he was here. Why would she be so afraid?"

"Maybe she's afraid because of what she saw at Doc's. Maybe she's afraid of everyone now."

Remembering the examination room, Anne shivered. That poor woman. Alone in a country where she didn't speak the language and didn't know whom to trust. Illegally in that country, so that out of fear, she might not go to the

authorities. With a newborn baby to care for. Still suffering
the effects of that difficult birth. Maybe ill. And maybe
terrified that what she had seen happen to Doc would happen to her. Or that the people who had done that would
find her.

So she had made her way to the only place where she
had believed she might find help, to the place where she
had found help once before. Undoubtedly, she had come
here looking for Rio. And untrusting of the Texas authorities, taught to be untrusting by the continuous border
games of hide-and-seek, she had now simply disappeared
again into the desert night.

"Let Rommel out," Rio said, breaking into that depress-
ing chain of thought, "and have Jenny call Chase."

Her eyes flicked up to his, a long way up. She realized
that she was still crouching on the ground, still lost in regret, while Rio had been thinking about what to do. She
stood up, brushing her dirty palms down the front of her
jeans.

"Rommel?" she repeated.

"Maybe he can find her."

"I thought you needed a hound for tracking."

"I don't know. I'm going to ask him," Rio said, and it
was only when he didn't smile, his eyes again on the terrain
beyond the backyard, that she realized he meant exactly
what he'd said. *"I'm going to ask him."* In Spanish, no
doubt.

"And Chase?" she asked.

"I'm going to ask him what the hell we do with her if
we find her."

WHEN SHE OPENED THE BACK door for the shepherd, she
heard Rio's low whistle, calling the dog to join him in the
darkness. Rom disappeared without a backward glance at
her for permission. Anne turned to where Jenny stood, the
phone at her ear.

Anne waited through the long seconds, and finally Jenny

shook her head. She punched the Off button and laid the portable back on the kitchen counter.

"They're not there," she said unnecessarily.

"Then maybe we ought to go out and help Rio look for her."

"He shouldn't be out there," Jenny said. "Despite the tough-guy routine, he shouldn't be wandering around out there in the dark. All kinds of things could happen. None of them good."

"He's got Rom," Anne said, fighting the images Jenny's worry had suggested. It was true, of course, despite the fact that they both knew Rio *was* tough, that his toughness was certainly no "routine." But for a man who should probably be in a hospital bed somewhere, his condition carefully monitored, given the severity of his injuries, wandering around at night in the desert wasn't exactly the smartest thing he'd ever done.

"Rom eat rattlesnakes?" Jenny asked. Her tone was almost sarcastic, but anxiety was clear in her dark eyes.

"Not that I know of," Anne said. "I'm going with them."

"Then take Mac's revolver. I'll keep trying to get Chase. It's possible they're there and are just..." She shrugged slightly, "Maybe they're outside, out at the stables."

It made sense, and Jenny had already started down the hall toward her bedroom to get the gun. Anne opened the back door, for some reason expecting to see Rommel and Rio still there. The backyard was as empty as it had seemed after the woman had disappeared.

She could see almost nothing beyond the reach of the two rectangles of light shining outward from the kitchen where she stood. And only a short distance beyond that, she knew, the relatively tame grounds around the ranch house very quickly became rugged, almost-wild desert grassland. And on the other side of the ranch was the river and Mexico. The two people she was looking for could be anywhere in that shadowed darkness.

The more she thought about it, the more she believed the woman would head for the Rio Grande. She had found the ranch. Obviously she had her bearings now, and so she would probably go home, simply disappear across the unguarded border. Just as Rio might have done if it hadn't been for her involvement in all this. As he still might do, she thought. If he followed the woman across—

"Here," Jenny said softly from behind her.

Turning, she found her hostess holding the revolver out to her. "It's loaded," Jenny said. "Be careful."

Anne nodded and took the gun, knowing that soft warning had had nothing to do with handling it, and then she slipped through the open door and out into the desert night.

SHE WAS HEADED FOR the river, Rio realized. It had taken Rommel only a few seconds to pick up the woman's trail. She had skirted around the other side of the ranch house and apparently waited there until they had moved out of the front yard, clearing the way to the Rio Grande.

Rio tried to hurry, his left arm bent and pressed tightly into his body, the fingers of that hand spread over his side, trying to protect his ribs. The dog forged ahead, running for a short distance, nose to the ground, and then turning impatiently to come back to him.

He knew he could have given the shepherd his head. Rommel wouldn't hurt the woman, but he might frighten her. She was carrying the baby, Anne had said, and considering all she'd been through, she didn't need to be terrorized by the unexpected appearance of the big dog, lunging at her out of the night.

Hurrying across this terrain as he was was dangerous, but Rio didn't feel that he had a choice. There was too much country out here that someone on the run could disappear into. He still might lose her, despite Rom's help. As Anne had reminded him, the shepherd wasn't trained to track. The river would add to the difficulty of what the dog was trying to do, as would the increasingly rocky expanse on the other side.

If the woman reached the river, then she would almost certainly be gone. Rio knew he had no choice but to move as quickly as he could force his abused body to go. He knew this country better than the woman he was following, but he also knew he couldn't afford a fall. Not now.

His breath had begun sawing painfully in and out of his gasping lungs before he spotted her, still too far ahead of him. She was a dark shape struggling toward the star-touched charcoal of the Rio Grande. Heading for the river. Heading for home.

His home, too, he thought. Perhaps they would both be better off if he simply followed her through the dark, shallow warmth of the water and disappeared.

Except, he thought, forced by exhaustion to pick his way with more caution over the ground leading down to the Rio Grande, there were a couple of people to whom he owed something better than that. Better than simply disappearing into the border darkness. He owed Doc the effort of trying to find his killer. And he owed Anne Richardson. If for nothing more, then at least for the trust she had given him.

He was close enough now to the struggling figure that he decided to risk calling to her. Even if she panicked and increased her speed, it probably wouldn't matter. He knew that he couldn't keep up this pace any longer. This morning he had thought he couldn't manage getting out of bed, and now he was almost running.

"I need to talk to you," he called. His voice was gasping, too soft and lacking any force. The woman didn't pause, but she must have heard some part of that. She threw a quick glance over her shoulder. It was obvious that she didn't recognize him because, as he had feared, she increased her speed. She was almost to the river now, still too far ahead of him.

"I took you to Doc Horn's that night," he called, still speaking in Spanish. He didn't have breath or strength enough to concentrate on making his tone reassuring as he had tried to do then. Now, just getting the words out at all was an effort. "I'm not going to hurt you," he gasped. "I need to talk to you about what happened to Doc."

She hesitated, moving more slowly now, either because she had recognized his voice or was thinking about what he'd said. He tried to increase his speed, but his side was a burning agony and his legs felt almost numb with fatigue.

He realized that Rommel had bounded out of the darkness and toward the woman only when he heard her terrified shriek. She had stopped, and he was near enough now that he could see her hold the baby up, away from what she probably imagined to be the snapping jaws of a wild animal.

He had lost track of the shepherd. He knew he hadn't been paying enough attention to what was going on, diverted instead by what seemed to be happening to his body. He was on the verge of collapse.

"He won't hurt you," he tried to tell her, but the words seemed to whisper away into the darkness. But he realized finally that the dog's ears were far more sensitive than hers, so he added the command he should have used instead of trying to explain to her. "Heel, Rommel."

The shepherd turned toward him, but Rio didn't even slow down, trying desperately to close the distance. It was obvious the big dog was pulled between staying with the woman he was trying to guard and obeying Rio's command.

Rommel looked from one to the other as if he were trying to make up his mind about which duty was more important. And then, seeming suddenly to decide, he charged back toward the man who had issued the command, barking wildly.

"It's all right. Nobody's going to hurt you. Just stay there," Rio begged the woman. "We need—"

He never completed the sentence. In shock, he saw Rommel's forward motion check. The dog staggered sideways, his body seeming to move in slow motion. Then he collapsed on the ground, midway between himself and the woman. Rio had watched it, but it wasn't until he put the crack of the rifle together with the dog's fall, that he realized what had happened. Someone had shot Anne's shepherd.

Chapter Twelve

"Don't take another step, Delgado. I'm warning you."

The voice came out of the darkness behind him. It was the unmistakable voice of authority. Despite his shock and horror over what had just happened, Rio automatically obeyed, having endured almost five years under that kind of authority. He stopped, his exhausted body trembling now with the monumental effort of remaining upright. His eyes hadn't left the dark form of the dog, which lay limp and unmoving where he had fallen.

"I thought you might try something like this," the voice behind him continued. "Only things ain't gonna go exactly like you planned. Now why don't you turn around, real slow and easy."

Rio lifted his eyes to the Mexican woman who stood as motionless as he was, as shocked, apparently, by the sudden violence. Her dark gaze met his, and it was filled with terror. He supposed he should be feeling that same terror, but instead all he felt was fury, a burning anger over the senseless death of the beautiful animal who had loved him. And who had trusted him to keep him safe.

Holding his arms slightly away from his body to indicate that he wasn't a threat, Rio began to turn slowly around to face the man who had shot Rommel. Every second he expected to feel the impact of a high-powered bullet slam into his own body.

The person who stood on the slight rise leading down to the river was Ray Morales, Buck Elkins's deputy. The butt of the rifle was still resting professionally against his shoulder, and he was sighting down the long barrel.

"What the hell did you shoot him for?" Rio asked. He was sickened by the senseless slaughter, sickened by the thought that anyone could do that to an animal.

"To stop that big son of a bitch from attacking me." The comment was almost offhand. There was no fear in his voice.

The deputy hadn't been afraid of the dog, so there had been no reason to shoot him. No reason, Rio knew, except that he'd wanted to.

"And to keep you from getting away," Morales added.

"I'm not going anywhere," Rio said. "You've got it all wrong. All of it."

"I know damn well where you're heading. Across that river," Morales said. "I told Buck you'd run. I told him not to let you out. Seems I was right."

"I'm not going anywhere," Rio said again. He could hear the resignation and exhaustion in his own voice. No one would believe him this time, either. No one would care about the truth.

He could no longer see the woman behind him. Morales could, but the deputy wouldn't know who she was. In spite of the situation, the rifle pointing unwaveringly at his heart, Rio hesitated to try to explain what he'd really been doing out here. Given the woman's terror, to tell her story felt like a betrayal.

"You're damn right you're not," Morales said softly.

There was a minute shift in the positioning of the rifle, the dark eye of the muzzle settling more firmly on the center of Rio's chest. He took a breath—maybe his last one, he had time to realize—as all the regrets ran through his head in a series of lightning images, just like that night in the line shack when he'd smelled the gasoline.

This is what they would tell Anne, he thought. What they

would tell everyone. That he'd been killed breaking parole, trying to run away. Trying to go home. Except that village in Mexico had never been home, despite the years he'd spent there. *Blood is thicker than water,* Mac had told him. Rio Delgado had always known where his home was. Through the long years of fighting that admission, somewhere inside he had always known.

He hadn't come back here to settle the score with Chase McCullar. That wasn't why he was here. He had always come back to this land. McCullar land.

And now he would die here, his blood mingling with the dry, alkaline soil that had never belonged to him in any sense except that. In no way had this land ever belonged to him except through the blood they all shared.

"What's going on?"

Rio's eyes flicked upward at the question, but he had already identified her voice before his gaze found her. Anne Richardson was standing slightly above Morales on the slope. She had Mac's big revolver in her hand, but she wasn't pointing it at anybody.

"I caught Delgado trying to get across the river," the deputy explained. "Sheriff Elkins told me to watch the place, to make sure he didn't try to get away."

Anne didn't say anything for a moment. She knew why he had come out here, of course. Not to escape. Not to disappear into Mexico. Rio knew that she, too, would be able to see the woman they'd been looking for behind him. And apparently, as he had, she was thinking about whether or not to identify her to the authorities.

The decision she reached was different from the one he'd come to, but his had been based on instinct, maybe, and not logic. It didn't make any sense *not* to explain what was going on, not considering the direction that rifle was pointed, not considering what the deputy thought. And Rio himself had admonished Anne because she *hadn't* told the sheriff about the woman earlier, so he wasn't surprised when she did it now.

"That's the woman we took to Doc Horn's clinic. She showed up at the McCullar ranch tonight. Rio was trying to stop her from disappearing. To stop her from going home. He wasn't running."

"The night before Doc was killed?" Morales asked. There was no element of shock or surprise in the question. Instead, its tone was considering.

"Sheriff Elkins will want to talk to her about what she might have seen," Anne said. "She's a material witness to the murder. Rio knew that. He wasn't trying to get away. He was only trying to keep her from disappearing."

The deputy didn't respond, but the rifle didn't falter from its focus on Rio's chest.

"You can ask the sheriff," Anne added. "We told him about her."

"Why don't you just put that gun down while I think about this?" Morales suggested. "You just lower it real easy down onto the ground."

Again Anne hesitated.

"Do it now, Ms. Richardson," Morales ordered softly. "I'm not real comfortable with women waggling around guns that might go off by accident."

"He shot Rom," Rio said softly.

It was a warning, he supposed. It still seemed to him there had been no sense in Morales's shooting the shepherd. The deputy had known the animal wasn't attacking him. That act, the fact that he'd been so eager to do that, seemed to Rio to say something important about Ray Morales. Maybe what it said was he'd be just as eager to pull that trigger again.

"Shot *Rommel?*" Anne repeated.

Rio knew she hadn't spotted the body in the darkness. The dog's death had been almost incomprehensible to him, and he had watched it happen. One minute Rom had been alive, vital, bounding to obey his command, and the next...

"Why would you shoot my dog?" she asked unbelievingly. She was still holding the revolver.

"He tried to attack me."

"That's not true," Rio said.

"What the hell difference does it make?" Morales asked angrily. "He was a dog. He was interfering in the apprehension of a criminal." His voice had been impatient with her demand for an explanation, too full of tension, and he must have become aware of it. Or maybe he had just remembered who Anne Richardson was.

When the deputy spoke again, his tone was much more conciliatory, just as the sheriff's had been on the phone that day. The day she'd called to report Doc's murder.

"You just drop that gun. You hear me now, Ms. Richardson? I promise you everything will be all right. We'll straighten this all out later on. The sheriff's department will reimburse you for the animal."

"I don't want you to *reimburse* me," Anne denied, clearly furious. "You shot my dog, damn it. I want to know why the hell you did that."

Rio watched, his heart suddenly moving into his throat, as she began to raise the revolver. He didn't blame her for being angry about Rommel. He'd like to have Morales's neck between his fingers right now.

And Rio couldn't understand, of course, that the tone of the deputy's voice, that same condescending tone she'd heard one time too often from the policemen she had dealt with, had simply fueled Anne's fury over Rom's death, her anger over everything that had happened. What Rio did understand, with crystal clarity, was that lifting the gun in this situation was very dangerous.

"I'll shoot him," Morales threatened softly. He was watching her slow, unthinking movement but the rifle he held was still pointed at Rio's heart. "I swear to God I'll shoot 'em both if you don't drop it. Drop the gun *now,* Ms. Richardson, before somebody gets hurt."

There was no doubt in Rio's mind that the deputy would do exactly what he said he'd do. He felt just as he had the day Anne had put the muzzle of the revolver she was holding against the underside of his jaw. He knew he was only one heartbeat away from being dead.

The revolver tilted, slowly pointing downward again. He watched Anne's knees bend, almost in slow motion, moving carefully now, finally realizing maybe what was going on here. Realizing that there was a very real possibility that Morales would do what he'd threatened. Maybe realizing that he might even get away with it. She put Mac's gun on the ground beside her and then stood again.

"Now you move away from it," Morales ordered.

Anne took a step to the side and then another, and finally Rio remembered to breathe. And to think again.

Maybe Morales could explain away his decision to shoot him, given the circumstances of where he was and given his background, but it made no sense for him to threaten the woman. He should know that he couldn't get away with shooting her.

Except for Anne's presence, of course, he probably could have. The woman would simply "disappear." She would become another illegal who didn't make it back home. There would be no questions asked about her disappearance. Just as there had been none about her husband's. Not unless Doc had for some reason asked them.

The question was not whether the deputy could get away with shooting them both, Rio realized, his brain finally beginning to work past the pain and exhaustion, past his fear about Morales doing something stupid that might get Anne hurt. The real question was why the deputy would even *threaten* to shoot the woman. Unless... *Unless Doc had for some reason asked them.* Rio finally realized the significance of that errant thought.

"Now you get down there by him," Morales ordered. The deputy's eyes were still focused on Anne.

There was no logical reason for that command, either, Rio realized. Anne wasn't a threat to Morales. But he wanted them all in one place, and if he got them together, all three of them lined up together, they'd be like ducks in a shooting gallery.

"AMPEX," Rio said softly, trying to distract Morales before Anne could obey. "You were involved in that, weren't you?"

If ever there had been a shot in the dark, he acknowledged, this was it. He didn't even know what the word meant. Or if—as he suspected—it was composed of initials, what they stood for. He was surprised he even remembered the word.

Chase had thought the notation he'd found in Doc's records might be important, connected somehow to his murder, and it was worth taking a chance. Especially since Rio hadn't been able to think of anything else that would give them a chance, a chance to keep Anne out of the line of fire.

The barrel of the rifle had been moving toward Anne, intended maybe to urge her along, but at Rio's words, the dark eye of its muzzle tracked back to its original focus on the center of Rio's chest.

"What the hell do you know about that?" Morales demanded. There was shock in his voice, and for the first time, Rio thought he could hear fear there as well.

"Enough to know you're involved."

"She tell you that?" the deputy asked.

Luckily the rifle had moved minutely, a silent identifying gesture toward the woman who was standing behind Rio. Morales's pronoun had not referred to Anne, but to the woman who had been at Doc's that night. And who had possibly been there the next morning, too. The morning someone had butchered Doc.

"Chase McCullar told me," Rio said. That was the truth, what little of it there was, and it might buy them some time. It might make Morales think about the idea that killing the three of them wouldn't make it all go away.

Even if it put Chase in danger, Rio knew McCullar could take care of himself. He wanted the deputy to realize that someone else knew about AMPEX, whatever the hell it was. Someone who wasn't an illegal alien. Or an ex-con. Or a woman who was involved with him. People in this county would listen to Chase McCullar, and Ray Morales had to realize that.

"Just exactly what did McCullar tell you?" the deputy asked carefully.

"That that's why her husband disappeared." Make it be enough, Rio prayed, at least enough to keep him talking. Every second mattered. He wondered if Anne had done what he'd told her to do. Had she asked Jenny to call Chase? If so, maybe…

"You got no proof I had anything to do with that."

"Maybe not," Rio said, trying desperately to figure out the next bluff. He'd gotten this far only on the word Chase had found penciled on Doc's records. He just needed to keep talking until he finally ran out of things to say. "But her husband's not the only one who disappeared. And those people have all got families, too. Somebody's going to be willing to talk. You know McCullar's not going to give up. Not until he's figured out who killed the old man."

He could almost see Morales thinking about that, turning it over in his mind. Examining the possibility.

"Murderer."

The soft Spanish word came from behind him, and the hatred in it chilled his blood. Rio didn't know if that whisper was loud enough for the others to hear. Anne might not understand the Spanish, but Morales would. He would know exactly what the woman had said. And what it meant—its implications for all of them.

Rio saw the muzzle of the rifle move again, tracking this time to a target behind him. Moving in response to that whispered accusation. He should have been relieved that the rifle was no longer focused on him, Rio supposed, but he wasn't, of course. In her terror the woman had just signed her own death warrant.

Doc or her husband? That was the question. Which one

was she accusing the deputy of murdering? Guess the
wrong one and the pretense that he really knew what was
going on would be over. Don't guess at all, and Morales
would kill the woman.

"Shooting her won't do you any good," Rio warned
softly. "She's not the only one who knows you killed Doc.
Not anymore."

The tracking movement hesitated and then stopped. The
muzzle of the rifle was brought slowly back to point again
at Rio's chest. "Damn bitch. I didn't have any idea she
was there. Everything would have been all right except for
her."

At the confirmation, Rio took a breath. Right guess. He
had to block the memory of the examination room. Block
the images of how Doc had died. Block the thought that
this was the animal who had done it, apparently with as
little feeling as when he'd shot Rommel.

"When I got out there," Morales said, a murderer's
compulsion to explain it all, to justify it to somebody,
working as it usually did, "I thought Doc was alone. When
he'd called the office, he'd said some woman had come in
with a story about her husband disappearing after he'd gone
to work for AMPEX. Doc wanted to file a report for her
about the man's disappearance.

"And he claimed it wasn't the first time he'd heard that
story. He wanted an investigation. He mentioned a couple
of other names. He was just going to stir up a bunch of
stuff. Get everybody in trouble. We couldn't let that happen. But I swear I didn't know she was still there. She must
have slipped out the back while…" The reasonable voice
faded, but it didn't matter. Rio already knew the rest.

While he was killing Doc.

"How'd you finally figure it out, that she *was* still
there?" Rio asked the question instead of saying any of the
things that were crowding his throat. He understood now
why the woman had had to give voice to that whispered

accusation, despite the danger. If he allowed himself to think about the way Doc had died—

"When I heard what the two of you told Buck. There was no way, knowing Doc, that he'd have let her leave. Not the next morning, anyway."

"And you've been looking for her. That's why you were out here. Not because Buck told you to watch me, but because you thought she might come back here."

That was why the woman had been so terrified at the ranch tonight, Rio realized. She must have seen Sheriff Elkins's car. She hadn't known that it wasn't being driven by the man who had come to the clinic that day. Raymond Morales had been driving an identical county car that morning, identical to the one the sheriff had parked in the ranch yard tonight.

"And I was right," Morales said smugly. "I knew if I just waited long enough, she'd show up."

"The smart thing to do is to let her go," Rio suggested. "She's not going to tell anybody what she saw. She'll just disappear. You know that. Just let her go. Let her cross the river, and you'll never see her again."

"The smart thing to do?" Morales mocked. "I think the smart thing to do would be to just get rid of all of you. Then nobody knows anything."

"Except McCullar. I told you he knows about AMPEX."

"There's nothing illegal about it," Morales said. "Everybody I send up there's legal. At least by the time they arrive," he added. His voice was relaxed now. No longer full of tension. He had made his decision. He was going to kill them all, and he didn't care if they knew what he'd done. He was enjoying letting them realize how clever he was.

"You're recruiting for them," Rio said, putting the clues together as he talked. "You're their coyote." Rio finally understood what had gone on. "Coyote" was the border term. Morales was recruiting illegals. Damn it, he should have figured it out a long time before now. Before it was too late.

"The people who go to work for AMPEX make more money than they've ever made in their lives," Morales said. "Your people, Delgado. You should be glad for them."

"Except when something goes wrong. Like it did with her husband. What happened, Morales? What went wrong with that one?"

"Stupid bastard," the deputy said, his voice full of disgust. "There was an accident at the plant. Just a freaking accident. Nothing like that had ever happened before."

"And somehow he ended up dead?" Rio asked, working to keep emotion out of his voice. It had to be a death. Nothing else would be serious enough to frighten the company into a cover-up. To frighten Morales into murder. "But the company didn't want anybody to know about it?"

"They couldn't afford to. There's been some trouble in the past with OSHA. Big fines. A couple of investigations. They don't want any more trouble. What happened wasn't their fault. It was his. Stupid Mexican bastard. I mean, maybe they break a few rules, but everybody does that. You got to make a profit."

"And occasionally people die," Rio said. "Or get injured so they can't work anymore."

He knew all about that kind of business. Illegal labor brought in to feed the relentless maw of the giant meatpacking plants of the Midwest. People like Morales recruited workers in Mexico and collected their bounties from the American companies. Maybe he even supplied the papers that would make those workers "legal." But if he didn't, someone else would.

The jobs were hard, the labor backbreaking and relentless, and the wages too low to attract American workers, but the companies didn't need to worry about that as long as there were people like Morales who would bring illegals across the border, Mexican men who were desperate to find work, to support the families they'd left in Mexico. That was what Doc had been talking about that night.

"And Doc?" Rio asked softly. "Doc's asking questions got him killed?"

"That wasn't supposed to happen," Morales said. "Doc just kept on. He wouldn't let it alone. He kept talking about families that had been deserted. I can't help it if the men don't want to come home. Most of them send money. And if they don't…" He shrugged away that concern. "Hell, once they get a taste of the life up there, they don't want to go back. And who can blame them? But Doc…" Morales shook his head in regret. "He just wouldn't let it go. I knew he was going to keep on until he stirred somebody up."

"That morning," Rio said softly, remembering. "You wanted something from Doc. You didn't let him die easy because he wouldn't tell you."

"I needed to know who else knew what he knew. I needed to know who he'd talked to."

And apparently the old man hadn't talked to anyone. Nobody except him and Anne. That night. *"Now that ain't the first time I've heard that story,"* Doc had said. Rio hadn't realized that muttered sentence was so significant, not even when he'd repeated it to Chase. He hadn't realized that that was what had gotten Doc killed.

"Did he tell you who he'd talked to?" Rio asked.

"That old bastard didn't say a thing," the deputy said. And, remembering, his voice was touched with admiration. "He sure was one tough old bastard."

If rage and adrenaline could have changed the situation, Rio knew, the sudden surge of both through his body should have been enough. But even if he hadn't been in the condition he was in, he probably couldn't do anything to change what was going to happen here.

"But it didn't matter," Morales continued. "As soon as you and Ms. Richardson talked to the sheriff the next day, I knew you were the only ones Doc could have told about

AMPEX. I figured she'd be gone as soon as her brother heard what was going on, and you… It wasn't too hard to figure out what to do about you.''

"You're the one who stirred them up," Rio said. "You were the one who instigated what happened out at the line shack."

"Folks don't like you too much, Delgado. It wasn't tough to get them to realize that this county would be better off without you in it."

Ray Morales had already killed once. And had tried to a second time. Maybe he even liked it. It sounded as if he did. He'd shot the shepherd without a second's hesitation. And he would never have confessed to Doc's murder if he intended for any of them to be left alive to tell about it. He was going to kill them all, and Rio didn't have any other questions to ask that might stop him. End of the line. He knew it all now, all that had happened that morning at the small clinic where Doc had died. And so did Anne Richardson.

With that thought, his eyes again moved to Anne. It was a mistake, but he didn't realize how serious a mistake until he saw Morales's gaze follow his. The rifle didn't move, but apparently the deputy finally remembered that he needed all of them together. All his ducks in a row, Rio thought again.

"You need to move on down there, Ms. Richardson," Morales said.

Anne's eyes were still on Rio. He could feel them there. And he understood the question that was in them.

But Rio also knew that Morales was too far away from him for any heroics to succeed. It was obvious that Morales was marksman enough to take them all out before Rio could even begin to cross the distance that stretched between them and try to take the rifle away from him. Which left only one option.

He had to give the two women a chance. If he could get his body to move, if he could find the strength to force his trembling legs up that slope, he might keep the focus of the powerful rifle on himself. At least for a little while. At least long enough to give the women an opportunity to run.

Unless Morales hit him dead center the first time, it might even take two shots to bring him down. Rio didn't know how long it would take to pump a couple of bullets into his body. A few seconds at most.

Maybe the woman behind him might not make it, then, because the deputy would surely try to take her out next, after he'd finished with Rio, while the gun was still pointed in that direction. It's what any good hunter would do. It was efficient and it made sense.

Maybe while Morales was occupied with the two of them, Anne could disappear into the darkness behind her. If she could hide and then eventually work her way back to the ranch... She'd be safe there. He didn't have any doubts about that.

"If Jenny had been there with a shotgun," Chase had assured him, *"we'd have never lost the Alamo."* He'd back Anne and Jenny McCullar against Morales any day, Rio thought, his mouth moving slightly in acknowledgment of that confidence. He just had to provide them that opportunity.

Anne was watching him. He was sure her eyes were on him, despite the distance that separated them. Maybe his certainty was the result of that connection that had been there from the beginning. Her eyes were locked on him. She wasn't even looking at the deputy, almost as if she considered him unimportant.

Rio bent his knees slightly, preparing. Morales was going to kill him anyway. And he would kill him first. Rio understood that. He had known the deputy was going to shoot him from the beginning, even before he'd realized that Morales had been involved in Doc's death. He was going to die, but maybe he could do something for Anne. For the woman behind him.

And Rio Delgado had nothing to lose. He'd never had

anything to lose. Nothing in his entire life. Except Diablo. Doc's love. And what Anne Richardson had given him. No matter what happened, no one could take that away from him.

I will protect you, my dearest heart. And keep you safe.

"Run," he yelled to Anne. And then Rio began to charge up the slope, toward the dark, waiting eye of the rifle.

Chapter Thirteen

Anne had known Rio was going to try something. He had been waiting for Chase, trying to delay until help arrived. He didn't know that Jenny hadn't been able to reach his half brother. And now they couldn't afford to wait any longer. If Morales got them all together, then time would have run out.

She understood that as well as Rio did. That was why she had hesitated, waiting for some indication of what he wanted her to do. Suddenly she had felt his determination, had almost been aware of the second when he'd made his decision.

She hadn't obeyed him, of course. She had never even thought about running. The only thing she considered in the split second it took her to realize what Rio was doing was how long it would take her to get to the revolver. How long to get her hand around the grip and her finger positioned over the trigger.

Even as she threw herself toward the .45, hitting the ground hard, flat on her stomach, her hand stretched out, reaching for and then closing around the grip of the gun, she knew it had taken too long. She had the revolver, but it was already too late. She had heard the shots ring out almost before she'd hit the ground. One shot while she'd been going for the gun, her fingers tightening around it. The second as she lifted her eyes and her right hand, lifting both of them at exactly the same moment, trying to line up on Morales.

It took her brain a second to accept the message her eyes were sending. There was no target. The deputy was no longer silhouetted where she'd expected him to be, no longer outlined, his county uniform light against the darkness of the night sky. She raised her upper body by pushing onto her elbows, searching desperately for the target that should have been there and for some reason wasn't. All that time she was listening for the next shot.

But Morales wasn't there. Morales and the rifle weren't there. Her eyes tracked toward the movement that she had been aware of, at least peripherally aware of, through the endless seconds she'd been trying to get to the revolver and get off a shot.

Rio was still on his feet, but he was no longer running. Even as she watched, he almost stumbled to a halt and stood, swaying slightly, a long, slow heartbeat before his knees folded. He put his left hand down on the ground.

She didn't remember getting up, but she was running, the revolver still held, almost forgotten, in her hand; that headlong journey checked briefly when she found Ray Morales's body.

She hadn't fired Mac's gun, so she didn't understand why the deputy was down, but she hesitated beside him only long enough to realize that he wasn't moving. And he wasn't going to. Raymond Morales was dead. She hadn't shot him, but that wasn't important. Or important only in context of the other.

She ran down the slope to where Rio was on his knees, still held upright by his left hand, its knuckles resting on the ground. She was too numbed by fear to even voice the prayers she should be praying. Too afraid to think about what she might find when she got there.

She went down on her knees in the dirt beside him. In the background she could hear the Mexican woman crying, a soft keening noise that was beginning to fade as she waded through the shallow water. She would cross the river and melt into the darkness on the Mexican side.

"Rio?" Anne whispered, terrified he wouldn't be able to answer her. She couldn't see any blood. That was how she had known Morales had been shot, she realized only now. There had already been a dark pool forming under the deputy's body. Thank God there was nothing like that here.

Rio's head lifted, slowly, as if the movement was possible only through the greatest effort. She watched his dark eyes find her face.

"All right?" he asked. His voice was a whisper, but he raised his right hand and touched her cheek. His fingers were trembling.

Wordlessly, she nodded. She caught his hand and gently enclosed the long, dark fingers, bringing them to her lips. She held them, savoring the incredible and unexpected miracle that he was alive.

She looked up at the sound of voices, neither of which she had identified. That didn't seem important, either. Obviously, it was whoever had taken care of Morales. Friend, then, and not foe.

She recognized Chase McCullar's big form only a fraction of a second before he slid to a stop beside them. He didn't say anything. He simply stood, looking down at the two of them, on their knees together in the dust. She was still holding Rio's hand against her lips.

She had never cared who knew how she felt about Rio. She didn't care now, but she couldn't help but be aware of the shock in McCullar's eyes.

"Are you all right, Ms. Richardson?"

That was Sheriff Elkins, who had followed Chase down the slope, moving less precipitously. He was holding a rifle across his body, and Anne realized that he must have been the one who'd shot Morales. He and Chase had come up from behind, their careful approach hidden by darkness and by the deputy's concentration on answering Rio's questions, on explaining it all away, trying to justify what he had done.

She nodded, not trusting her voice. She remembered how angry Elkins's condescension had made her at the clinic that day. She'd be damned if she'd give him the satisfaction of knowing how terrified she was, now that it was all over.

"How about you, Mr. Delgado?" the sheriff asked.

"I just ran out of steam," Rio said, his voice still ragged. "I don't think he got off a shot."

"There were two shots," Anne said, reliving those nightmare seconds while she had believed those had been directed at Rio. "I heard two shots."

"Both were mine," Buck Elkins said. "You were right, then. He never had time to fire."

"Did you hear him?" Rio whispered. His eyes were on his brother's now. "About Doc?"

"Enough," Chase said. "Enough to know that he killed Doc and to know why."

"That stupid son of a bitch," Elkins said softly. "Sorry, ma'am," he added automatically.

Even now, he was considering who she was. Or rather, who her brother was. "It's all right," she assured him, so grateful for what he had done. He could say anything he wanted to in front of her. Especially about Raymond Morales. "And you're right. He was."

There was no reason for what had happened, for what Morales had done. That was the real tragedy. There had been no reason to kill the old man. The Mexican woman would have disappeared. She would never have brought charges against the company, and even if Doc had tried, he couldn't have proved anything. The records of the man's employment would surely have been destroyed. In all likelihood, nothing would ever have come of Doc's accusations. And instead...

"Let's get you back to Jenny's," Chase said.

Anne looked up again, thinking he was talking to her.

Instead he had stooped to help Rio stand by slipping a hand under his elbow.

Rio accepted Chase's support to get to his feet because he probably didn't have a choice, but he didn't head up the slope. Instead he turned and made his way slowly back to the body of the dog.

Anne didn't follow him. She didn't want to see Rom. She didn't want to be haunted by the memory of what had been done to the shepherd as she had been haunted by Doc's death.

She turned to Chase. "He doesn't need to see that," she said softly. "He needs to go home."

Chase nodded, but he held her eyes for a moment, searching them, before he moved to join his half brother.

Anne turned away, unwilling to think about the cold brutality of Rommel's death. He was just a dog, she told herself. He had died doing what he had been trained to do. She should be grateful they weren't *all* lying dead beside the river. They would have been, she knew, if it hadn't been for Rio's quick thinking. And for the arrival of Chase McCullar and the sheriff.

"He's not dead," Rio said softly. He was standing beside her again, and she hadn't been aware of his approach. He took her elbow and squeezed it gently. "Not yet, anyway."

Chase walked by, carrying the big shepherd in his arms as carefully as he would have carried his own daughter.

"Chase says there's a vet who's not too far away. His practice is mostly cows and horses, but we're going to take Rommel there. He's going to have Samantha call and tell him we're coming. The Kincaid connection will make sure he'll at least open up."

"Does Chase think—"

"Don't get your hopes up. It's just a chance."

She nodded, reading the warning in his eyes.

"Thank you for taking him."

Rio nodded. Then he turned and began to follow Chase

up the slope, moving far more slowly than his half brother. As he had while he'd talked to her, he was holding his arm pressed tightly across his midsection. She knew that the broken ribs must be agonizing.

She looked back toward the river, but there was no sign of the woman. She had been lost to the darkness that stretched beyond it. Anne shook her head, wishing she had been able to do something to help her. And to help the baby she had held that night in Doc's clinic.

Finally she, too, turned and began to follow Rio's slow, uncertain steps. She caught up with him, and as she had this morning, she slipped under his shoulder, and put her arm around his waist.

"If you don't need us anymore," she said, glancing up at the sheriff when they reached him, "we're going home."

Even Elkins realized the significance of that, it seemed. At least he didn't protest. He nodded slightly, moving out of their way. He walked over to the body of the man he'd shot and stood watching the others disappear over the slight rise to be swallowed up by the darkness. Only then did Buck Elkins look down at the body sprawled in the dirt at his feet.

"You poor, stupid son of a bitch," he said softly. This time there was no one to apologize to, no one left in the desert night to hear that profanity except Raymond Morales.

WHEN RIO OPENED HIS EYES, it was almost dawn. The faint, silvered gray of sunrise was just beginning to filter into the dark room. He didn't know what had awakened him. Maybe he'd been dreaming. There had been enough in the last few days to cause all sorts of nightmares. He closed his eyes again, thinking about what had happened last night.

Jenny had adamantly refused to let him go to the vet's with Chase, and by the time he'd made it back to the ranch, he'd had to admit she was right. He wasn't in any shape to go anywhere.

Surprisingly, Anne had chosen to stay at the ranch with him instead of going with the shepherd. He had seen the speculation in Jenny McCullar's eyes. She understood that something had happened between them. Hopefully, she didn't understand everything.

He took a breath, thinking how impossible the situation was. He understood why Anne Richardson had responded to him as she had. She had known instinctively that he would never hurt her. She had read him that well from the very beginning.

He knew that now, because of what had happened to her, that was really all she wanted. Just the assurance that she wouldn't be hurt again. But eventually she would want more, and he had nothing else to offer her.

He had always known that his compassion wouldn't be enough. There would be other men, far more suitable men.... He blocked those images, hating the thought of another man with Anne. But not every man was like the one who had raped her. Gradually she would learn to trust again. Only…it wouldn't be him who would be allowed to teach her. It couldn't be him.

A penniless ex-con, with no skills and no prospects. Few prospects, he amended. He could get a job, of course. Some rancher would hire him, even given his record. Maybe not around here, not where Mac McCullar was so well beloved, but somewhere.

He would make a few hundred dollars a month and live in a place like the line shack. That was his future. Nothing had changed about that. And it was better, he supposed, than his past had been. But it wasn't any kind of life for someone like Anne Richardson.

He took a deep breath, fighting the familiar bitterness. He had Diablo, he reminded himself. That was more than he'd started with. And a couple of friendships. Those had been unexpected. Maybe even worth the trip back here. Worth the pain of leaving again.

"Rio?" Anne said softly. "Are you awake?"

Her voice was very near. He opened his eyes and turned his head. She was on the narrow bed beside him. She was lying on top of the sheet that covered the lower half of his body. She was on her side, propped on one elbow, her upper body slightly raised above his, looking down on him.

She was so damn beautiful. Her hair was loose, curling softly as it fell against her shoulder, its fairness silvered with the thin light of dawn. But her eyes were dark, still shadowed with the night, and fastened on his face.

She was in the same bed with him, something he had only dreamed about, and that realization caught him off guard. Without thinking, simply reacting to the pleasure of that, he smiled at her.

There must have been provocation in it. Or maybe invitation. As she had in the barn, Anne leaned toward him, her mouth slightly open. When her lips touched his, he was not physically capable of denying her. His tongue slipped into her mouth. Familiar. Belonging. He had known for a couple of days now that she was his. If he wanted her. She had made her feelings about him clear, and he would always cherish that.

So this kiss was different from the other they had shared. Deeper and infinitely more satisfying, but more tantalizing, too, because it promised things they both wanted. Both needed. But could never have.

Except here. Now. Thinking that, he deepened the contact, consciously allowing his mouth to plunder the sweet softness of hers, savoring her immediate response. No one could ever take this away from him. When it was over, at least he would have this.

But creating this kind of memory would only make it harder. On him, certainly, but more importantly, harder on her. He moved his head back slightly, but her lips clung to his for an instant, the dampness of the kiss holding the skin together a heartbeat longer than he intended.

He watched her eyes open, the dark lashes drifting upward to reveal what was in them. Exactly what he had known would be there.

Almost against his will, trying to memorize each detail, his eyes traced over the perfection of her face. Her cheeks were slightly flushed now with emotion. Her lips were still open, and the moisture his tongue had left touched the bottom one with a shimmer of light. His eyes moved lower, to the soft cream of her throat and then downward to the shadowed recess between her breasts.

She was wearing a nightgown, pale blue with a wide band of white lace around the low, square neckline. He could see the outline of her breasts moving against the thin material as she breathed. His body hardened, tightening impossibly with the expansion of blood that rushed so hotly, painfully, into his groin.

What was happening between them now was nothing like what had occurred in the dark barn. That had been something entirely different. A different part of his feelings for her, the protective part, which was more important than this, perhaps, for someone like Anne.

This was undeniably the other. Feelings that were inherent in any normal relationship. Sexual feelings. A natural aspect of any man-woman relationship. And he had always been very normal in that regard.

His lips moved, remembering what Chase had said, mocking his reputation. His *gift*. Maybe some of that was even true. He'd never had any complaints. And making love to Anne would be something he would give half of his life to be able to do. Just once, to be allowed to show her what making love should be. *"Thank you for making that what it should always be,"* she had said to him in the barn. What it should *always* be…

"What are you doing here?" he asked, forcing his gaze away from the small, regular lift and fall of her breasts and back to her face. Her eyes were almost black, the pupils widely distended in the dimness, but there was enough light to watch her slow smile.

"I needed to sleep. I couldn't do that in my room. And I suppose I just…wanted to be with you."

"You slept here all night?"

She nodded. "I felt safe here. Protected."

His lips tightened against the emotion that invoked, and he felt the familiar pain of moving his damaged mouth. At least that gave him something else to feel, something else to think about besides what she had said. A welcome distraction from those whispered words that only echoed his own. *I will keep you safe, my dearest heart.* As always, it seemed she had known everything he thought.

"What about Rom?" he asked. He needed time to remind himself of all the very valid reasons why this couldn't be allowed to go any further. Time for the hard, aching desire to fade. The physical one. The other, he would never lose. Not until he died, still loving her.

"I don't know," she said. "I don't think Chase came back. I didn't hear him if he did."

"He probably went home to check on his family."

She nodded again.

"You'd better go," he suggested softly. "Before Jenny gets up."

"I told you," she said, smiling at him. "I don't *care* if Jenny knows."

He hesitated, trying to find a way to allow this to happen. A way to make it right. A way to justify what he wanted.

Which made him no better than Ray Morales, he realized. Trying to make something so monumentally wrong make sense because he wanted it to.

"And I told you that you weren't the only one involved in that decision," he reminded her.

He could see the quick shock fill her eyes, and then he was forced to watch that give way to hurt, more pain growing in the blue depths. Her mouth flattened with the pressure she exerted, but she didn't cry. Despite all that had happened to her, he had never seen her cry except when he'd kissed her the first time.

"Why?" she asked softly. "Why not?"

"Your brother can probably give you a thousand reasons."

"I don't care about my brother's reasons. It's *my* life, Rio."

"And mine," he said inexorably, knowing that he was destroying what she felt about him. Deliberately destroying.

She waited for a long time before she spoke again. She had held his eyes, trying to read them, maybe, but he'd had a lot of practice at hiding what he was feeling.

"You don't understand..." she began, and the words faded at the sudden coldness that was allowed to invade the black eyes.

"Somebody hurt you. You know I won't. That's all this is, Anne. All it's ever been."

"No," she denied.

"You just want some kind of guarantee that no one will hurt you again. Only, there are a hundred men who will gladly give you that. A thousand. Any one of them will be better for you than me."

"Is that what this is? Some kind of misplaced nobility?" she asked. "Because if it is, I have to tell you—"

"Reality," he said, interrupting. That was the only thing he *needed* to know, needed to recognize. The reality of their situation. If he let this go any further, there would be plenty of people who would be more than happy to point out to her all the reasons it couldn't work. And worse than that, what he couldn't face, was that one day he would see disappointment in her eyes, and the slow, painful admission that they all had been right.

He couldn't be the kind of man she needed. He had nothing to offer her but his love. His "gift." And he was realist enough to know that that was never enough. Life had made him a realist, and he might as well face up to what he knew before he hurt her anymore.

"You don't want..." she began.

"I'm not the man you need," he said, his voice almost harsh. "I can't *be* that man."

She held his eyes, and this time he let her see what was there. Surety. And denial. There was nothing else in the coal black depths because Rio Delgado was also very good at control. After all, he had learned that lesson early, and he had learned it well.

Finally Anne nodded. He turned his eyes toward the ceiling, and he listened to her leave. He didn't watch. The image of Anne leaving his bed was not a memory he wanted.

WHEN JENNY CAME TO CALL her for breakfast, Anne was packing. She was methodically folding one garment after another and laying them with careful precision in the suitcase she'd brought with her from San Antonio. Her hands moved quickly and competently.

"I didn't know you were leaving," Jenny said.

Anne didn't look up. Instead she chose a blouse from the pile on the bed and folded it neatly and put it on top of the others in the suitcase. It was only with the appearance of a small dark spot on the navy cotton that Jenny realized why she hadn't looked up. Anne Richardson was crying. As Jenny watched, another tear rolled to the edge of her chin and dropped silently onto the clothes in the bag.

"What's wrong?" Jenny asked. This couldn't be about Rommel. Chase had talked to her when he'd called this morning, and the news from the vet was as good as they could hope for. The shepherd was still holding on, still clinging to that slim thread of life that was all Ray Morales's bullet had left him.

Anne shook her head—a quick, determined movement, obviously denying—and folded another garment, a pair of cotton shorts this time.

"Rio's all right," Jenny reassured. "He's tough. He was exhausted last night, to the point of collapse and beyond, but I don't think..." She hesitated, watching a teardrop spot the shorts.

When Anne had placed them on top of the neat stack in the suitcase, she raised her hand and wiped her nose. She took a small shuddering breath, but she picked up another item from the pile on the bed and began to fold it also.

"Stop it," Jenny said. "Either cry or pack, but don't do both. I need to know what's wrong. What happened?"

"I called Trent. He'll be here before lunch to pick me up."

"And you told him about Rio," Jenny guessed. Poor Trent, she thought again. Obviously he'd said all the wrong things.

Anne turned at that, meeting Jenny's dark eyes, the gentle concern in them. "Told him *what* about Rio?" she asked very distinctly. "What do you think I told Trent about Rio?"

Jenny couldn't read the exact tone of that question, but it wasn't what she'd expected. Not anger at her brother. Not defense of the man she was in love with.

"How you feel about him?" Jenny suggested carefully. "How he feels about you."

"And how is that?" Anne's hands found another garment on the bed and picked it up.

"I thought..." Jenny paused again, trying to find the right words.

"Yeah. Me, too," Anne said, turning back to put the knit top in the suitcase. "Obviously we were both wrong."

"What did he say?"

She couldn't have been mistaken, Jenny thought. She had seen that look too many times, the one that had been in Rio's eyes every time he looked at Anne Richardson. It was the same way Mac had once looked at her—a long time ago. Like Chase looked at Samantha now. She *couldn't* be that wrong about what she had seen.

"Not much," Anne said softly. "But he didn't have to. Some men can't deal with it. I understand that. I certainly don't blame him."

"Deal with what?" Jenny asked. Trent's office? The difference in their social positions? The ethnic differences? Economics? She didn't believe either one of them was foolish enough to care about any of those things.

"It doesn't matter," Anne said. She folded the last of the clothing and closed the lid, snapping the locks into place. "I appreciate your hospitality, Jenny. I really hope Trent can talk you into marrying him. It will be nice to have you in San Antonio. Especially nice to have you as my sister." As she talked, the short sentences almost staccato, she picked up the suitcase and put it down decisively next to the door. "I'm going to take a shower now. My hair feels like it's got half the desert still in it."

Anne smiled at her, despite the tearstains on her pale cheeks, but that had clearly been dismissal. A No Trespassing sign had been put up, and Jenny McCullar had never intruded on someone else's grief. She understood all the tormenting nuances of the emotion too well to ever do that.

So she nodded, and she closed the door behind her when she went out. It was always better, she knew, to be allowed to do your grieving in private.

As Jenny watched Trent load Anne's suitcases into the trunk that afternoon, she tried to think if there was anything she could say to change what was happening.

"I left a signed check on the kitchen table," Anne said as she came out of the house. "It's for the vet bill. If you'll keep Rom here for a while when they release him... If he makes it..." Anne's voice faltered, but then she took a quick, determined breath and went on. "Just let him stay with you until we can come back and pick him up. He loves it out here, and we'll be so tied up with the trial. Would you mind keeping him for me, Jenny? Just for a little while?''

"Of course, I don't mind. I'll be glad to look after Rom. And glad of the company. I'm going to miss you."

"Thanks," Anne said softly. "Thanks for everything."

Finally she gave in and put her cheek against Jenny's warm one. Jenny caught her hands and held them.

"Call me if you need to," she said. "Let me know how things are going." It was an opportunity, if Anne wanted it, to make the same request: *Let me know how things are going.*

But Anne didn't respond to that offer, simply nodding and then walking down the steps to climb into the passenger seat of her brother's car. Trent's eyes met Jenny's over the top of the car, but she had no answer for the question that was in them.

Finally Trent smiled at her and got behind the wheel. The car pulled out of the yard, leaving the ubiquitous dust trail behind. Jenny watched until it disappeared down the dirt road. When she finally turned around, Rio was standing on the porch, leaning against the low railing.

"Did you do something stupid?" she asked. She had never seen his eyes this dark, glittering like jet in the sculptured bronze of his face.

His gaze remained fixed in the direction the car had taken for a moment longer before he looked down at her. "I guess that depends on whose definition you use," he said.

"Let's use mine," Jenny said. "It's pretty simple, despite how long it took me to figure it out."

"I don't need a lecture, Mrs. McCullar," he said quietly.

"It's not a lecture," she said. "Maybe a lesson. And it's really very short. There aren't that many people in this world who will ever really love you. Your mother and father…" she began. When she remembered Rio's father, she was sorry for the unthinking cruelty of that. But there had been no change in the cold, black emptiness of his eyes. No reaction. "Your brothers," she continued, remembering

Mac's love and concern for this brother he had never really known. "And then occasionally," she said softly, again remembering, "occasionally, if you're very lucky, you may find someone who…"

Her throat closed, blocking the words. For years she had tried *not* to remember Mac, tried not to ever think about him, about the way he moved or the way he laughed or the way his big hands touched her in the darkness. But sometimes that was impossible. Sometimes the memories of what they had shared, those few short years they had had together, overwhelmed her.

She felt her eyes brim with sudden tears, and she blinked them away, angry with herself. She was done with crying. It was time to get on with whatever came next. Another good man loved her. It was time to consider applying the lesson she had been about to share with Rio to her own life.

When she had cleared the unexpected blur of moisture from her eyes, the porch was empty. Rio had already disappeared back inside, letting the screen door slam behind him.

Chapter Fourteen

Rio watched the shepherd carefully climb the steps of the back porch. When he reached the top, the big dog stood trembling for a moment before he looked up, pain and uncertainty at his body's betrayal in the dark eyes.

"I know just how you feel, amigo," Rio said softly. It had been over a month since the beating the good citizens of this county had seen fit to inflict, and he was just beginning to be able to get out of bed in the morning without having to dread those first movements. There were even long stretches of the day now when nothing hurt at all. Then he would turn too suddenly or bend the wrong way and be reminded all over again.

He meant what he'd said to the dog. He remembered exactly how those first couple of weeks had felt. He had been so damn frustrated by the pain and traitorous weakness of his own body. Now he could see that same frustration in Rommel's eyes.

He hadn't expected the big shepherd to make it. He didn't think the vet had, either, despite his optimistic reassurances. Rio had visited the dog almost every morning, driving the thirty miles there and back in Jenny's truck. He would sit on the floor beside the shepherd and talk to him. Talking nonsense, he supposed, although the intelligent eyes never left his face as he whispered. And Rommel was the only one to whom Rio had ever tried to justify what he had done.

He had been aware after Anne left of the question in Jenny's eyes, and he'd even caught Chase looking at him too intently on a couple of occasions when her name had come up, but no one had asked what had gone wrong between them. And, of course, Rio hadn't volunteered any information.

After his visits to the vet's, he had spent the rest of his days methodically doing the jobs around the ranch that had been neglected during the last five years. The signs of that neglect, the unmistakable evidence that there had been no man around to take care of the things that needed a masculine hand, were plain. To him, at least. He had lived around ranches all his life, and he knew very well what needed to be done here.

He had cleaned and painted and repaired. At first he'd worked only a few hours a day because that was all he could hold out for. But gradually he'd gotten his strength back and things had gone faster, maybe faster than he'd wanted them to.

The last project he'd undertaken was to reroof the barn, learning as he went, with only the patient instructions of the man at the lumber supply store where he'd bought the roofing materials. Jenny had paid for the materials, of course. She had tried to pay him for the labor, but he hadn't even listened to that offer. Or to any of the other things she'd tried to pay him for.

He wasn't doing any of this for money. She was already providing him with room and board. A home. That was something he needed right now far more than he needed Jenny McCullar's money.

He knew that eventually he'd run out of things to do around the ranch, and then it would be time to move on. He was certainly physically capable of doing that now, despite the occasional twinge, but for some reason he didn't yet seem emotionally able to leave.

McCullar land, he thought, raising his eyes from Rom to look out over the grayish brown landscape. No one else would understand how he felt about this barren expanse. Maybe Chase, he amended. But they had never talked about it, of course. This wasn't his land or his ranch, and it never would be. But he would leave it better than he'd found it.

"Well, look at you," Jenny said softly.

Rio turned and found her bending down to speak to Rom. This was the first time the shepherd had ventured so far from the bed Rio had made for him in the barn when he'd brought him home. Rommel had been tottering around the yard for a couple of days now, trying not to let Rio out of his sight, but the shepherd hadn't tried to follow him up on the porch until today.

"Would you like to come inside?" Jenny invited. Rommel and not him, Rio realized with amusement. "You, too," she said, raising her eyes to include him in the invitation, as if she'd read his mind. "I've made lemonade, and Samantha brought over half a pound cake this morning. It's her first, and it's got a sad streak a mile wide, but I have to confess that's always been my favorite part. Want a slice with your lemonade?"

It would probably be a long time before he got another offer as good as that one. "I'd like that," he said, "if you don't mind a little dirt in your kitchen sink. Or I can wash up out back."

"You can wash inside. The day my kitchen gets too fine for a man to wash his hands in…" For some reason she hesitated, maybe thinking about all the times it had been Mac's hands that had been scrubbed clean at her sink. "It's nice to have a man around again. I don't think I've told you that often enough," she said. Even her eyes were smiling.

She had never told him that. He had known he was welcome. Jenny had made him feel welcome here almost from the beginning, but still it was nice to hear her say the words.

He followed her inside, holding the door open for the shepherd's slow entrance. Jenny had already poured the lemonade and was unwrapping the cake to cut when the phone rang.

Rio had begun to lather his hands at the sink, so Jenny laid down the knife she was using to answer it. He was not even conscious of listening to the conversation. Listening with half an ear only, thinking about how much he was going to miss all this. The weeks he'd spent at the McCullar ranch were as close to having a home, as near to belonging somewhere, as he'd been in almost twenty years.

He cut his own slice of cake while Jenny listened to whoever was on the other end of the call. He put the cake on a paper towel instead of dirtying a plate she'd have to wash. He carried it and his glass to the table and sat drinking his lemonade and breaking off pieces of the cake with his fingers. Jenny had been right about the width of the sad streak.

When she hung up, she turned around and looked at him. He lifted his eyes and knew immediately from her expression that something was wrong.

"They lost the case," Jenny said. "*Damn* it. Damn them all. Damn *him*."

Rio's hand had hesitated, halfway to his mouth, and then he put the piece of cake back down on the napkin. "What case?" he asked carefully. There was no one to be tried for Doc's murder, so he didn't have any idea what Jenny was talking about.

Her eyes came up, dark and wide, filled with anger. "The rape," she said.

He shook his head, but he was beginning to put it together. Anne's rape? "Anne?" he asked, fighting down the coiling sickness the thought of her being raped always stirred in his gut. "Are you talking about Anne?"

"They knew going in the chances weren't good. Acquaintance rape, his apartment, his family's position. That rich bastard was almost certain to get away with it. Trent tried to talk Anne out of it."

"But she didn't listen?"

"She said she couldn't let him get away with it. Even if she lost, maybe someone else would be warned. Some other woman would know what she hadn't known about him."

"She told me she didn't even like to talk about it. I never thought…" He shook his head again, remembering the pain in Anne's eyes the day she had been forced to tell him what had happened to her. "She said people always changed when they knew. Even the way they looked at her changed."

Suddenly it all made sense to Jenny. *"Some men can't deal with it,"* Anne had said the day she'd left. Jenny hadn't known what she was talking about, had never put those words together with the rape, because the idea was so foreign to how the men she had known would have reacted.

Mac might have killed someone for touching her, but the fact that it had happened would never have made any difference in the way he felt about her.

"Is that what you did?" Jenny asked. The question was very low, but accusation was there, clear in the soft voice.

"What *I* did?"

"Some men can't deal with it. Anne said that the day she left. I didn't have any idea what she meant. I thought you were letting other things stand in your way."

"Things?"

"Money. Position. *Things,*" Jenny finished, her disdain for those also clear in the mocking emphasis she put on the word.

"A couple of those *things* should be considerations," Rio said, his tone as mocking.

"No," Jenny denied. "You're smarter than that. You

have to know that those never really matter. She didn't care what you'd been accused of. Or that you'd been in prison. That you didn't have two cents.''

"She should have.''

"You don't really believe that. And I can't believe that you'd let *her* believe the other. I can't believe you're that kind of man.''

"What the hell are you—'' he began to question, but Jenny didn't stop.

"She thought you didn't want her because she'd been raped. That's why she was crying that morning. That's what she meant,'' Jenny spoke her realizations aloud. "I just hope to God she wasn't right,'' she added softly.

The black eyes were suddenly glittering with rage. "You know better than that,'' he said. "You *have* to know me better than that.''

"Does Anne?'' Jenny asked. "I guess that's the important question. Are you absolutely certain that Anne knows better than that?''

"SOMEONE'S HERE TO SEE you,'' Peg Harris said. She was standing in the hall, leaning slightly into the doorway of Anne's office at the mission museum.

Anne looked up in surprise and then glanced at her watch. "It's too early for the group from Miss Claire's school,'' she said. "If they're here already, they'll just have to wait a couple of minutes until I finish up.''

"This is definitely not anybody from Miss Claire's,'' Peg said. "But if those girls arrive while *he's* standing around out there, then the school's liable to become Miss Claire's School for Wayward Girls, and we'll probably all get sued. I have to confess I'm feeling a little wayward myself.''

Peg Harris, one of the museum's docents, was in her late sixties. She was still slim, always elegant and usually very southern-lady reserved.

"What in the world?" Anne asked, laughing. "Who's out there?"

"He said his name's Rio. We didn't get much past that. I have to confess I got a little tongue-tied just looking at him."

"Rio," Anne repeated softly.

Apparently there was enough revealed in Anne's soft repetition of the name to make one of Peg's carefully shaped brows arch and the shrewd brown eyes stretch a little. "Definitely larger than life," she agreed. She tilted her head toward the reception area. "You want me to send him back here?"

Wordlessly, Anne nodded. It didn't seem she had much of an alternative. And besides, despite what she knew and had even accepted about Rio's feelings, she couldn't deny that she wanted to see him.

Trent had been right. Apparently she *was* a glutton for punishment. Her brother had been talking about the trial, about pursuing a date-rape case they both knew they would probably lose, but the phrase applied here just as well. But she didn't think she could have refused to see Rio Delgado any more than she could have not pressed charges against the son of a bitch who had raped her.

However, when she remembered the painful outcome of that almost-quixotic crusade, she decided she didn't have to be that big a glutton. She stood, hurrying around her desk toward the door in hopes of catching Peg to tell her she'd changed her mind. When she looked up, Rio was standing in the doorway.

He was wearing jeans that had been washed so often the thin material was shaped to the strong muscles of his legs. A denim work shirt was neatly tucked into their waistband. He had polished his boots, but they were the same ones he'd been wearing since she'd met him, old and scuffed with years of hard wear. His blue-black hair was longer than the close-cropped prison cut he'd worn then, and for the first time, its slight curl was obvious. And his face...

She took an involuntary breath. She had almost forgotten what he had looked like before Chase McCullar and then a bunch of cowards of the county had tried rearranging his features.

This was exactly the way he'd looked that first night, the night they'd gone to Doc's. Maybe the aquiline nose was a little crooked, but everything else was the same. Beautiful, she thought again, but incredibly and intensely masculine. And still just as compelling as he had always been to her.

"Rio," she said. Greeting. Acknowledgment.

He didn't say anything for a moment, his eyes intent on her face. They had focused on her mouth when she said his name, and she watched as they moved slowly upward to meet hers.

"Jenny said you believed it made a difference to me. That you'd been raped. That it made a difference in the way I feel about you."

She thought that had been the heart of what they had talked about that morning, the quiet dawn conversation they'd had in his bed the day she'd left the McCullar ranch. Only...why would he come all the way to San Antonio now to tell her what Jenny thought?

"Is that true?" he asked softly, still watching her.

She didn't want him to think she didn't understand. She did. She had always understood when people found it difficult to get past what had happened. She found it difficult herself to accept that she had been that stupid. That she'd let something like that happen to her. And she knew that most men had a hard time dealing with the aftereffects of someone they loved having been raped.

That was the other thing she had come to realize during the month they'd been apart. Rio *had* cared about her. She hadn't been mistaken about that. Somehow, however, that realization hadn't made what he'd said that morning any easier to bear. *"I'm not the man you need. I can't be that man."*

"It's not that I don't understand," she said. "I do. I've always understood."

"Understood what?" he asked. His voice was still low, as intimate as it had been in the barn. The first time he'd kissed her. Or rather, the first of the two times she had kissed him.

"I know how hard it is to get past...all that. How hard it is to forget it ever happened. Believe me, it's hard for me to forget."

She saw the depth of the breath he took. His chest expanded, stretching against the worn cotton of his shirt.

"Is that what you think about me?" he asked.

"I don't blame you. I don't want you to think that I blame you for...how you feel. No one can help the way they feel."

He waited for a moment, his eyes still studying hers.

"What will it take for you to leave?"

"To leave?" she repeated.

"You have to get permission? Tell somebody?"

"That I'm leaving the museum?"

He nodded.

"Why am I leaving?" she asked. Her heart had begun to pound in her chest, so strongly it crowded her lungs. Making it too hard to breathe.

His eyes moved past her, and then came back to her face. Somehow they had changed. The black was soft. And heated. They were luminous with intent and even touched with amusement when he answered her.

"Because it's going to be damned uncomfortable making love to you on that desk. I mean, I don't mind if you don't, but I just think we might shock sweet little Ms. Harris out there with the sound effects."

One corner of his mouth moved, tilting upward. She had

never noticed how sensuous his mouth was. Not even when she had kissed him. She noticed it now.

"I don't think so," she said.

His dark head cocked, questioning.

"I don't think she'd be very shocked at all," she clarified.

THEY DIDN'T USE THE DESK, of course. She took him home to the house she shared with her brother. Trent was in Austin, playing catch-up for the time he'd missed with the trial.

"Would you like something to drink?" she had asked when they arrived. They were standing in the den, and the awkwardness that he had made disappear at the museum was back.

Rio's eyes finished their contemplation of the room before he turned to answer her. "No, thanks. I'm fine."

She nodded and took off the jacket of her ivory suit. She threw it over the back of the couch. When she looked up, she realized he'd been watching her.

"This is a nice house," he said.

"Thank you."

"Did you decorate it?"

She shook her head, a little embarrassed to admit to him that she hadn't, that their home had been professionally done.

"Trent thought…" She hesitated, knowing it didn't matter what Trent thought. And that Rio didn't really care who had decorated the place. They were simply making conversation, strained and awkward as it was.

"Nothing's going to happen that you won't want to happen, Anne," he said into the silence. "I promise you that."

Her smile was involuntary. "I know. I've always known that."

"You're not afraid of me."

That was statement and not question, but she shook her head anyway. "I'm not afraid of you," she agreed.

"You'll probably be relieved to know that I'm supposed to be pretty good at this." The amusement that had been in his voice when he'd suggested the desk was back, and her tension loosened minutely.

The comment had been self-mocking rather than boastful, and for some reason it *was* reassuring. She was glad Rio was so confident everything would be all right. She needed him to be confident, given the scope of her own uncertainties.

"That's good to know," she said softly. He was smiling at her, a smile that was slightly one-sided and more seductive than she would have believed a smile could be.

"I'm going to make love to you. You know that and I know it. We might as well get beyond whatever discomfort thinking about that generates."

She nodded because her mouth was suddenly too dry to speak.

"Your brother's not coming back today?" he asked.

"No," she whispered.

"Or tonight?"

Wordlessly, she shook her head.

SHE TOOK A SHOWER. A delaying tactic, she supposed, but she had to admit there had been something infinitely relaxing about the familiar ritual. She had moved the soap slowly over her body, anticipating his hands moving across the same places hers were touching.

It would be no different than this, she told herself. Her body belonged to him. Intellectually, she knew that. She wanted him to make love to her, had wanted it for a long time, and so she didn't understand the sense of dread that thinking about it created in the pit of her stomach.

This was Rio. She concentrated on that, and on remembering his hands. How they felt, his thumb caressing slowly up and down her spine or wiping a teardrop from her cheek. She remembered how they had looked, cupping the protrusion that was the last baby Doc Horn ever delivered. Or caressing Rommel, clearly conveying Rio's love to the animal.

There was nothing to dread about what was about to happen. She turned her body under the spray of the shower, letting the heat of the water cascade over the tightness in her back and shoulders. Nothing to dread. Nothing to worry about. This was Rio. And he would take care of her. He would keep her safe.

Finally, after a long time, she turned off the water. She dried her body as carefully as she had bathed it. Occasionally her eyes would lift to the woman revealed in the fogged mirror. The figure there was familiar and yet somehow, today, a stranger.

When she opened the bathroom door, the bedroom had been darkened to an artificial twilight. Rio had pulled the draperies across the windows and the dimness was pleasant. It was less frightening to her than the revealing glare of the afternoon sun might have been, and she was grateful that he understood that.

It took a moment for her eyes to find him. He was already in her bed, his broad shoulders propped against the pillows he had stacked against the headboard. The sheet was across his lower body, hiding it. His chest was dark, the skin smooth and deeply bronzed with the sun and with his heritage, its color a stark contrast to the delicate, feminine paleness of her sheets.

"I saved room for you," he said. Again his smile was invitation, but there was no amusement now in his eyes, despite the fact that she had put on the white terry robe that usually hung behind the bathroom door and had even belted it, tying the sash into a knot. She had not been conscious of the significance of that until after it was done. But then she hadn't undone it.

She swallowed, gathering her courage because she had never been a coward, not about anything but this, and she took the first steps toward him, feeling the familiar softness of the carpet under her bare feet. It was better that they were here, surrounded by her things. Home. Safe at home.

When she finally reached the bed, she had no idea what she wanted to do next. Rio took her hand and held it loosely in his strong brown fingers. His eyes were on her face, and in them she saw what she had seen there from the beginning. Something to hold on to. Something she could always trust.

"Would you like to come to bed with me, my heart?" he asked.

Yes, her own heart answered. Her mind had long ago accepted that desire, and so it echoed now its own affirmation. And then finally her body agreed, still trembling, but feeling the force of need push through to fight the months-long anxiety.

She held his eyes, allowing the tension to drift out of her consciousness and the slow heat she found in their blackness to flood in. She pulled her fingers from his and began to work at the knot she had tied in the belt of the robe. Her hands were shaking so much that it took too long, and finally *his* fingers completed the task. That was kindness. And they were unhurried in their movements. Supremely confident.

His hand brushed past the edge of the open robe, slipping inside. His thumbnail skimmed across the bare skin of her stomach, and although she had been aware of what he was doing, had been expecting him to touch her, she flinched.

"Easy, my dear heart," he said softly. The caress that had been in the slow movement of his thumb across her belly was in his voice now. The words were Spanish and she didn't even think about the translation. She knew what he was saying; knew it in her heart, where it mattered.

He sat up, pulling his shoulders away from their calm relaxation against the stacked pillows. He touched the sides of the opening of the robe, one lapel caught in each hand.

He smiled at her before he pushed the fabric apart, knuckles deliberately trailing across her shivering skin. His hands increased the width of the gap between the parted edges of the robe, finally revealing her naked body. She heard the depth of the breath he took. And that, too, was reassurance.

His hands moved upward to her shoulders, and he pushed the robe off, allowing it to drop over her arms and down to the floor where it pooled around her feet. She was standing before him, totally nude. His dark eyes held hers, giving her time to adjust, to respond, if she wished, to what he had done.

Then his gaze traveled down the length of her body and back up, taking an eternity for the journey. When he met her eyes again, she answered his slow smile with her own—tremulous, perhaps, but still a smile. He held out his hand, palm upward. Without any hesitation now, holding on to what was in the black eyes, she placed her hand over his.

He lifted the sheet with his other hand. Inviting her again. "Come with me, my heart," he said, "and I will show you my soul. And yours." The soft Spanish was seductive, promising, and the words were unimportant. It was the tone that mattered. That was the magic Rio had always possessed. His gift.

She put her knee on the edge of the bed and his arms reached upward to enfold her. And keep her safe.

NIGHT WAS FALLING, and the twilight in the bedroom was no longer artificial. But the long, dark nightmare that had held her victim was over at last. Never again would it have the power to steal what belonged to her—this, which was her right. Every woman's right.

Rio had given that back to her. The ability, the freedom, to lose any consciousness of self. To trust enough to let him control. To let him possess her. And to know as he did that she had lost nothing. And had regained her birthright.

There was an old song. She remembered the lyrics only vaguely. Something about slow hands. Her lips moved, almost smiling, except it was too hard to move. Too much trouble. She was *exhausted.* Wrong word, she decided. Not exhausted. *Sated. Fulfilled. Languid.* She tried them out one by one before she decided none was exact enough. Or expressive enough.

The first time Rio had made love to her, she had not been able to stop shivering. Not for a long time after she had slipped under the sheet he had raised invitingly. He hadn't hurried her. She remembered him telling her at some point that there was all the time in the world. They had all of time to make it right.

His hands had touched her first, feathering lightly over her skin as he held her eyes. He had smiled at her as his fingers began to explore. Drifting aimlessly at first. Seemingly without intent. Certainly without demand.

Gradually, she had relaxed into that gentle drift. Minutely, without her being really aware of it, at some point the pressure of them against her skin had increased. Tracing the blue-marked pathway of a vein. Sliding to circle around a delicate wrist bone. Dipping into the small, damp hollow at the base of her throat. Following the shaped cartilage of her ear, as his breath fluttered nearby, almost inside.

There was no demand. Still no demand. No echo of the threat that had haunted her heart. Only pleasure and its sensations. For a long time he did not touch her with any real intimacy, and when finally he did, his thumb brushing lightly across her nipple, it created no uneasiness.

She had already been drugged into relaxation by the slow glide of his fingers, a willing partner now. A co-conspirator to his sensual examination of her body. And to his enjoyment of what he was doing. That had also been made obvious to her. Even without her participation, even with her shivering fear, he enjoyed touching her. Just touching her.

Finally, after hours it seemed, his hands had grown

bolder, and by that time, she had ached for them. The pressure inside her body, deep and low, had expanded until she wanted release from its tension now. The other tensions had been forgotten, or had been lost in the slow, seductive movement of his hands.

When his mouth and tongue finally joined the caress of his fingers, the intense, wet heat of their stroking had been almost more than she thought she could bear.

The whispered word had escaped before she had been aware it was formed. "Yes," she said softly. Permission or entreaty. She didn't know, and he didn't care.

His response was made only to the need her mind had expressed and to her body. Her mouth formed no more words, gasping instead, breath slowly hissing inward, with the sheer pleasure of what he was doing. After a long time, his mouth fit over hers again. She could taste the moisture of her body on his tongue, and her awareness of that held no trace of embarrassment.

There was only one more wall, one more barrier to be overcome. When she acknowledged that they were finally, after an eternity, at that point, she felt the small tightness begin to creep into her muscles, the memories edging toward her consciousness.

"No, my heart," he said softly, his mouth against her cheek, his breath warm and moist against her skin. "No," he whispered again.

His entrance was silken. Her body had been so ready for him, made ready by his endless patience, that there was no hesitation, no tension. He was there, already moving inside her, before she had even had time to be afraid.

And now there was nothing to fear. There was only the strong, sure power of his body moving above hers in the growing darkness. Moving for a long time. All the time in the world.

"Open your eyes," he commanded finally.

And when she did, she felt almost immediately the

heated jet of his seed bursting into her warmth. His eyes closed, clenched tight, and the muscles of his hard stomach jerked uncontrollably against the yielding softness of hers.

There was nothing to fear in this. Nothing but wonder beginning to tremble though her frame. It began deep within, responding automatically to his loss of control after the endless hours of deliberate control. There was nothing to fight against. Nothing to resist. No need any longer of his protection. And the small earthquake of sensation swelled upward, forever burying the past in its molten heat.

SHE TURNED TO SEE his face, shadowed by the twilight. He was watching her, and so she smiled at him. A slow, intimate smile, comfortable with the fact that they were in bed together. Had been in bed together for most of the afternoon and well into the night.

"We didn't…" She hesitated, wondering why she was bringing this up. It was far, far too late to worry about what they hadn't done.

"Yes, we did," he corrected her softly, and then his smile broadened into a grin. "I believe we did everything. Several times."

She laughed. That was something else she had learned today. Something else she had reclaimed. The ability to laugh. To laugh while making love. Rio had also given her that rare and precious gift because he understood its importance.

"We didn't what, my heart?" he whispered. His hand found hers and his thumb caressed across the back. "What did I fail to do for you?"

"It doesn't matter," she said. She put her lips against the dark, lean cheek. She could feel the stubble of his whiskers as she had felt them that day in the barn. As she had felt them today, moving across her body, over her stomach, and the electrifying sensation of their erotic roughness against the soft, silken skin of her thighs.

"It matters to me," he said. He turned his head and put his lips against her forehead. "Every thought of yours matters to me."

"We didn't use anything," she said. The words were wrong, too stark after the poetry he had breathed against her body all afternoon.

"Birth control?" he asked.

She nodded, forehead moving against his mouth.

"I'm a very good Catholic, *querida*," he said. His voice was amused, but she didn't know if that was because what he had said was true or because what he had said was such a blatant lie. She couldn't read the tone he'd used well enough to guess.

"Are you really?" she whispered.

"I like children."

She smiled, remembering the baby she had held. The baby who had looked like Rio. As his babies would. Unexpectedly, her eyes filled, the moisture hot and stinging.

He leaned away from her to see her face, seeming again to sense her every mood. "Don't you like children, my heart?"

She nodded again, fighting the tears.

"But you'll have to marry me. None of my sons will ever be called bastard."

The tears brimmed and escaped.

"I realize that's asking a great deal. After all," he said, smiling at her, "I don't have a job. I don't even have a home to take you to. I don't have two cents," he said, using Jenny's words. Remembering all of Jenny McCullar's hard earned lessons that she had so generously shared with him.

"That doesn't matter," Anne said.

"I know," he agreed softly. "Just *things.*" The mocking emphasis he gave the word was also learned.

"I love you," she whispered. She had wanted to say that to him for an eternity.

"And I love you. And soon you will marry me and then we will have babies."

"Yes," she said, smiling through her tears, her heart lifting with the incredible promise of that. It sounded so ordinary. So...normal. And she truly knew as well as he did that none of the rest of it would ever matter. "I will marry you," she promised, "and then we will have babies."

Epilogue

"Texas, right?" the orderly asked.

The man seated at the table looked up, revealing features that were too strong, almost harsh under the stretched tautness of his skin. His right eye was covered by a black patch, and the skin that surrounded it was subtly different in texture than that on the other side of his face.

"You're from Texas, aren't you?" the orderly asked again.

The gaze of the single blue eye held on the questioner a moment, and then the seated man nodded. "I used to be," he said. "A long time ago."

"Somebody left a newspaper downstairs. San Antonio. The doc said to give it to you. He thought you might like to see what's happening at home."

The steady regard of that blue eye didn't falter, and the orderly grinned. "Okay, what he really said was that turning the pages would be great therapy." The orderly's eyes moved down to the drawn fingers of the hand that rested unmoving on the top of the table.

"If the two of you aren't careful," the seated man said softly, "I'm gonna be forced to tell you exactly what you can do with that newspaper."

The orderly's grin spread, undeterred by the threat. "He

said to tell you to read the sports. He has a couple of questions for you about something in there."

He took the newspaper from under his arm and unfolded it on the table. The blue eye of the seated man didn't look down on the printed words, and thin lips hadn't responded to the orderly's grin, which spread slightly as he walked away.

When the orderly disappeared, the man finally glanced down at the paper. It wasn't the sports section. That was the whole purpose behind this. He'd have to turn the flimsy pages to get to the sports. Manipulate them with a hand that didn't work. That hadn't worked in five years.

This was what they called "therapy," and he was familiar with all their tricks. He damn well ought to be. He resisted the urge to lift that nearly useless right hand and push the paper forward with its heel until it fell off the far edge of the table.

Except he was too stubborn for that. And they all understood that around here. He was too damn stubborn to give up. That was the only thing that had kept him alive. The only thing that had gotten him this far.

Even as he thought it, he knew it was a lie. There was something else. Something that he only allowed himself to think about late at night when he was alone, away from these too-familiar sights and sounds and smells that had been all he'd known for five years.

But those memories weren't for the light of day. The thin lips tightened, less mobile on the right side where the nerves had been irreparably damaged.

He didn't think about his face much anymore. Occasionally, he'd catch a glimpse of it in a mirror somewhere and wonder who that stranger was. It didn't happen often. He'd learned five years ago to avoid mirrors. And despite the miracles the plastic surgeons had wrought in the time since, that wasn't a habit he'd ever broken. Or ever wanted to.

He looked down again at the paper in front of him, preparing to meet the newest challenge they'd devised for him. Challenge? he thought, amusement touching the thin lips for the first time. He guessed he'd come a long way, then. He used to consider all this simply torture. Something to be endured. Another day to be gotten through.

Read the sports section, he'd been told. The doctor would ask him a question about something that was there. Another damn game. He could refuse, of course. There was nothing at stake but his pride. Only, he had always had a lot of that. Too damn much.

He finally managed to grasp the corner of the top page with the unresponsive fingers. He began to lift it, some society crap, and the flimsy paper slipped out of his grip, fluttering back to the table.

His expletive was explicit and highly reflective of his background, but too soft to carry to anyone else in the big room. His mouth tightened, and again he captured the elusive corner between his fingers and again it fluttered away as he tried to lift it.

He could feel the frustration building as he tried the simple task again and again, but he tamped it down, fighting against thinking about anything except compelling his fingers to obey the command of his brain. Getting frustrated didn't change anything. Nothing *could* change except him. No one could do anything about his situation except him. They had already done all they could for him.

He had carefully grasped the corner again, maybe the fifteenth or sixteenth attempt, when his eyes rested briefly on the printed page in front of him. He hadn't been thinking about the words there. He had simply been willing his fingers to hold this time. But for some reason the import of the small headline registered.

"Senator Trent Richardson is pleased to announce the engagement of his sister, Anne, to Roderigo Delgado."

Rio? he wondered unbelievingly. Could that possibly be Rio? He read the headline again. And then once again before his eyes skimmed quickly down the rest of the column, which was maybe three inches long. They came back to the top, and he began to read the short announcement with careful concentration.

It was in the last paragraph. The columnist's opinion, obviously, and not part of whatever had been sent to the paper. There were just a couple of sentences, almost a teaser. Some of the stuff they did to imply they knew more than the reader, to imply what an insider they were. This one was about the senator's own impending nuptials. To Jenny McCullar. To the widow of slain lawman Mac McCullar.

Slowly the damaged fingers released the corner of the page and closed, almost into a fist. And with the heel of that fist, he pushed the paper he'd been brought off the edge of the table. The pages separated as they fell, and scattered, fluttering outward across the shining tile floor. Mac McCullar didn't watch them.

Chase had tried to warn him the last time he was here. To prepare him for this, he supposed. But despite what Chase had said then, Mac had never believed it would happen. He had never believed Jenny would even think about marrying someone else.

"She believes you're dead, Mac. That's what you wanted her to believe," Chase had said. "What the hell did you think she was going to do for the rest of her life? Grieve for you?"

Is that what he'd thought? He closed his eye, knowing now that Chase had been right. *"Now or never,"* his brother had warned. *"Do it now, or it's too late. It will forever be too late."*

"Come home," Chase had said. Only, Mac had known he wasn't ready. He opened his eye and looked down on the big fingers lying uselessly on the table now. And there were other things, of course. Things that… He took a breath, trying to think. He had never intended to go back until...

Until everything was like it had been before? his intellect mocked. Somewhere inside, he had admitted a long time ago that things would never be the same. Never be what they had been before. He would never be the man he had been then. The man who had once been married to Jenny McCullar.

"Come home, or it will forever be too late." Maybe it already was. Maybe...

There was no point in that kind of thinking. Surely that was one thing he had learned. Trying to figure out what was going to happen was worse than useless. Just like trying to reason his way past what had already happened.

Home. He had fought those images for five long years, had denied them because he wanted better for her than what he had to offer. And now he was going to lose Jenny forever through his own cowardice.

Mac McCullar had never considered himself to be a coward, but he knew that what he wanted to do would take more sheer, raw courage than he probably possessed. Only he didn't have any choice. Not the way he wanted Jenny. Not if there was the slightest possibility that she would still want him.

Come home, he thought again. And for Mac McCullar that would literally mean coming back from the dead.

The three McCullar brothers once stood strong against the lawlessness on their ranches. Then the events of one fateful night shattered their bond and sent them far from home. But their hearts remained with the ranch—and the women—they left behind. And now all three are coming

HOME TO TEXAS

Gayle Wilson has written a romantic, emotional and suspenseful new trilogy and created characters who will touch your heart. Don't miss any of the cowboy McCullar brothers in:

#461 RANSOM MY HEART
April

#466 WHISPER MY LOVE
May

#469 REMEMBER MY TOUCH
June

These are three cowboys' stories you won't want to miss!

Looking For More Romance?

Visit Romance.net

Look us up on-line at: http://www.romance.net

Check in daily for these and other exciting features:

Hot off the press

View all current titles, and purchase them on-line.

What do the stars have in store for you?

Horoscope

Hot deals

Exclusive offers available only at Romance.net

Plus, don't miss our interactive quizzes, contests and bonus gifts.

PWEB

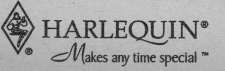

DEBBIE MACOMBER

invites you to the

HEART OF TEXAS

Join Debbie Macomber as she brings you the lives
and loves of the folks in the ranching community
of Promise, Texas.

If you loved Midnight Sons—don't miss
Heart of Texas! A brand-new six-book series
from Debbie Macomber.

Available in February 1998
at your favorite retail store.

Heart of Texas by Debbie Macomber

Lonesome Cowboy	February '98
Texas Two-Step	March '98
Caroline's Child	April '98
Dr. Texas	May '98
Nell's Cowboy	June '98
Lone Star Baby	July '98

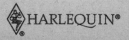

HARLEQUIN®

HPHRT1

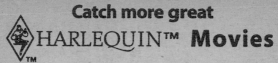 

 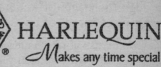

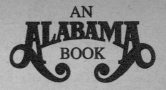

MEN at WORK

All work and no play? Not these men!

April 1998

KNIGHT SPARKS by Mary Lynn Baxter

Sexy lawman Rance Knight made a career of arresting the bad guys. Somehow, though, he thought policewoman Carly Mitchum was framed. Once they'd uncovered the truth, could Rance let Carly go...or would he make a citizen's arrest?

May 1998

HOODWINKED by Diana Palmer

CEO Jake Edwards donned coveralls and went undercover as a mechanic to find the saboteur in his company. Nothing— or no one—would distract him, not even beautiful secretary Maureen Harris. Jake had to catch the thief—*and* the woman who'd stolen his heart!

June 1998

DEFYING GRAVITY by Rachel Lee

Tim O'Shaughnessy and his business partner, Liz Pennington, had always been close—but never *this* close. As the danger of their assignment escalated, so did their passion. When the job was over, could they ever go back to business as usual?

MEN AT WORK™

Available at your favorite retail outlet!

 HARLEQUIN®   Silhouette®

Look us up on-line at: http://www.romance.net

PMAW1

HARLEQUIN®
INTRIGUE®

COMING NEXT MONTH

#469 REMEMBER MY TOUCH by Gayle Wilson
Home to Texas

Five years after her husband's murder, Jenny McCullen's life was
turned upside down by Matt Dawson, who aroused familiar passions.
Matt claimed to be a DEA agent on the trail of Mac's killer—but
Jenny's heart told her he was keeping more than his share of secrets.

#470 THE MISSING HOUR by Dawn Stewardson

P.I. Cole Radford worked alone—until Beth Gregory asked him to
solve a twenty-two-year-old murder case. She'd finally remembered
witnessing the murder, but insisted her memory was wrong. Now only
Cole stood between Beth and someone who wanted her dead....

#471 JODIE'S LITTLE SECRETS by Joanna Wayne

Single mom of twin baby boys, Jodie Gahagen saw her ordered life
destroyed when a stalker sent her running home. But once there, she
couldn't avoid Ray Kostner's probing questions. He knew Jodie was
hiding two secrets...but he never guessed he was their father.

#472 RUNAWAY HEART by Saranne Dawson

When C. Z. Morrison found by-the-book cop Zach Hollis as a fugitive,
she left behind her button-down ways and went on the run with him to
clear his name. With no safe haven except in each other's arms, would
their love overcome the odds?

AVAILABLE THIS MONTH:

Look us up on-line at: http://www.romance.net